One of the s⬚⬚⬚⬚⬚⬚⬚⬚⬚⬚⬚⬚⬚e chlorine breather's pressu⬚⬚⬚⬚⬚⬚⬚e, ripping it open along the entire length of the body. Keeping his mouth and nostrils sealed with one hand, MacEwan used the other to feel along the Illensan's body and pressure envelope. His eyes were stinging even though they were now tightly shut. The sound of the pulse in his head was incredible, like a thudding explosion, and the constriction in his chest was fast reaching the stage where he was ready to inhale even chlorine to stop that fiery, choking pain in his lungs. But he fought desperately not to breathe . . .

Also from Futura by James White:

ALL JUDGEMENT FLED
AMBULANCE SHIP
MAJOR OPERATION
STAR SURGEON
HOSPITAL STATION

JAMES WHITE

Sector General

Futura

An Orbit Book

Copyright © 1983 by James White

First published in Great Britain in 1987
by Futura Publications, a Division of
Macdonald & Co (Publishers) Ltd
London & Sydney

ISBN 0 7088 8186 6

Reproduced, printed and bound in Great Britain by
Hazell Watson & Viney Limited,
Member of the BPCC Group,
Aylesbury, Bucks

Futura Publications
A Division of
Macdonald & Co (Publishers) Ltd
Greater London House
Hampstead Road
London NW1 7QX
A BPCC plc Company

Dedicated to The Friends of Kilgore Trout,
who treat the impossible with the contempt
it deserves

CONTENTS

ACCIDENT

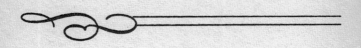

R̲ETLIN complex was Nidia's largest air terminal, its only spaceport, and, MacEwan thought cynically, its most popular zoo. The main concourse was thronged with furry native airline passengers, sightseers, and ground personnel, but the thickest crowd was outside the transparent walls of the off-planet departure lounge where Nidians of all ages jostled each other in their eagerness to see the waiting space travelers.

But the crowd parted quickly before the Corpsmen escorting MacEwan and his companion—no native would risk giving offense to an offworlder by making even accidental bodily contact. From the departure lounge entrance, the two were directed to a small office whose transparent walls darkened into opacity at their approach.

The man facing them was a full Colonel and the ranking Monitor Corps officer on Nidia, but until they had seated themselves he remained standing, respectfully, as befitted one who was meeting for the first time the great Earth-human MacEwan and the equally legendary Orligian Grawlya-Ki. He remained on his feet for a moment longer while he looked with polite disapproval at their uniforms, torn and stained relics of an

3

almost forgotten war, then he glanced toward the solidograph that occupied one corner of his desk and sat down.

Quietly he began, "The planetary assembly has decided that you are no longer welcome on Nidia, and you are requested to leave at once. My organization, which is the closest thing we have to a neutral extraplanetary police force, has been asked to implement this request. I would prefer that you leave without the use of physical coercion. I am sorry. This is not pleasant for me, either, but I have to say that I agree with the Nidians. Your peacemongering activities of late have become much too . . . warlike."

Grawlya-Ki's chest swelled suddenly, making its stiff, spikey fur rasp dryly against the old battle harness, but the Orligian did not speak. MacEwan said tiredly, "We were just trying to make them understand that—"

"I know what you were trying to do," the Colonel broke in, "but half wrecking a video studio during a rehearsal was not the way to do it. Besides, you know as well as I do that your supporters were much more interested in taking part in a riot than in promulgating your ideas. You simply gave them an excuse to—"

"The play glamorized war," MacEwan said.

The Monitor's eyes flickered toward the solidograph, then back to Grawlya-Ki and MacEwan again. His tone softened. "I'm sorry, believe me, but you will have to leave. I cannot force it, but ideally you should return to your home planets where you could relax and live out your remaining years in peace. Your wounds must have left mental scars and you may require psychiatric assistance; and, well, I think both of you deserve some of the peace that you want so desperately for everyone else."

When there was no response, the Colonel sighed and said, "Where do you want to go this time?"

"Traltha," MacEwan said.

The Monitor looked surprised. "That is a hot, high-gravity, heavily industrialized world, peopled by lumbering, six-legged elephants who are hardworking, peaceloving, and culturally stable. There hasn't been a war on Traltha for a thousand years. You would be wasting your time there, and feeling very uncomfortable while doing so, but it's your choice."

"On Traltha," MacEwan said, "commerical warfare never stops. One kind of war can lead to another."

The Colonel made no attempt to disguise his impatience. "You are frightening yourselves without reason and, in any case, maintaining the peace is our concern. We do it quietly, discreetly, by keeping potentially troublesome entities and situations under observation, and by making the minimum response early, before things can get out of control. We do a good job, if I do say so myself. But Traltha is not a danger, now or in the foreseeable future." He smiled. "Another war between Orligia and Earth would be more likely."

"That will not happen, Colonel," Grawlya-Ki said, its modulated growling forming a vaguely threatening accompaniment to the accentless speech coming from its translator pack. "Former enemies who have beaten hell out of each other make the best friends. But there has to be an easier way of making friends."

Before the officer could reply, MacEwan went on quickly, "I understand what the Monitor Corps is doing, Colonel, and I approve. Everybody does. It is rapidly becoming accepted as the Federation's executive and law-enforcement arm. But it can never become a truly multispecies service. Its officers, of necessity, will be almost entirely Earth-human. With so much power entrusted to one species—"

"We are aware of the danger," the Colonel broke in. Defensively he went on, "Our psychologists are working on the problems and our people are highly trained in e-t cultural contact procedures. And we have the authority to ensure that the members of every ship's crew making other-species contacts are similarly trained. Everyone is aware of the danger of uttering or committing an unthinking word or action which could be construed as hostile, and of what might ensue. We lean over backward in our efforts not to give offense. You know that."

The Colonel was first and foremost a policeman, MacEwan thought, and like a good policeman he resented any criticism of his service. What was more, his irritation with the two aging war veterans was rapidly reaching the point where the interview would be terminated. *Take it easy,* he warned himself, *this man is not an enemy.*

Aloud he said, "The point I'm trying to make is that leaning

over backward is an inherently unstable position, and this hy-
perpoliteness where extraterrestrials are concerned is artificial,
even dishonest. The tensions generated must ultimately lead to
trouble, even between the handpicked and highly intelligent
entities who are the only people allowed to make off-planet
contacts. This type of contact is too narrow, too limited. The
member species of the Federation are not really getting to know
and trust each other, and they never will until contact becomes
more relaxed and natural. As things are it would be unthinkable
to have even a friendly argument with an extraterrestrial.

"We must get to really know them, Colonel," MacEwan
went on quickly. "Well enough not to have to be so damnably
polite all the time. If a Tralthan jostles a Nidian or an Earth-
human, we must know the being well enough to tell it to watch
where it's going and to call it any names which seem appro-
priate to the occasion. We should expect the same treatment
if the fault is ours. Ordinary people, not a carefully selected
and trained star-traveling elite, must get to know offworlders
well enough to be able to argue or even to quarrel nonviolently
with them, without—"

"And that," the Monitor said coldly, rising to his feet, "is
the reason you are leaving Nidia. For disturbing the peace."

Hopelessly, MacEwan tried again. "Colonel, we must find
some common ground on which the ordinary citizens of the
Federation can meet. Not just because of scientific and cultural
exchanges or interstellar trade treaties. It must be something
basic, something we all feel strongly about, an idea or a project
that we can really get together on. In spite of our much-vaunted
Federation and the vigilance of your Monitor Corps, perhaps
because of that vigilance, we are *not* getting to know each other
properly. Unless we do another war is inevitable. But nobody
worries. You've all forgotten how terrible war is."

He broke off as the Colonel pointed slowly to the solidograph on his desk, then brought the hand back to his side again.
"We have a constant reminder," he said.

After that the Colonel would say no more, but remained
standing stiffly at attention until Grawlya-Ki and MacEwan left
the office.

The departure lounge was more than half filled with tight,
exclusive little groups of Tralthans, Melfans, Kelgians, and

Illensans. There was also a pair of squat, tentacular, heavy-gravity beings who were apparently engaged in spraying each other with paint, and which were a new life-form to MacEwan. A teddybearlike Nidian wearing the blue sash of the nontechnical ground staff moved from behind them to escape the spray, but otherwise ignored the creatures.

There was some excuse for the chlorine-breathing Illensans to keep to themselves: the loose, transparent material of their protective envelopes looked fragile. He did not know anything about the paint-spraying duo, but the others were all warmblooded, oxygen-breathing life-forms with similar pressure and gravity requirements and they should, at least, have been acknowledging each others' presence even if they did not openly display the curiosity they must be feeling toward each other. Angrily, MacEwan turned away to examine the traffic movements display.

There was an Illensan factory ship in orbit, a great, ungainly nonlander whose shuttle had touched down a few minutes earlier, and a Nidian ground transporter fitted with the chlorine breathers' life-support was on the way in to pick up passengers. Their Tralthan-built and crewed passenger ship was nearly ready to board and stood on its apron on the other side of the main aircraft runway. It was one of the new ships which boasted of providing comfortable accommodation for six different oxygen-breathing species, but degrees of comfort were relative and MacEwan, Grawlya-Ki, and the other non-Tralthans in the lounge would shortly be judging it for themselves.

Apart from the Illensan shuttle and the Tralthan vessel, the only traffic was the Nidian atmosphere craft which took off and landed every few minutes. They were not large aircraft, but they did not need to be to hold a thousand Nidians. As the aircraft differed only in their registration markings, it seemed that the same machine was endlessly taking off and landing.

Angry because there was nothing else in the room to engage his attention fully, and because it occupied such a prominent position in the center of the lounge that all eyes were naturally drawn to it, MacEwan turned finally to look once again at that frightful and familiar tableau.

Grawlya-Ki had already done so and was whining softly to itself.

It was a life-sized replica of the old Orligian war memorial, one of the countless thousands of copies which occupied public places of honor or appeared in miniature on the desks or in the homes of responsible and concerned beings on every world of the Federation. The original had stood within its protective shield in the central Plaza of Orligia's capital city for more than two centuries, during which a great many native and visiting entities of sensitivity and intelligence had tried vainly to describe its effect upon them.

For that war memorial was no aesthetic marble poem in which godlike figures gestured defiance or lay dying nobly with limbs arranged to the best advantage. Instead it consisted of an Orligian and an Earthman, surrounded by the shattered remnants of a Control Room belonging to a type of ship now long obsolete.

The Orligian was standing crouched forward, the fur of its chest and face matted with blood. A few yards away lay the Earth-human, very obviously dying. The front of his uniform was in shreds, revealing the ghastly injuries he had sustained. Abdominal organs normally concealed by skin, layers of subcutaneous tissue and muscle were clearly visible. Yet this man, who had no business being alive much less being capable of movement, was struggling toward the Orligian.

Two combatants amid the wreckage of a warship trying to continue their battle hand-to-hand?

The dozens of plaques spaced around the base of the tableau described the incident in all the written languages of the Federation.

They told of the epic, single-ship duel between the Orligian and the Earth-human commanders. So evenly matched had they been that, their respective crew members dead, their ships shot to pieces, armaments depleted and power gone, they had crashlanded close together on a world unknown to both of them. The Orligian, anxious to learn all it could regarding enemy ship systems, and driven by a more personal curiosity about its opponent, had boarded the wrecked Earth ship. They met.

For them the war was over, because the terribly wounded Earth-human did not know when he was going to die and the Orligian did not know when, if ever, its distress signal would bring rescuers. The distant, impersonal hatred they had felt toward each other was gone, dissipated by the six-hour period of maximum effort that had been their duel, and was replaced by feelings of mutual respect for the degree of professional competence displayed. So they tried to communicate, and succeeded.

It had been a slow, difficult, and extraordinarily painful process for both of them, but when they did talk they held nothing back. The Orligian knew that any verbal insubordination it might utter would die with this Earth-human, who in turn sensed the other's sympathy and was in too much pain to care about the things he said about his own superiors. And while they talked the Earth-human learned something of vital importance, an enemy's-eye view of the simple, stupid, and jointly misunderstood incident which had been responsible for starting the war in the first place.

It had been during the closing stages of this conversation that an Orligian ship which chanced to be in the area had landed and, after assessing the situation, used its Stopper on the Earth wreck.

Even now the operating principles of the Orligian primary space weapon were unclear to MacEwan. The weapon was capable of enclosing a small ship, or vital sections of a large one, within a field of stasis in which all motion stopped. Neither the ships nor their crew were harmed physically, but if someone so much as scratched the surface of one of those Stopped hulls or tried to slip a needle into the skin of one of the Stopped personnel, the result was an explosion of near-nuclear proportions.

But the Orligian stasis field projector had peaceful as well as military applications.

With great difficulty the section of Control Room and the two Stopped bodies it contained had been moved to Orligia, to occupy the central square of the planetary capital as the most gruesomely effective war memorial ever known, for 236 years. During that time the shaky peace which the two frozen beings had brought about between Orligia and Earth ripened into friendship, and medical science progressed to the point where the terribly injured Earth-human could be saved. Although its injuries had not been fatal, Grawlya-Ki had insisted on being Stopped with its friend so that it could see MacEwan cured for itself.

And then the two greatest heroes of the war, heroes because they had ended it, were removed from stasis, rushed to a hospital, and cured. For the first time, it was said, the truly great of history would receive the reward they deserved from posterity—and that was the way it had happened, just over thirty years ago.

Since then the two heroes, the only two entities in the whole Federation with direct experience of war, had grown increasingly monomaniacal on the subject until the honor and respect accorded them had gradually changed to reactions of impatience and embarrassment.

"Sometimes, Ki," MacEwan said, turning away from the frozen figures of their former selves, "I wonder if we should give up and try to find peace of mind like the Colonel said. Nobody listens to us anymore, yet all we are trying to tell them is to relax, to take off their heavy, bureaucratic gauntlets when extending the hand of friendship, and to speak and react honestly so that—"

"I am aware of the arguments," Grawlya-Ki broke in, "and the completely unnecessary restatement of them, especially to one who shares your feelings in this matter, is suggestive of approaching senility."

"Listen, you mangy, overgrown baboon!" MacEwan began furiously, but the Orligian ignored him.

"And senility is a condition which cannot be successfully treated by the Colonel's psychiatrists," it went on. "Neither, I submit, can they give psychiatric assistance to minds which are otherwise sane. As for my localized loss of fur, you are so lacking in male hormones that you can only grow it on your head and—"

"And your females grow more fur than you do," MacEwan snapped back, then stopped.

He had been conned again.

Since that first historic meeting in MacEwan's wrecked Control Room they had grown to know each other very well. Grawlya-Ki had assessed the present situation, decided that MacEwan was feeling far too depressed for his own good, and instituted curative treatment in the form of a therapuetic argument combined with subtle reassurance regarding their sanity. MacEwan smiled.

"This frank and honest exchange of views," he said quietly, "is distressing the other travelers. They probably think the Earth—Orligian war is about to restart, because they would never dream of saying such things to each other."

"But they do dream," Grawlya-ki said, its mind going off at one of its peculiarly Orligian tangents. "All intelligent lifeforms require periods of unconsciousness during which they dream. Or have nightmares."

"The trouble is," MacEwan said, "they don't share our particular nightmare."

Grawlya-Ki was silent. Through the transparent outer wall of the lounge it was watching the rapid approach of the ground transporter from the Illensan shuttle The vehicle was a great, multiwheeled silver bullet distinctively marked to show that it was filled with chlorine, and tipped with a transparent control module whose atmosphere was suited to its Nidian driver. MacEwan wondered why all of the smaller intelligent lifeforms, regardless of species, had a compulsion to drive fast. Had he stumbled upon one of the great cosmic truths?

"Maybe we should try a different approach," the Orligian said, still watching the transporter. "Instead of trying to frighten them with nightmares, we should find them a pleasant and inspiring dream to—What is that idiot *doing*?"

The vehicle was still approaching at speed, making no attempt to slow or turn so as to present its transfer lock to the lounge's exit port for breathers of toxic atmospheres. All of the waiting travelers were watching it now, many of them making noises which did not translate.

The driver is showing off, MacEwan thought. Reflected sunlight from the canopy obscured the occupant. It was not until the transporter ran into the shadow of the terminal building that MacEwan saw the figure of the driver slumped face downward over its control console, but by then it was too late for anyone to do anything.

Built as it was from tough, laminated plastic nearly a foot thick, the transparent wall bulged inward but did not immediately shatter as the nose of the vehicle struck. The control module and its occupant were instantly flattened into a thin pancake of riven metal, tangled wiring, and bloody Nidian fur. Then the transporter broke through.

When the driver had collapsed and lost control, the automatic power cutoff and emergency braking systems must have been triggered. But in spite of its locked wheels the transporter skidded ponderously on, enlarging the original break in the transparent wall and losing sections of its own external plating in the process. It plowed through the neat rows of Tralthan, Melfan, Kelgian, and Illensan furniture. The heavy, complex structures were ripped from their floor mountings and hurled aside along with the beings unfortunate enough to still be occupying them. Finally the transporter ground to a halt against one of the building's roof support pillars, which bent alarmingly but did not break. The shock brought down most of the lounge's ceiling panels and with them a choking, blinding cloud of dust.

All around MacEwan extraterrestrials were coughing and floundering about and making untranslatable noises indicative of pain and distress, Grawlya-Ki included. He blinked dust out of his eyes and saw that the Orligian was crouched, apparently uninjured, beside the transporter. Both of its enormous, furry hands were covering its face and it looked as if it would shake itself apart with the violence of its coughing. MacEwan kicked loose debris out of the way and moved toward it. Then his eyes began to sting and, just in time, he covered his mouth and nose to keep from inhaling the contaminated air.

Chlorine!

With his free hand he grasped the Orligian's battle harness and began dragging it away from the damaged vehicle, wondering angrily why he was wasting his time. If the internal pressure hull had been ruptured, the whole lounge would be rendered uninhabitable to oxygen breathers within a few minutes—the Illensans' higher-pressure chlorine atmosphere would see to that. Then he stumbled against a low, sprawling, membraneous body which was hissing and twitching amid the debris and realized that it was not only the damaged vehicle which was responsible for the contamination.

The Illensan must have been hit by the transporter and flung against a Kelgian relaxer frame, which had collapsed. One of the support struts had snagged the chlorine breather's pressure envelope, ripping it open along the entire length of the body. The oxygen-rich atmosphere was attacking the unprotected body, coating the skin with a powdery, sickly blue organic corrosion which was thickest around the two breathing orifices. All body movement ceased as MacEwan watched, but he could still hear a loud hissing sound.

Still keeping his mouth and nostrils sealed with one hand, he used the other to feel along the Illensan's body and pressure envelope. His eyes were stinging even though they were now tightly shut.

The creature's skin felt hot, slippery, and fibrous, with patterns of raised lines which made it seem that the whole body was covered by the leaves of some coarse-textured plant, and there were times when MacEwan did not know whether he was touching the skin or the ruptured pressure suit. The sound of the pulse in his head was incredible, like a constant, thudding explosion, and the constriction in his chest was fast reaching the stage where he was ready to inhale even chlorine to stop that fiery, choking pain in his lungs. But he fought desperately not to breathe, pressing his hand so tightly against his face that his nose began to bleed.

After what seemed like a couple of hours later, he felt the shape of a large cylinder with a hose connection and strange-feeling bumps and projections at one end—the Illensan's air tank. He pulled and twisted desperately at controls designed for the spatulate digits of an Illensan, and suddenly the hiss of escaping chlorine ceased.

He turned and staggered away, trying to get clear of the localized cloud of toxic gas so he could breathe again. But he had gone only a few yards when he tripped and fell into a piece of broken e-t furniture covered by a tangle of plastic drapery which had been used to decorate the lounge. His free arm kept him from injuring himself, but it was not enough to enable him to escape from the tangle of tubing and plastic which had somehow wrapped itself around his feet. He opened his eyes and shut them again hastily as the chlorine stung them. With such a high concentration of gas he could not risk opening his mouth to shout for help. The noise inside his head was unbelievable. He felt himself slipping into a roaring, pounding blackness, and there was a tight band gripping and squeezing his chest.

There *was* something gripping his chest. He felt it lifting him, shaking him free of the debris entangling his arm and legs, and holding him aloft while it carried him for an unknown distance across the lounge. Suddenly he felt his feet touch the floor and he opened his eyes and mouth.

The smell of chlorine was still strong but he could breathe and see. Grawlya-Ki was standing a few feet away, looking concerned and pointing at the blood bubbling from his nose, and one of the two paint-spraying extraterrestrials was detaching one of its thick, iron-hard tentacles from around his chest. He was too busy just breathing again to be able to say anything.

"I apologize most abjectly and sincerely," his rescuer boomed over the sounds being made by the injured all around them, "if I have in any fashion hurt you, or subjected you to mental trauma or embarrassment by making such a gross and perhaps intimate physical contact with your body. I would not have dared touch you at all had not your Orligian friend insisted that you were in grave danger and requested that I lift you clear. But if I have given offense—"

"You have not given offense," MacEwan broke in. "On the contrary, you have saved my life at great risk to your own. That chlorine is deadly stuff to all us oxygen breathers. Thank you."

It was becoming difficult to speak without coughing because the cloud of gas from the dead Illensan's suit was spreading, and Grawlya-Ki was already moving away. MacEwan was about to follow when the creature spoke again.

"I am in no immediate danger." Its eyes glittered at him from behind their hard, organic shields as it went on. "I am a Hudlar, Earthperson. My species does not breathe, but absorbs sustenance directly from our atmosphere, which, near the planetary surface, is analogous to a thick, high-pressure, semigaseous soup. Apart from requiring our body surface to be sprayed at frequent intervals with a nutrient paint, we are not inconvenienced by any but the most corrosive of atmospheres, and we can even work for lengthy periods in vacuum conditions on orbital construction projects.

"I am glad to have been of assistance, Earthperson," the Hudlar ended, "but I am not a hero."

"Nevertheless I am grateful," MacEwan shouted, then stopped moving away. He waved his hand, indicating the lounge which resembled a battlefield rather than a luxurious departure point for the stars, and started coughing. Finally he was able to say, "Pardon me, please, if I am being presumptuous, but is it possible for you to similarly assist the other beings who have been immobilized by their injuries and are in danger of asphyxiation?"

The second Hudlar had joined them, but neither spoke. Grawlya-Ki was waving at him and pointing toward the transparent wall of the Colonel's office where the Monitor Corps officer was also gesticulating urgently.

"Ki, will you find out what he wants?" MacEwan called to the Orligian. To the first Hudlar he went on, "You are understandably cautious in the matter of physically handling members of another species, lest you inadvertently give offense, and in normal circumstances this would be wholly admirable and the behavior of a being of sensitivity and intelligence. But this is not a normal situation, and it is my belief that any accidental physical intimacy committed on the injured would be forgiven when the intention is purely to give assistance. In these circumstances a great many beings could die who would otherwise—"

"Some of them will die of boredom or old age," the second Hudlar said suddenly, "if we continue to waste time with unnecessary politeness. Plainly we Hudlars have a physical advantage here. What is it you wish us to do?"

"I apologize most abjectly for my lifemate's ill-considered and hasty remarks, Earth-human," the first Hudlar said quickly. "And for any offense they may have given."

"No need. None taken," MacEwan said, laughing in sheer relief until the chlorine turned it into a cough. He considered prefacing his instructions with advance apologies for any offense he might inadvertently give to the Hudlars, then decided that that would be wasting more time. He took a deep, careful breath and spoke.

"The chlorine level is still rising around that transporter. Would one of you remove heavy debris from casualties in the area affected and move them to the entrance to the boarding tunnel, where they can be moved into the tunnel itself if the level continues to rise. The other should concentrate on rescuing Illensans by lifting them into their transporter. There is a lock antechamber just inside the entry port, and hopefully some of the less seriously injured chlorine breathers will be able to get them through the lock and give them first aid inside. The Orligian and myself will try to move the casualties not immediately in danger from the chlorine, and open the boarding tunnel entrance. Ki, what have you got there?"

The Orligian had returned with more than a dozen small cylinders, with breathing masks and straps attached, cradled in both arms. It said, "Fire-fighting equipment. The Colonel directed me to the emergency locker. But it's Nidian equipment. The masks won't fit very well, and with some of these beings they won't fit at all. Maybe we can hold them in position and—"

"This aspect of the problem does not concern us," the first Hudlar broke in. "Earthperson, what do we do with casualties whose injuries might be compounded by the assistance of well-meaning rescuers ignorant of the physiology of the being concerned?"

MacEwan was already tying a cylinder to his chest, passing the attachment over one shoulder and under the opposite armpit because the Nidian straps were too short to do otherwise. He said grimly, "We will have that problem, too."

"Then we will use our best judgment," the second Hudlar said, moving ponderously toward the transporter, followed closely by its lifemate.

"That isn't the only problem," Grawlya-Ki said as it, too, attached a cylinder to its harness. "The collision cut our communications and the Colonel can't tell the terminal authorities about the situation in here, nor does he know what the emergency services are doing about it. He also says that the boarding tunnel entrance won't open while there is atmospheric contamination in the lounge—it is part of the safety system designed to contain such contamination so that it won't spread along the boarding tunnel to the waiting ship or into the main concourse. The system can be overridden at this end, but only by a special key carried by the Nidian senior ground staff member on duty in the lounge. Have you seen this being?"

"Yes," MacEwan said grimly. "It was standing at the exit port just before the crash. I think it is somewhere underneath the transporter."

Grawlya-Ki whined quietly, then went on, "The Colonel is using his personal radio to contact a docked Monitor Corps vessel to try to patch into the port network that way, but so far without effect. The Nidian rescue teams are doing all the talking and are not listening to outsiders. But if he gets through he wants to know what to tell them. The number and condition of the casualties, the degree of contamination, and optimum entry points for the rescue teams. He wants to talk to you."

"I don't want to talk to him," MacEwan said. He did not know enough to be able to make a useful situation report, and until he did their time could be used to much better effect than worrying out loud to the Colonel. He pointed to an object which looked like a gray, bloodstained sack which twitched and made untranslatable sounds, and said, "That one first."

The injured Kelgian was difficult to move, MacEwan found, especially when there was just one Orligian arm and two human ones to take the weight. Grawlya-Ki's mask was such a bad fit that it had to hold it in position. The casualty was a caterpillar-like being with more than twenty legs and an overall covering of silvery fur now badly bloodstained. But the body, although no more massive than that of a human, was completely flaccid. There seemed to be no skeleton, no bony parts at all except possibly in the head section, but it felt as though there were wide, concentric bands of muscle running the length of the body just underneath the fur.

It rolled and flopped about so much that by the time he had raised it from the floor, supporting its head and midsection between his outstretched arms and chest—Grawlya-Ki had the tail gripped between its side and free arm—one of the wounds began bleeding. Because MacEwan was concentrating on holding the Kelgian's body immobile as they moved it toward the boarding tunnel entrance, his mind was not on his feet; they became tangled in a piece of decorative curtain, and he fell to his knees. Immediately the Kelgian's blood began to well out at an alarming rate.

"We should do something about that," the Orligian said, its voice muffled by the too-small mask. "Any ideas?"

The Service had taught MacEwan only the rudiments of first

aid because casualties in a space war tended to be explosive
decompressions and rarely if ever treatable, and what little he
had learned applied to beings of his own species. Serious bleeding was controlled by cutting off the supply of blood to the
wound with a tourniquet or local pressure. The Kelgian's cir-
culatory system seemed to be very close to its skin, possibly
because those great, circular bands of muscle required lots of
blood. But the position of the veins were hidden by the being's
thick fur. He thought that a pad and tight bandages were the
only treatment possible. He did not have a pad and there was
no time to go looking for one, but there was a bandage of sorts
still wrapped loosely around his ankle.

He kicked the length of plastic curtain off his foot, then
pulled about two meters free of the pile of debris which had
fallen with it. The stuff was tough and he needed all his strength
to make a transverse tear in it, but it was wide enough to cover
the wound with several inches to spare. With the Orligian's
help he held the plastic in position over the wound and passed
the two ends around the cylindrical body, knotting them very
tightly together.

Probably the makeshift bandage was too tight, and where
it passed around the Kelgian's underside it was pressing two
sets of the being's legs against the underbelly in a direction
they were not, perhaps, designed to bend, and he hated to think
of what the dust and dirt adhering to the plastic might be doing
to that open wound.

The same thought must have been going through the Orligian's head, because it said, "Maybe we'll find another Kelgian
who isn't too badly hurt and knows what to do."

But it was a long time before they found another Kelgian—
at least, it felt like an hour even though the big and, strangely,
still-functioning lounge clock, whose face was divided into
concentric rings marked off in the time units of the major
Federation worlds, insisted that it was only ten minutes.

One of the Hudlars had lifted wreckage from two of the
crablike Melfans, one of whom was coherent, seemingly uninjured but unable to see because of the chlorine or dust. Grawlya-Ki spoke reassuringly to it and led it away by grasping a
thick, fleshy projection, purpose unknown, growing from its

head. The other Melfan made loud, untranslatable noises. Its carapace was cracked in several places and of the three legs which should have supported it on one side, two were limp and useless and one was missing altogether.

MacEwan bent down quickly and slipped his hands and lower arms under the edge of the carapace between the two useless legs and lifted until the body was at its normal walking height. Immediately the legs on the other side began moving slowly. MacEwan sidled along at the same pace, supporting the injured side and guiding the Melfan around intervening wreckage until he was able to leave it beside its blinded colleague.

He could think of nothing more to do for it, so he rejoined the Hudlar excavating among the heavier falls of debris.

They uncovered three more Melfans, injured but ambulatory, who were directed to the boarding tunnel entrance, and a pair of the elephantine, six-legged Tralthans who appeared to be uninjured but were badly affected by the gas which was still leaking steadily from the transporter. MacEwan and Grawlya-Ki each held a Nidian breathing mask to one breathing orifice and yelled at them to close the other. Then they tried desperately not to be trampled underfoot as they guided the Tralthans to the casualty assembly point. Then they uncovered two more of the Kelgian caterpillars, one of whom had obviously bled to death from a deep tear in its flank. The other had five of its rearmost sets of legs damaged, rendering it immobile, but it was conscious and able to cooperate by holding its body rigid while they carried it back to the others.

When MacEwan asked the being if it could help the earlier Kelgian casualty he had tried to bandage, it said that it had no medical training and could think of nothing further to do.

There were more walking, wriggling, and crawling wounded released from the wreckage to join the growing crowd of casualties at the tunnel entrance. Some of them were talking but most were making loud, untranslatable noises which had to be of pain. The sounds made by the casualties still trapped by fallen wreckage were slight by comparison.

The Hudlars were working tirelessly and often invisibly in a cloud of self-created dust, but now they seemed to be un-

covering only organic wreckage of which there was no hope
of salvage. There was another Kelgian who had bled spectac-
ularly to death; two, or it may have been three, Melfans with
crushed and shattered carapaces and broken limbs, and a Tralthan who had been smashed flat by a collapsing roof beam and
was still trying to move.

MacEwan was afraid to touch any of them in case they fell
apart in his hands, but he could not be absolutely sure that they
were beyond help. He had no idea of their ability to survive
major injury, or whether specialized medical intervention could
save them if taken in time. He felt angry and useless and the
chlorine was beginning to penetrate his face mask.

"This being appears to be uninjured," the Hudlar beside
them said. It had lifted a heavy table from a Tralthan who was
lying on its side, its six massive legs twitching feebly and its
domelike brain casing, multiple eye-trunk, and thick, leathery
hide free of any visible signs of damage. "Could it be that it
is troubled only by the toxic gas?"

"You're probably right," MacEwan said. He and Grawlya-
Ki pressed Nidian masks over the Tralthan's breathing orifices.
Several minutes passed with no sign of improvement in its
condition. MacEwan's eyes were stinging even though he, like
the Orligian, was using one hand to press the mask tightly
against his face. Angrily, he said, "Have you any other ideas?"

The anger was directed at his own helplessness, and he felt
like kicking himself for taking it out on the Hudlar. He could
not tell the two beings apart, only that one tended to sound
worried, long-winded, and overly polite, while its lifemate was
more forthright. This one, luckily, was the former.

"It is possible that its injuries are to the flank lying against
the floor and are presently invisible to us," the Hudlar said
ponderously. "Or that the being, which is a squat, heavy-gravity
creature with certain physical similarities to myself, is seriously
inconvenienced by being laid on its side. While we Hudlars
can work comfortably in weightless conditions, gravity if present must act downward or within a very short time serious and
disabling organ displacement occurs. There is also the fact that
all Tralthan ships use an artificial gravity system with multiple
failsafe backup, which is just one of the reasons for the de-
pendability and popularity of Tralthan-built ships. This suggests

that a lateral gravity pull must be avoided by them at all costs, and that this particular being is—"

"Stop talking about it," the second Hudlar said, joining them, "and lift the thing."

The Hudlar extended its forward pair of tentacles and, bracing itself with the other four in front of the Tralthan's weakly moving feet, slid them over the creature's back and insinuated them between the floor and its other flank. MacEwan watched as the tentacles tightened, took the strain, and began to quiver. But the body did not move, and the other Hudlar positioned itself to assist.

MacEwan was surprised, and worried. He had seen those tentacles, which served both as ambulatory and manipulatory appendages, lifting beams, major structural members, and large masses of wreckage seemingly without effort. They were beautifully evolved limbs, immensely strong and with thick, hardened pads forming a knuckle on which the being walked while the remainder of the tentacle—the thinner, more flexible half tipped with a cluster of specialized digits—was carried curled inward against its underside. The Tralthan they were trying to move was roughly the mass of an Earthly baby elephant, and the combined efforts of both Hudlars were shifting it only slightly.

"Wait," MacEwan said urgently. "Both of you have lifted much heavier weights. I think the Tralthan is caught, perhaps impaled on a structural projection, and you cannot move it because—"

"We cannot move it," the polite Hudlar said, "because we have been expending large amounts of energy after insufficient sustenance. Absorption of our last meal, which was overdue in any case, was halted by the accident after the process was scarcely begun. We are as weak as infants, as are you and your Orligian friend. But if you would both go to the other side of the being and push, your strength, puny as it is, might make a difference."

Perhaps it wasn't the polite one, MacEwan thought as he and Grawlya-Ki did as suggested. He wanted to apologize to the Hudlars for assuming that they were simply organic pieces of heavy rescue machinery whose capabilities he had taken for granted. But he and Grawlya-Ki had their shoulders under the side of the Tralthan's cranial dome, their puny efforts *were* making a difference, and, unlike Hudlars, MacEwan needed breath with which to speak.

The Tralthan came upright, rocked unsteadily on its six, widely spaced feet, then was guided toward the other casualties by the Orligian. Sweat as well as chlorine was in MacEwan's eyes so he did not know which Hudlar spoke, but presumably it had been the one engaged in lifting injured Illensans into the damaged transporter.

"I am having difficulty with a chlorine breather, Earthperson," it said. "The being is abusive and will not allow me to touch it. The circumstances call for a very close decision, one I am unwilling to make. Will you speak to it?"

The area around the transporter had been cleared of casualties with the sole exception of this Illensan, who refused to be moved. The reason it gave MacEwan was that while its injuries were not serious, its pressure envelope had suffered two small ruptures. One of these it had sealed, after a fashion, by grasping the fabric of its envelope around the tear in both manipulators and holding it tightly closed, while the other one it had sealed by lying on it. These arrangements had forced it to increase the internal pressure of the envelope temporarily, so that it no longer had any clear idea of the duration of its chlorine tank and asphyxiation might be imminent. But it did not want to be moved to the relative safety of the transporter, which was also leaking, because that would allow the lethal atmosphere of the lounge to enter its envelope.

"I would prefer to die of chlorine starvation," it ended forcefully, "than have my breathing passages and lungs instantly corroded by your oxygen. Stay away from me."

MacEwan swore under his breath but did not approach the Illensan. Where were the emergency rescue teams? Surely they should have been there by now. The clock showed that it had been just over twenty-five Earth minutes since the accident. He could see that the sightseers had been cleared from the lounge's inner wall, to be replaced by a Nidian television crew and some uninformed ground staff who did not appear to be doing anything at all. Outside there were heavy vehicles drawn up and Nidians with backpacks and helmets scurrying around, but his constantly watering eyes and the ever-present plastic hangings kept him from seeing details.

MacEwan pointed suddenly at the hangings and said to the Hudlars, "Will you tear down a large piece of that plastic material, please, and drape it over the Illensan. Pat it down flat around the being's suit and smooth the folds out toward the edges so as to exclude our air as much as possible. I'll be back in a minute."

He hurried around the transporter to the first Illensan casualty, whose body had turned a livid, powdery blue and was beginning to disintegrate, and tried to look only at the fastenings of the chlorine tank. It took him several minutes to get the tank free of the body harness, and several times his bare hands touched the dead Illensan's flesh, which crumbled like rotting wood. He knew that oxygen was vicious stuff where chlorine breathers were concerned, but now he could really sympathize with the other Illensan's panic at the thought of being moved in a leaking suit.

When he returned it was Grawlya-Ki who was smoothing out the plastic around the Illensan while the two Hudlars were standing clear. One of them said apologetically, "Our movements have become somewhat uncoordinated and the chlorine breather was worried lest we accidentally fall on it. If there is something else we can do—"

"Nothing," MacEwan said firmly.

He turned on the tap of the chlorine tank and slipped it quickly under the plastic sheet and pushed it close to the Illensan. The extra seepage of the gas would make little difference, he thought, because the whole area around the transporter was fast becoming uninhabitable for oxygen breathers. He pressed the tiny mask hard against his face and took a long, careful breath through his nose, and used it to speak to the Hudlars.

"I have been thoughtless and seemingly ungrateful for the fine work you have been doing here," he said. "There is nothing more that you can do. Please go at once and spray yourselves with the necessary nutrient. You have acted most unselfishly, and I am, as are we all, most grateful to you."

The two Hudlars did not move. MacEwan began placing

pieces of debris around the edges of the plastic and the Orligian, who was quick on the uptake, began doing the same. Soon the edges were held tightly against the floor, the gas escaping from the tank was beginning to inflate the plastic, and they had the Illensan in a crude chlorine tent. Still the Hudlars had not moved.

"The Colonel is waving at you again," Grawlya-Ki said. "I would say with impatience."

"We cannot use our sprayers here, Earthperson," one of the Hudlars said before MacEwan could reply. "The absorption mechanism in our tegument would ingest the toxic gas with our food, and in our species trace amounts of chlorine are lethal. The food sprayers can only be used in a beneficent atmosphere or in airless conditions."

"Bloody *hell*!" MacEwan said. When he thought of the way the Hudlars had worked to free the casualties, knowing that their time and available energy was severely limited and letting him assume that they had no problems, he should have had more to say—but that was all that came out. He looked helplessly at Ki, but the Orligian's face was covered by its furry hand holding the ridiculously small mask.

"With us," the other Hudlar added, "starvation is a rapid process, somewhat akin to asphyxiation in a gas breather. I estimate that we should lose consciousness and die in just under eight of our small time divisions."

MacEwan's eyes went to the concentric circles of the lounge clock. The Hudlar was talking about the equivalent of about twenty Earth minutes. Somehow they had to get that boarding tunnel open.

"Go to the tunnel entrance," he said, "and try to conserve your strength. Wait beside the others until—" He broke off awkwardly, then said to the Orligian, "Ki, you'd better get over there as well. There's enough chlorine in the air here to bleach your fur. Keep passing the masks around and—"

"The Colonel," Grawlya-Ki reminded him as it turned to follow the Hudlars. MacEwan waved acknowledgment, but before he could leave the Illensan began speaking, its voice muffled by the fabric of the makeshift chlorine tent.

"That was an ingenious idea, Earthperson," it said slowly. "There is now a beneficent atmosphere surrounding my pressure envelope, which will enable me to repair the torn fabric and survive until Illensan assistance arrives. Thank you."

"You're welcome," MacEwan said, and began picking his way over the debris toward the gesticulating figure of the Colonel. He was still several meters from the wall when the officer pointed to his ear, then rapped with a knuckle on the interior surface. MacEwan obediently unfastened his mask on one side and pressed an ear against the transparent wall. The other's voice was low and indistinct, even though the color of the Colonel's face showed that he was shouting.

"Listen, MacEwan, and don't try to answer yet," the Colonel shouted.

"We'll have you out of there in fifteen, twenty minutes at most, and you'll have fresh air in ten. Medical help for all of the casualty species is on the way. Everybody on the planet knows about the accident because the TV channels were covering your deportation as a news item, and now this is big news indeed. Their contact mikes and translators are bringing us every word said in there, and the authorities are insisting that every effort be made to speed up the rescue. . . ."

Across the lounge Grawlya-Ki was waving a mask and air tank above his head. When the Orligian was sure that MacEwan had seen it, he threw it away. None of the other casualties were wearing masks so obviously they were useless, their air tanks empty. He wondered how long his own tank would last.

The equipment had been designed for the diminuitive Nidians, whose lungs were less than half the capacity of an Earthperson's. A lot of air had been wasted during the continual passing of masks between the casualties, and the furry face of the Orligian would have allowed air to leak past the edges of its mask, especially if Grawlya-Ki had increased the pressure to exclude the chlorine.

The Colonel had seen the Orligian's action and must have arrived at the same conclusion.

"Tell them to hang on for just a few more minutes," he went on. "We can't cut a way in from the main concourse because there are too many unprotected people out there. That plastic wall is tough and needs special, high-temperature equipment to cut it, and it won't be available soon enough. Anyway, it reacts with the plastic to produce large quantities of highly toxic fumes, bad enough to make your chlorine problem seem like a bad smell.

"So they're going in through the hole made by the transporter. There is only a few inches clearance around the vehicle's hull now, but they're going to pull the transporter out backward and you will be brought out through the hole it made and into the fresh air, where the medics will be standing by—"

MacEwan began banging with his fist and a foot against the plastic to attract the Colonel's attention, and breathing as deeply as he could through the mask. He had some shouting to do himself.

"*No!*" MacEwan said loudly, putting his mouth as close to the wall as the mask would allow. "All but one of the injured Illensans are inside the transporter. The structure was damaged in the collision and is leaking chlorine from every seam. If you drag it out like that it is likely to fall apart and the air will get to the casualties. I've seen what exposure to oxygen did to one of them."

"But if we don't go in there fast the oxygen breathers will die," the Colonel replied. His face was no longer red now, but a sickly white.

MacEwan could almost see the way the officer's mind was working. If the transporter with the chlorine-breathing casualties on board was hauled out and it broke up, the Illensan authorities would not be amused. But neither would the governments of Traltha, Kelgia, Melf, Orligia, and Earth if they did not act quickly to save those people.

This was how an interstellar war could start.

With the media covering every incident as it occurred, with their contact mikes picking up every translated word as it was spoken, and with fellow beings of the casualties' species on Nidia watching, judging, feeling, and reacting, there was no possibility of this incident being hushed up or diplomatically smoothed over. The decision to be taken was a simple one: Certain death for seven or eight chlorine-breathing Illensans to possibly save triple that number of Tralthans, Hudlars, Kelgians, Melfans, many of whom were dying anyway. Or death by chlorine poisoning for the oxygen breathers.

MacEwan could not make the decision and neither, he saw, could the pale, sweating, and silent Colonel trapped inside his office. He banged for attention again and shouted, "Open the boarding tunnel! Blast it open from the other side if you have to. Rig fans or pump in fresh air from the ship to raise the tunnel pressure and keep back this chlorine. Then send the emergency team to this end of the tunnel and open it from the inside. Surely the wiring of the safety system can be short-circuited and—"

While he was talking, MacEwan was thinking about the distance between the tunnel entrance and the take-off apron. It would take a long time to traverse the tunnel if the fast walkway was not operating. And explosives might not be quickly available in an air and space terminal. Maybe the Monitor Corps vessel in dock could provide some, given time, but the time they had was to be measured in minutes.

"The safety system is triggered from your end," the Colonel broke in. "The other end of the tunnel is too close to the ship for explosives to be used. The vessel would have to take off first and that would waste more time. The system can only be overriden at your end by a special key, carried by the Nidian on lounge duty, which unlocks the cover of the tunnel controls. The cover is transparent and unbreakable. You see, contamination can be a killer in a big complex like this one, especially when you consider that chlorine is mild compared with the stuff some of the offworlders breathe—"

MacEwan thumped the wall again and said, "The Nidian with the key is buried under the transporter, which can't be moved. And who says the cover is unbreakable? There is bar metal, furniture supports, among the wreckage. If I can't unlock the cover then I'll try levering or bashing it off. Find out what I'm supposed to do when it is off."

But the Colonel was ahead of him. He had already asked the Nidians that same question. In order to make accidental operation impossible for non-Nidian digits, the tunnel controls were in the form of six recessed buttons, which had to be depressed in a certain sequence. MacEwan would have to use a stylus or something similar to operate them because his Earthly fingers were too thick. He listened carefully, signaled that he understood, then returned to the casualties.

Grawlya-Ki had heard MacEwan's half of the shouted conversation and had found two lengths of metal. It was using one

of them to attack the console when he arrived. The metal was
a strong-enough alloy, but lacked the necessary weight and
inertia. The metal bounced or skidded off the cover every time
they swung at it, without leaving a mark.

Damn the Nidians and their superhard plastics! MacEwan
raged. He tried to lever off the cover, but the join was almost
invisible and the fastenings were flush with the console ped-
estal. He swore and tried again.

The Orligian did not speak because it was coughing all the
time now, and the chlorine was affecting its eyes so badly that
more often than not its blows missed the console altogether.
MacEwan was beginning to feel an impairment in his own air
supply, as if the tank were nearly empty and he was sucking
at air which was not there, instead drawing in the contaminated
air of the lounge through the edges of his mask.

Around them the casualties were still moving, but jerkily,
as if they were struggling in the final stages of asphyxiation.
The movements were not helping their injuries. Only the two
Hudlars were motionless; their six tentacular limbs supported
them just a few inches above the floor. MacEwan raised the
metal bar high, stood on his toes, and brought it down as hard
as he could.

He grunted in pain as the shock jarred his arms from wrist
to shoulders and the bar slipped out of his hands. He swore
again and looked around helplessly.

The Colonel was watching him through his glass-walled
office. Through the inner wall of the lounge MacEwan could
see the cameras of the Nidian TV networks watching him,
listening and recording every word and cough and groan of
those inside. Beyond the outer wall, now that the dust had
settled and most of the intervening draperies had been pulled
down, he could see the crews of the heavy Nidian towing
vehicles watching him. He had only to signal to the Colonel
and the emergency team would drag out the damaged transporter and medics would be attending the casualties within a
few minutes.

But how would the Illensans as a species react to that? They
were highly advanced technologically, occupying scores of colony worlds which they had had to adapt to their environmental
needs, and, despite being the most widely traveled race in the

Federation, they were a virtually unknown quantity because
their worlds were so dangerous and unpleasant that few, indeed,
were the visitors they received. Would they hold Nidia responsible for the accident and the deaths of their people? Or
the worlds of the other warm-blooded, oxygen breathers whose
people had survived at the expense of the Illensans?

And if everybody dithered and remained undecided until all
but the Illensans had died, how would the world governments
of Kelgia, Traltha, Melf, Orligia, and Earth react?

They would probably not gang up on Illensa, nor would the
war start over this incident—not officially. But the seeds would
have been planted no matter which races were saved or sac-
rificed, or even if all of them died. It would start, not because
anyone wanted it, but because of a highly improbable accident
with a number of contributing factors most of which could have
been avoided.

Even the sudden collapse of the Nidian driver at the controls
of the transporter could have been avoided by keeping closer
medical checks on the ground staff. It had been sheer bad luck
that the incident had happened when it did, and then the too
rigidly designed safety system had done the rest. But most of
the deaths would occur, MacEwan thought angrily, because of
ignorance and fear—everyone was too frightened and over-
polite to have asked the offworlders for a few basic lessons in
first aid.

Beside him Grawlya-Ki was on its knees, coughing but still
gripping its metal bar. At any moment the Colonel would make
his decision because MacEwan, the Earth-being on the spot,
was too much of a moral coward to make it. But whether the
Colonel decided to save the Illensans or the others he would
be wrong. MacEwan moved closer to one of the motionless
Hudlars and waved a hand in front of one of its large, widely
spaced eyes.

For several interminable seconds there was no response. He
was beginning to wonder if the being was already dead when
it said, "What is it, Earthperson?"

MacEwan took a deep breath through his nose and found
that his air had run out. For a moment he panicked and almost
inhaled through his mouth, but stopped himself in time. Using
the air remaining in his nearly empty lungs, he pointed to the

console cover and said, "Are you able to break open the cover? Just the cover. I can . . . operate . . . controls . . ."

Desperately he fought the urge to suck the chlorine-laden air into his deflated lungs as the Hudlar slowly extended a tentacle and curled it around the cover. It slipped off the smooth, hemispheric surface. The Hudlar tried again without success, then it withdrew the tentacle slightly and jabbed at it with its sharp, steel-hard digits. A small scratch appeared on the cover but the material showed no sign of cracking. The tentacle withdrew, farther this time.

There was a roaring in MacEwan's head which was the loudest sound he had ever heard, and big, throbbing patches of darkness obscured the Hudlar as it made another attempt to break through the cover. MacEwan shrugged off his tunic, bunched it tightly in his fist and pressed it against his mouth as a makeshift filter. With his other hand he pressed the Nidian mask against his face to protect his eyes, at least, from the chlorine. He inhaled carefully and tried not to cough as the Hudlar swung its tentacle back for another try.

This time it struck like a battering ram and the cover, console, and even the floor supports exploded into their component parts.

"I am sorry for my clumsiness," the Hudlar said slowly. "Food deprivation impairs my judgment—"

It broke off as a loud, double chime sounded and the boarding tunnel doors slid open, bathing them suddenly in a wash of cool, pure air. A recorded voice was saying, "Will passengers please mount the moving way of the boarding tunnel and have their travel documents ready for inspection."

The two Hudlars found enough strength between them to lift the heavier casualties onto the moving way before they got on themselves, after which they began spraying each other with nutrient and making untranslatable noises. By then members of the Nidian emergency services, followed by a couple of Illensan and other offworlder medics, were hurrying in the opposite direction along the static borders of the moving way.

The incident had placed a six-hour hold on the Tralthan ship's departure, time for the less severe casualties to be treated and taken on board while the others were moved to the various offworlder accommodations in the city where they could be under the close supervision of medics of their own species. The transporter, empty of its Illensan casualties, had been withdrawn and a cold wind from the field blew through the gap in the transparent wall.

Grawlya-Ki, MacEwan, and the Colonel were standing beside the entrance to the boarding tunnel. The multichronometer above them indicated that take-off was less than half an Earth hour away.

The Colonel touched a piece of the demolished console with his boot and did not look at them when he spoke. "You were lucky. We were all lucky. I hate to think of the repercussions if you had failed to get all the casualties away. But you, both of you and the Hudlars, were instrumental in saving all but five of them, and they would have died in any case."

He gave an embarrassed laugh and looked up. "The offworld medics say some of your ideas on first aid are horrendous in their simplicity, but you didn't kill anybody and actually saved lives. You did it in full view of the media, with all of Nidia and its offworld visitors looking on, and you made your point about closer and more honest contact between species in a way that we are not going to forget. You are heroes again and I think—no, damn it, I'm sure—that you have only to ask and the Nidians will rescind their deportation order."

"We're going home," MacEwan said firmly. "To Orligia and Earth."

The Colonel looked even more embarrassed. He said, "I can understand your feelings about this sudden change in attitude. But now the authorities are grateful. Everybody, Nidians and offworlders alike, wants to interview you, and you can be sure that your ideas will be listened to. But if you require some form of public apology, I could arrange something."

MacEwan shook his head. "We are leaving because we have the answer to the problem. We have found the area of common interest to which all offworlders will subscribe, a project in which they will gladly cooperate. The answer was obvious all along but until today we were too stupid to see it.

"Implementing the solution," he went on, smiling, "is not a job for two tired old veterans who are beginning to bore people. It will take an organization like your Monitor Corps to coordinate the project, the technical resources of half a dozen planets, more money than I can conceive of, and a very, very long time. . . ."

As he continued, MacEwan was aware of excited movement among the members of the video team who had stayed behind hoping for an interview with Grawlya-Ki and himself. They would not get an interview but they were recording his final words to the Colonel. And when the Orligian and the Earth-person turned to leave they also got a not very interesting picture of the ranking Monitor Corps officer on Nidia standing very still, with one arm bent double so that the hand was held stiffly against the head. There was an odd brightness in the Earth-person's eyes and an expression on the pink, furless face which they were, naturally, unable to read.

It took a very long time, much longer than the most generous estimates. The original and relatively modest plans had to be continually extended because scarcely a decade passed without several newly discovered intelligent species joining the Federation and these, too, had to be accommodated. So gigantic and complex was the structure required that in the end hundreds of worlds had each fabricated sections of it and transported them like pieces of a vast, three-dimensional jigsaw puzzle to the assembly area.

The tremendous structure which had finally taken shape in Galactic Sector Twelve was a hospital, a hospital to end all hospitals. In its 384 levels were reproduced the environments of all the different life-forms who comprised the Galactic Federation—a biological spectrum ranging from the frigid, methane life-forms through the more normal oxygen and chlorine-breathing types, up to the exotic beings who existed by the direct conversion of hard radiation.

Sector Twelve General Hospital represented a twofold miracle of engineering and psychology. Its supply, maintenance, and administration were handled by the Monitor Corps, but the traditional friction between the military and civilian members of the staff did not occur. Neither were there any serious disagreements among its ten thousand-odd medical personnel, who were composed of over sixty differing life-forms with the same number of mannerisms, body odors, and life views.

Perhaps their only common denominator, regardless of size, shape, and number of legs, was their need to cure the sick.

And in the vast dining hall used by the hospital's warm-blooded, oxygen-breathing life-forms there was a small dedication plaque just inside the main entrance. The Kelgian, Ian, Melfan, Nidian, Etlan, Orligian, Dwerlan, Tralthan, and Earth-human medical and maintenance staff rarely had time to look at the names inscribed on it, because they were all too busy talking shop, exchanging other-species gossip, and eating at tables with utensils all too often designed for the needs of an entirely different life-form — it was a very busy place, after all, and one grabbed a seat where one could. But then that was the way Grawlya-Ki and MacEwan had wanted it.

SURVIVOR

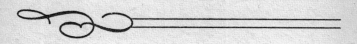

FOR more than an hour Senior Physician Conway had been dividing his attention between the interstellar emptiness outside the direct vision port and the long-range sensor display, which showed surrounding space to be anything but empty, and feeling more depressed with every minute that passed. Around him the officers on *Rhabwar's* Control Deck were radiating impatience—but inaudibly, because they all knew that when their ship was at the scene of a disaster it was the senior medical officer on board who had the rank.

"Only one survivor," he said dully.

From the Captain's position, Fletcher said, "We've been fortunate on previous missions, Doctor. More often than not this is all an ambulance ship finds. Just think of what must have happened here."

Conway did not reply because he had been thinking of little else for the past hour.

An interstellar vessel of unknown origin and fully three times the mass of their ambulance ship had suffered a catastrophic malfunction which had reduced it to finely divided and widely scattered wreckage. Analysis of the temperature

37

and relative motions showed the debris to be much too cool to have been at the center of a nuclear explosion less than seven hours earlier, when the distress beacon had been automatically released. It was obvious, therefore, that the ship had lost one of its hypergenerators and it had not been of a sufficiently advanced design for the occupants, with one exception, to have any chance of surviving the accident.

On Federation ships, Conway knew, if one of the matched set of hyperdrive generators failed suddenly, the others were designed to cut out simultaneously. The vessel concerned emerged safely into normal space somewhere between the stars, to sit there helplessly, unable to make it home on impulse drive, until it either repaired its sick generator or help arrived. But there were times when the safety cutoffs had failed or been late in functioning, which meant that while a part of the ship had continued for a split second at hyperspeed the remainder was braked instantaneously to sublight velocity. The effect on the early hyperships had been, to say the least, catastrophic.

"The survivor's species must be relatively new to hypertravel," Conway said, "or they would be using the modular design philosophy which we, from long experience, know to be the only structural form which enables a proportion of a ship's crew to survive when a sudden hypergenerator imbalance tears the vessel apart around them. I can't understand why the section containing the survivor wasn't fragmented like the rest."

The Captain was visibly controlling his impatience as he replied, "You were too busy getting the survivor out before the compartment lost any more air and decompression was added to its other problems, Doctor, to have time for structural observations. The compartment was a separate unit, purpose unknown, which was mounted outboard of the main hull and joined by a short access tube and airlock, and it simply broke away in one piece. That beastie was very lucky." He gestured toward the long-range sensor displays. "But now we know that the remaining pieces of wreckage are too small to contain survivors and frankly, Doctor, we are wasting time here."

"I agree," Conway said absently.

"Right," Fletcher said briskly. "Power Room, prepare to Jump in five—"

"Hold, Captain," Conway broke in quietly. "I hadn't fin-

ished. I want a scoutship out here, more than one if they can
be spared, to search the wreckage for personal effects, pho-
tographs, solid and pictorial art, anything which will assist in
reconstructing the survivor's environment and culture. And
request Federation Archives for any information on an intelligent life-form of physiological classification EGCL. Since
this is a new species to us, the cultural contact people will want
this information as soon as possible, and if our survivor continues to survive, the hospital will need it the day before yesterday.

"Tag the signals with Sector General medical first-contact
priority coding," he went on, "then head for home. I'll be on
the Casualty Deck."

Rhabwar's communications officer, Haslam, was already
preparing for the transmission when Conway stepped into the
gravity-free central well and began pulling himself toward the
Casualty Deck amidships. He broke his journey briefly to visit
his cabin and get out of the heavy-duty spacesuit he had been
wearing since the rescue. He felt as though every bone and
muscle in his body was aching. The rescue and transfer of the
survivor to *Rhabwar* had required intense muscular activity,
followed by a three-hour emergency op, and another hour sit-
ting still in Control. No wonder he felt stiff.

Try to think about something else, Conway told himself
firmly. He exercised briefly to ease his cramped muscles but
the dull, unlocalized aching persisted. Angrily he wondered if
he was becoming a hypochondriac.

"Subspace radio transmission in five seconds," the muted
voice of Lieutenant Haslam said from the cabin speaker. "Expect the usual fluctuations in the lighting and artificial gravity
systems."

As the cabin lights flickered and the deck seemed to twitch
under his feet, Conway was forced to think of something else—
specifically, the problems encountered in transmitting intelligence over interstellar distances compared with the relative
simplicity of sending a distress signal.

Just as there was only one known method of traveling faster
than light, there was only one way of calling for help when an
accident left a ship stranded between the stars. Tight-beam
subspace radio could rarely be used in emergency conditions

since it was subject to interference from intervening stellar material and required inordinate amounts of a vessel's power— power which a distressed ship was unlikely to have available. But a distress beacon did not have to carry intelligence. It was simply a nuclear-powered device which broadcast its location, a subspace scream for help which ran up and down the usuable frequencies until it died, in a matter of a few hours. And on this occasion it had died amid a cloud of wreckage containing one survivor who was very lucky indeed to be alive.

But considering the extent of the being's injuries, Conway thought, it could not really be described as lucky. Mentally shaking himself loose of these uncharacteristically morbid feelings, he went down to the Casualty Deck to check on the patient's condition.

Typed as physiological classification EGCL, the survivor was a warm-blooded, oxygen-breathing life-form of approximately twice the body weight of an adult Earth-human. Visually it resembled an outsize snail with a high, conical shell which was pierced around the tip where its four extensible eyes were located. Equally spaced around the base of the shell were eight triangular slots from which projected the manipulatory appendages. The carapace rested on a thick, circular pad of muscle which was the locomotor system. Around the circumference of the pad were a number of fleshy projections, hollows and slits associated with its systems of ingestion, respiration, elimination, reproduction, and nonvisual sensors. Its gravity and atmospheric pressure requirements had been estimated but, because of its severely weakened condition, the artificial gravity setting had been reduced to assist the heart and the pressure increased so that decompression effects would not aggravate the bleeding.

As Conway stood looking down at the terribly injured EGCL, Pathologist Murchison and Charge Nurse Naydrad joined him at the pressure litter. It was the same litter which had been used to move the casualty from the wreck, and, because the patient should not be subjected to unnecessary movement, it would be used again to transfer the EGCL into the hospital. The only difference was that for the second trip the casualty had been tidied up.

In spite of his considerable experience with spacewreck casualties of all shapes, sizes, and physiological classifications, Conway winced at the memory of what they had found. The compartment containing the EGCL had been spinning rapidly when they discovered it, and the being had been rolling about inside and demolishing furniture and equipment with its massive body for many hours before it had lodged itself in a corner under some self-created debris.

In the process its carapace had sustained three fractures, one of which was so deeply depressed that the brain had been involved. One of the eyes was missing, and two of the thin, tentacular manipulators had been traumatically severed by sharp-edged obstructions—these limbs had been retrieved and preserved for possible rejoining—and there were numerous punctured and incised wounds to the base pad.

Apart from carrying out the emergency surgery to relieve some of the cranial pressure, controlling the major areas of bleeding with clamps and temporary sutures, and assisting the patient's breathing by applying positive pressure ventilation to the remaining undamaged lung, there had been very little that they could do. Certainly there was no way of treating the brain damage aboard *Rhabwar*, and their efforts at charting the extent of that damage had resulted in conflicting indications from the biosensors and Doctor Prilicla's empathic faculty. The sensor indications were that cerebral activity had virtually ceased, while the little empath insisted, insofar as the timid, shy, self-effacing Prilicla could insist, otherwise.

"No physical movement and no change in the clinical picture since you left," Murchison said quietly, anticipating his question. She added, "I'm not at all happy about this."

"And I am far from happy, Doctor," the Charge Nurse joined in, its fur twitching and rippling as if it was standing in a strong wind. "In my opinion the being is dead and we are simply insuring that Thornnastor receives a fresher than usual specimen to take apart.

"Doctor Prilicla," the Kelgian went on, "is often guilty of saying things which are not completely accurate just so long as they make the people around it happy, and the predominant emotional radiation it detected from the patient was of pain.

The feeling was so intense, you will remember, that Prilicla asked to be excused as soon as the operation was completed. In my opinion, Doctor, this patient is no longer capable of cerebration but it is, judging by Prilicla's response, suffering intense pain. Surely your course is clear?"

"Naydrad!" Conway began angrily, then stopped. Murchison and the Charge Nurse had expressed exactly the same sentiments. The difference was that the Kelgian, in common with the rest of its species, was incapable of using tact.

Conway stared for a moment at the two-meters-long, caterpillar like life-form whose coat of silvery fur was in constant, rippling motion. This motion was completely involuntary among Kelgians, triggered by their reactions to external and internal stimuli, and the emotionally expressive fur complemented the vocal apparatus which lacked flexibility of tone. But the patterns of movement in the fur made it plain to any Kelgian what another felt about the subject under discussion, so that they always said exactly what they meant. The concepts of diplomacy, tact, and lying were therefore completely alien to them. Conway sighed.

He tried to conceal his own doubts about the case by saying firmly, "Thornnastor much prefers putting together a live speciment than taking apart a dead one. As well, on a number of occasions Prilicla's empathy has proved more trustworthy than medical instrumentation, so we cannot be absolutely sure that this case is hopeless. In any event, until we reach the hospital its treatment is my responsibility.

"Let's not become too emotionally involved with this patient," he added. "It is unprofessional and not like either of you."

Naydrad, its fur twitching angrily, made a sound which did not register on Conway's translator, and Murchison said, "You're right, of course. We've seen much worse cases and I don't know why I feel so badly about this one. Maybe I'm just growing old."

"The onset of senility could be one explanation for such uncharacteristic behavior," the Kelgian said, "although this is not so in my case."

Murchison's face reddened. "The Charge Nurse is allowed

to say things like that but you, Doctor, had better not agree with it," she said crossly.

Conway laughed suddenly. "Relax. I wouldn't dream of agreeing with such a blatantly obvious misstatement," he said. "And now, if you have everything you think Thorny will need on our friend here, both of you get some rest. Emergence is in six hours. If you can't sleep, please try not to worry too much about the casualty or it will bother Prilicla."

Murchison nodded and followed Naydrad from the Casualty Deck. Conway, still feeling more like a not very well patient than a medic in charge, set the audible warning which would signal any change in the EGCL's condition, lay down on a nearby litter, and closed his eyes.

Neither the Earth-human DBDG or the Kelgian DBLF classifications were noted for their ability to exercise full control over their mentation, and it was soon obvious that Murchison and Naydrad had been worrying and, in the process, producing some unpleasant emotional radiation. With his eyes still closed he listened to the faint tapping and plopping sounds which moved along the ceiling toward him and came to a halt overhead. There was a burst of low, musical clicks and trills which came through his translator as "Excuse me, friend Conway, were you sleeping?"

"You know I wasn't," Conway said, opening his eyes to see Prilicla clinging to the ceiling above him, trembling uncontrollably as it was washed by his own and the patient's emotional radiation.

Doctor Prilicla was of physiological classification GLNO— an insectile, exoskeletal, six-legged life-form with two pairs of iridescent and not quite atrophied wings and possessing a highly developed empathic faculty. Only on Cinruss, with its dense atmosphere and one-eighth gravity, could a race of insects have grown to such dimensions and in time developed intelligence and an advanced civilization.

But in both the hospital and *Rhabwar*, Prilicla was in deadly danger for most of its working day. It had to wear gravity nullifiers everywhere outside its own special quarters because the gravity pull which the majority of its colleagues considered normal would instantly have crushed it flat. When Prilicla held a conversation with anyone it kept well out of reach of any thoughtless movement of an arm or tentacle which would easily have caved in its eggshell body or snapped off one of the incredibly fragile limbs.

Not that anyone would have wanted to hurt the little being— it was far too well liked. The Cinrusskin's empathic faculty forced it to be considerate to *everyone* in order to make the emotional radiation of the people around it as pleasant for itself as possible—except when its professional duties exposed it to pain and associated violent emotion in a patient or to the un-intentionally unpleasant feelings of its colleagues.

"You should be sleeping, Prilicla," Conway said with con-cern, "or are Murchison and Naydrad emoting too loudly for you?"

"No, friend Conway," the empath replied timidly. "Their emotional radiation troubles me no more than that of the other people on the ship. I came for a consultation."

"Good!" Conway said. "You've had some useful thoughts on the treatment of our—"

"I wish to consult you about myself," Prilicla said, com-mitting the—to it—gross impoliteness of breaking in on an-other's conversation without prior apology. For a moment its pipestem legs and body shook with the strength of Conway's reaction, then it added, "Please, my friend, control your feel-ings."

Conway tried to be clinical about the little Cinrusskin who had been his friend, colleague, and invaluable assistant on virtually every major case since his promotion to Senior Phy-sician. His sudden concern and unadmitted fear of the possible loss of a close friend were not helping that friend and were, in fact, causing it even greater distress. He tried hard to think of Prilicla as a patient, only as a patient, and slowly the em-path's trembling abated.

"What," Conway said in time-honored fashion, "seems to be the trouble?"

"I do not know," the Cinrusskin said. "I have no previous experience and there are no recorded instances of the condition among my species. I am confused, friend Conway, and fright-ened."

"Symptoms?" Conway asked.

"Empathic hypersensitivity," Prilicla replied. "The emotional radiation of yourself, the rest of the medical team, and the crew is particularly strong. I can clearly detect the feelings of Lieutenant Chen in the Power Room and those of the rest of the crew in Control with little or no attenuation with distance. The expected, low-key feelings of disappointment and sorrow caused by the unsuccessful rescue bid are reaching me with shocking intensity. We have encountered these tragedies before now, friend Conway, but this emotional reaction to the condition of a being who is a complete stranger is—is—"

"We do feel bad about this one," Conway broke in gently, "perhaps worse than we normally do, and the feelings are cumulative. And you, as an emotion-sensitive, could be expected to feel them much more strongly. This might explain your apparent hypersensitivity."

The empath trembled with the effort needed to express disagreement. It said, "No, friend Conway. The condition and emotional radiation of the EGCL, highly unpleasant though it is, is not the problem. It is the ordinary, everyday radiation of everyone else—the minor embarrassments, the bursts of irritation, the odd emotions associated with the feeling you Earth-humans call humor and the like, are registering so strongly with me that I find difficulty in thinking clearly."

"I see," Conway said automatically, although he could not see at all. "Apart from the hypersensitivity, are there any other symptoms?"

"Some unlocalized discomfort in the limbs and lower thorax," Prilicla replied. "I checked the areas with my scanner but could find no obstructions or abnormalities."

Conway had been reaching for his own pocket scanner but thought better of it. Without taking a Cinrusskin physiology tape he would have only a vage idea of what to look for, and besides, Prilicla was a first-class diagnostician and surgeon and if it said that there were no abnormalities then that was good enough for Conway.

"Cinrusskins are susceptible to illness only during childhood," Prilicla went on. "The adults do occasionally suffer from nonphysical disturbances, and the onset of symptoms, as is expected with psychological disorders, takes many forms, some of which resemble my present—"

"Nonsense, you're not going insane!" Conway broke in. But he did not feel as sure as he sounded, and he was uncomfortably aware that Prilicla knew his feelings and was beginning to tremble again.

"The obvious course," Conway said, trying to regain his clinical calm, "is to desensitize you with a hefty sedative shot. You know that as well as I. But you are too good a doctor to self-administer the indicated medication which would, we both realize, simply be treating the symptoms, without first doing something about the disease, like reporting it to me. Isn't that so?"

"That is so, friend Conway."

"Right, then," Conway said briskly. "You also realize that we can't do anything about curing the condition until we have you back in the hospital. In the meantime we'll treat the symptoms with heavy sedation. I want you completely unconscious. You are relieved of all medical duties, naturally, until we have the answer to your little problem."

Conway could almost feel the little empath's objections while he was lifting it gently into a pressure litter fitted with gravity nullifiers and the incredibly soft restraints required by this ultrafragile species. Finally Prilicla spoke.

"Friend Conway," it said weakly, "you know that I am the only medically trained empath on the staff. Our patient will require extensive and delicate cerebral surgery. If my condition precludes me from taking a direct part in the operation, I wish to be treated in an adjacent ward where this abnormal hypersensitivity will better enable me to monitor the EGCL's unconscious emotional radiation.

"You know as well as I do," it went on, "that brain surgery in a hitherto unknown life-form is largely exploratory and very, very risky, and my empathic faculty enables me to sense when surgical intervention in any area is right or wrong. By becoming a patient I have lost none of my abilities as a diagnostic empath, and for this reason, friend Conway, I want your promise that I will be placed as close as possible to the patient and restored to full consciousness while the operation is in progress."

"Well—" Conway began.

"I am not a telepath, as you know," Prilicla said, so weakly that Conway had to increase the gain on his translator to hear it. "But your feelings, if you do not intend to keep this promise, will be clear to me."

Conway had never known the normally timid Prilicla to be so forthright in its manner. Then he thought of what the empath was asking him to do—to subject it, in its hypersensitive state, to the emotional trauma of a lengthy operation during which, because of the patient's strange physiological classification and metabolism, the effectiveness of the anesthetics could not be guaranteed. His hard-held clinical detachment slipped for a moment and he felt like any concerned friend or relative watching a patient whose prognosis was uncertain.

Prilicla began to shake in its harness, but the sedative was taking effect, and very soon it was unconscious and untroubled by Conway's feelings for it.

"This is Reception," a flat, translated voice said from the Control Deck's main speaker. "Identify yourself, please. State whether visitor, patient, or staff and give physiological classification. If unable to do so because of physical injury, mental confusion, or ignorance of the classification system, please make vision contact."

Conway cleared his throat and said briskly, "Ambulance ship *Rhabwar*, Senior Physician Conway. Staff and two patients, all warm-blooded oxygen breathers. Staff classifications are Earth-human DBDG, Cinrusskin GLNO, and Kelgian DBLF. One patient is an EGCL, origin unknown, spacewreck casualty in condition nine. The second patient is also staff, a GLNO in condition three. We need—"

"Prilicla?"

"Yes, Prilicla," Conway said. "We need matching environment OR and postop intensive care facilities for the EGCL, treatment to begin on arrival, and adjacent accommodation for the GLNO whose empathic faculty may be required during the operation. Can do?"

There was silence for a few minutes, then Reception said, "Use Entry Lock Nine into Level One Six Three, *Rhabwar*. Your traffic coding is Priority Red One. ETA?"

Fletcher looked across at his astrogator, and Lieutenant Dodds said, "Two hours, seven minutes, sir."

"Wait," Reception said.

There was another silence, much longer this time, before the voice returned. "Diagnostician Thornnastor wishes to discuss the patient's condition and metabolic profile with Pathologist Murchison and yourself as soon as possible. Senior Physician Edanelt has been assigned to assist Thornnastor during the operation. Both require information on the type and extent of the EGCL's injuries and want you to transmit surface and deep-scan pictures at once. Until otherwise instructed you are assigned to the Cinrusskin patient. As soon as possible Chief Psychologist O'Mara wants to talk to you about Prilicla."

It promised to be a very busy two hours and seven minutes.

In *Rhabwar*'s forward viewscreen the hospital grew from a fuzzy smear of light against the stellar background until it seemed to fill all of space like a gigantic, cylindrical Christmas tree. Its thousands of viewports blazed with light in the dazzling variety of color and intensity necessary for the visual equipment of its patients and staff.

Within a few minutes of *Rhabwar* docking at Lock Nine, the EGCL and Prilicla had been moved into Operating Room Three and Ward Seven respectively on Level 163. Conway was not familiar with this particular level because it had still been in the process of conversion from the old FROB, FGLI, and ELNT medics' quarters when he had been detached for ambulance ship duty. Now the Tralthans, Hudlars, and Melfans had more spacious accommodations and their old abode had become the emergency admission and treatment level for warm-blooded oxygen breathers, with its own operating theaters, intensive care units, observation and recovery wards, and a diet kitchen which could reproduce the staples of every known warm-blooded, oxygen-breathing race.

While Naydrad and Conway were transferring the EGCL casualty from the litter's portable life-support and biosensor systems to those of the operating room, Thornnastor and Edanelt arrived.

Senior Physician Edanelt had been the natural if not the inevitable choice for this case. Not only was it one of the hospital's top surgeons, the permanent possessor of four physiology tapes and, according to the grapevine, a being shortly to be elevated to Diagnostician status, the crablike Melfan's physiological classification of ELNT was perhaps the closest of all the life-forms on the medical staff to that of the EGCL survivor—a vitally important factor when no physiology tape was available for the patient being treated. Where Thornnastor, the elephantine Diagnostician-in-Charge of Pathology, was concerned there were no physical similarities to the patient at all, other than that they breathed the same air.

In spite of being a Tralthan FGLI and as such one of the more massive intelligent species in the Federation, Thornnastor was no mean surgeon itself. But on this case its primary responsibility was the rapid investigation of the survivor's physiology and metabolism and, using its own vast experience in the field of e-t pathology together with the facilities available in its department, the synthesizing of the required medication which would include a safe anesthetic, coagulant, and tissue regenerative.

Edanelt and Conway had already discussed the case in detail on the way in, as had Murchison and her chief, Thornnastor. He knew that their initial efforts would be directed toward repairing the grosser structural damage, after which would come the extremely delicate, dangerous, and perhaps impossible operation to relieve the pressure on and repair the damage to the brain and adjacent organs caused by the extensive depressed fracturing of the carapace. At that stage the assistance of Prilicla and its wonderfully sensitive and precise empathic faculty would be required to monitor the operation if the EGCL was to continue to survive as something more than a vegetable.

Conway's presence was no longer needed, and he would be more usefully employed discussing Prilicla's condition with O'Mara.

As he excused himself and left, Edanelt waved a pincer which it was spraying with the fast-setting plastic film favored by the Melfan medics instead of surgical gloves, but Thornnastor's four eyes were on the patient, Murchison, and two separate pieces of its equipment so that it did not see him leave.

In the corridor Conway stopped for a moment to work out the fastest route to the Chief Psychologist's office. The three levels above this one, he knew, were the province of the chlorine-breathing Illensans, and if he had not known that then the anticontamination warnings above the interlevel airlocks would have told him. There was no danger of contamination from the

levels below since they housed the MSVK and LSVO life-
forms, each of which breathed oxygen, required a gravity pull
of one-quarter Earth normal, and resembled thin, tripedal storks.
Below them were the water-filled wards of the Chalders and
then the first of the nonmedical treatment levels where O'Mara's
department was situated.

On the way down a couple of the Nallajim MSVK medics
chirped a greeting at him and a recuperating patient narrowly
missed flying into his chest before he reached the lock into the
AUGL section. For that leg of the journey he had to don a
lightweight suit and swim through the vast tanks where the
thirty-meters long, water-breathing inhabitants of the water world
of Chalderscol drifted ponderously like armorplated crocodiles
in their warm, green wards. With his suit still beaded with
Chalder water, he was in O'Mara's office just twenty-three
minutes later.

Major O'Mara indicated a piece of furniture designed for
the comfort of a DBLF and said sourly, "No doubt you have
been too busy in your professional capacity to contact me,
Doctor, so don't waste time apologizing. Tell me about Prilicla."

Conway insinuated himself carefully into the Kelgian chair
and began describing the Cinrusskin's condition, from the
symptoms at onset to their intensification to the degree where
complete sedation was indicated, and the relevant circumstance
pertaining at the time. While he was speaking, the Chief Psychologist's craggy features were still and his eyes, which opened
into a mind so keenly analytical that it gave O'Mara what
amounted to a telepathic faculty, were likewise unreadable.

As Chief Psychologist of the Federation's largest multienvironment hospital, he was responsible for the mental well-
being of a staff of several thousand entities belonging to more
than sixty different species. Even though his Monitor Corps
rank of Major did not place him high in the hospital's Service
chain of command, and anyway had been given for purely
administrative reasons, there was no clear limit to O'Mara's
authority. To him the medical staff were patients, too, regardless of seniority, and an important part of his job was to ensure
that the right doctor was assigned to each of the weird and
often wonderful variety of patients who turned up at the hos-

pital, and that there was no xenophobic complications on either side.

He was also responsible for the hospital's medical elite, the Diagnosticians. According to O'Mara himself, however, the real reason for the high level of mental stability among the diverse and often touchy medical staff was that they were all too frightened of him to risk his displeasure by going mad.

O'Mara watched him closely until Conway had finished, then he said, "A clear, concise, and apparently accurate report, Doctor, but you are a close friend of the patient. There is the possibility of clouded judgment, exaggeration. You are not a psychologist but an e-t physician and surgeon who has apparently already decided that the case is one which should be treated by my department. You appreciate my difficulty? Please describe for me your feelings during this mission from the rescue until now. But first, are *you* feeling all right?"

All that Conway could feel just then was his blood pressure rising.

"Be as objective as possible," O'Mara added.

Conway took a deep breath and let it out again slowly through his nose. "After our very fast response to the distress signal there was a general feeling of disappointment at the rescue of just one survivor, a survivor who was barely alive. But you're on the wrong track, Major. The feeling was shared by everyone on the ship, I believe, but it was not strong enough to explain the Cinrusskin's hypersensitivity. Prilicla was picking up emotional radiation of distressing intensity from crew members stationed at the other end of the ship, a distance at which emoting would normally be barely detectable. And I am given neither to maudlin sentimentality nor exaggeration of symptoms. Right at this moment I feel the way I usually do in this blasted office and that is—"

"Objectively, remember," O'Mara said dryly.

"I was not trying to do your diagnostic work for you," Conway went on, bringing his voice back to a conversational level, "but the indications are that there *is* a psychological problem. The result, perhaps, of an as yet unidentified disease, or organic malfunction or an imbalance in the endocrine system. But a purely psychological reason for the condition is also a possibility which—"

"Anything is *possible*, Doctor," O'Mara broke in impatiently. "Be specific. What are you going to do about your friend, and what exactly do you want me to do about it?"

"Two things," Conway said. "I want you to check on Prilicla's condition yourself—"

"Which you know I will do anyway," O'Mara said.

"—and give me the GLNO physiology tape," he went on, "so that I can confirm or eliminate the nonpsychological reasons for the trouble."

For a moment O'Mara was silent. His face remained as expressionless as a lump of basalt, but the eyes showed concern. "You've carried Educator tapes before now and know what to expect. But the GLNO tape is . . . different. You will feel like a very unhappy Cinrusskin indeed. You are no Diagnostician, Conway—at least, not yet. Better think about it."

The physiology tapes, Conway knew from personal experience, fell somewhere between the categories of mixed blessing and necessary evil. While skill in e-t surgery came with aptitude, training, and experience, no single being could hope to hold in its brain the vast quantity of physiological data needed for the treatment of the variety of patients encountered in a hospital like Sector General. The incredible mass of clinical and anatomical information needed to take care of them had therefore to be furnished, usually on a temporary basis, by means of the Educator tapes, which were the brain recordings of the great medical specialists belonging to the species concerned. If an Earth-human doctor had to treat a Kelgian patient, he took one of the Kelgian physiology tapes until treatment was completed, after which he had it erased. But for the medic concerned, whether the tape was being carried for as long as it took to perform an other-species operation or for a teaching project lasting several months, the experience was not a pleasant one.

The only good thing about it from the medic's point of view was that he was much better off than one of the Diagnosticians.

They were the hospital's elite. A Diagnostician was one of those rare entities whose mind had proved itself stable enough to retain up to ten physiology tapes simultaneously. To their data-crammed minds was given the work of original research in xenological medicine and the diagnosis and treatment of disease and injury in hitherto unknown life-forms. There was a saying current in the hospital, reputed to have originated with O'Mara himself, that anyone sane enough to be a Diagnostician was mad.

For it was not only physiological data which the tapes imparted; the complete memory and personality of the entity who had possessed that knowledge was impressed on the receiving mind as well. In effect, a Diagnostician subjected himself or itself voluntarily to a form of multiple schizophrenia, with the alien personalities sharing its mind so utterly *different* that in many cases they did not have even a system of logic in common. And all too frequently the foremost medical authorities of a planet, despite their eminence in the field of healing, were very bad-tempered, aggressive, and unpleasant people indeed.

Such would not be the case with the GLNO tape, Conway knew, because Cinrusskins were the most timid, friendly, and likable beings imaginable.

"I've thought about it," Conway said.

O'Mara nodded and spoke into his desk set. "Carrington? Senior Physician Conway is approved for the GLNO tape, with compulsory postimpression sedation of one hour. I'll be in Emergency Admissions on Level One Six Three—" he grinned suddenly at Conway "—trying not to tell the medics their business."

Conway woke to see a large, pink balloon of a face hanging over him. Instinctively he tried to scramble up the wall beside his couch in case the enormous, heavily muscled body supporting the face fell and crushed the life out of him. Then suddenly there was a mental shift in perspective as the features registered concern and withdrew and the slim, Earth-human body in Monitor Corps green straightened up.

Lieutenant Carrington, one of O'Mara's assistants, said, "Easy, Doctor. Sit up slowly, then stand. Concentrate on putting your two feet onto the floor and don't worry because they aren't a Cinrusskin's six."

He made good time back to 163 in spite of having to walk around a large number of beings who were much smaller than himself just because the Cinrusskin component of his mind insisted that they were big and dangerous. From Murchison he learned that O'Mara was in Prilicla's ward, having first called in to the OR to discuss the EGCL's basic physiology and probable environmental and evolutionary influence with Thornnastor and Edanelt, both of whom had been too busy to speak to him.

They would not speak to Conway, either, and he could see why. The operation on the EGCL had become an emergency with an unknown but probably extremely short time limit.

When the splinters of depressed carapace had been removed from the brain over an hour earlier, Murchison explained quietly between rumbled instructions from Thornnastor, there had been a sudden and surprising deterioration in the EGCL's condition. The change had been detected by Prilicla who, because of its condition, had been excluded from any part of the operation. But the Cinrusskin had continued to act like a doctor by making use of its abnormally heightened emotion-detection faculty. Prilicla had pulled rank to send Ward Seven's duty nurse to the operating theater with its empathic findings and a diffident suggestion that if they were to relay the operational proceedings to Seven's viewscreen, it would be able to assist them.

The cause of the deterioration was a number of large blood vessels in the cerebral area which had ruptured when the pressure from the depressed fracture had been removed. The two surgeons had been forced to accede to Prilicla's request because, without the empath's monitoring of the patient's level of consciousness, they had no way of knowing whether the delicate, dangerous, and perforce hurried repair work in the cerebral area was having a good or bad effect—if any.

"Prognosis?" Conway murmured. But before Murchison could reply, one of Thornnastor's eyes curled backward over its head to glare down at him.

"If this patient does not succumb to a massive cerebral hemorrhage within the next thirty minutes," the Diagnostician said crossly, "it is probable that it will perish, in time, from the degenerative diseases associated with extreme old age. Now stop distracting my assistant, Conway, and tend to your own patient."

On the way to Seven Conway wondered briefly how the empath's emotion sensitivity could detect the unconscious level

of emoting of the EGCL without the signals beings swamped
by the emotional radiation of dozens of fully conscious entities
in the area. Maybe Prilicla's recent hypersensitivity was responsible, but there was a niggling doubt at the back of his
mind which suggested that there was another reason.

O'Mara was still in the ward, steadying himself in the close
to zero-gravity conditions with a hand on an equipment rack
while he and Prilicla watched the scene in the operating theater.

"Conway, stop that!" O'Mara said sharply.

He had tried not to react when he had seen the empath's
condition. But half his mind belonged to a Cinrusskin, a member of a species acknowledged to be the most sensitive and
sympathetic intelligent life-form known to the Federation who
was regarding a brother in extreme distress while the Earth-
human half was feeling for a friend in the same condition, and
it was difficult to be cool and clinical for both of them.

"I'm sorry," he said inadequately.

"I know you are, friend Conway," Prilicla said, turning
toward him. "You should not have taken that tape."

"He was warned," O'Mara said gruffly, but his expression
showed concern.

Conway was a member of an empathic race. All the memories and experience of his GLNO life were those of a normally
healthy and happy empath, but now he was no longer an empath. He could see, hear, and touch Prilicla, but the faculty
was missing which enabled him to share the other's emotions
and which subtly colored every word, gesture, and expression
so that for two Cinrusskins to be within visual range was un-
alloyed pleasure for both. He could remember experiencing
empathic contact, remember having the ability all his life, but
now he was little more than a deaf-mute. What he was feeling
from Prilicla so strongly was a product of his imagination: It
was sympathy, not empathy.

His human brain did not possess the empathic faculty, and
it was not bestowed by filling his mind with memories of having
had it. But there were other memories as well, covering a
lifetime's experience of Cinrusskin clinical physiology, and
these he could use.

"If you don't mind, Doctor Prilicla," Conway said with cool
formality, "I would like to examine you."

"Of course, friend Conway." Prilicla's uncontrollable shaking had diminished to a steady, continuous trembling, an indication that Conway's emotional radiation was under control. "There are more symptoms, Doctor, which are causing severe discomfort."

"I can see that," Conway said as he gently moved aside one of the incredibly fragile wings to place his scanner against the empath's thorax. "Describe them, please."

In the two hours since Conway had last seen it, Prilicla had changed in ways which were individually subtle but cumulatively marked. There was a strange lack of animation and concentration in the large, triple-lidded eyes; the delicate structure which supported the wing membranes had softened and warped so that the translucent and iridescent membrane had fallen into unsightly folds and wrinkles; its four tiny, wonderfully precise manipulators, which should one day make it one of the finest surgeons in the hospital, were quivering in spite of being gripped tightly together, and the overall aspect was of a GLNO who was old and grievously ill.

While Conway continued the examination, the Cinrusskin part of his mind shared his bafflement at the findings and described symptoms. They were both sure, and in this their agreement was based on the GLNO tape donor's personal experience and Conway's knowledge acquired over many years in Sector General, that Prilicla was close to death.

The empath's trembling increased sharply, then diminished as Conway once again forced a feeling of clinical detachment on himself. He said calmly, "There is no evidence of deformation, obstruction, lesion, or infection which might cause the symptoms you describe. Neither can I see any cause for the respiratory difficulty you are experiencing. Some degree of empathic hypersensitivity occurs in adolescents of your species, my Cinrusskin alter ego tells me, but in nothing like the intensity you describe. It is possible, I suppose, that there is a nonpathogenic and nontoxic involvement with the central nervous system."

"You think it's psychosomatic?" O'Mara said harshly, jabbing a finger toward Prilicla. "This?"

"I would like to eliminate that possibility," Conway replied calmly. To Prilicla, he said, "If you don't mind I would like to discuss your case with Major O'Mara outside."

"Of course, friend Conway," the empath said. The constant trembling seemed as if it would shake the fragile body apart. "But please have that Cinrusskin tape erased as quickly as possible. Your heightened levels of concern and sympathy are helping neither of us. And consider, friend Conway, your tape was donated by a great Cinrusskin medical authority of the past. In all modesty, I can say that, before coming to Sector General and in preparation for my work here, I had reached a similar degree of eminence in the field.

"There is nothing in the clinical history of our species which even approximates this condition," it went on, "and absolutely no precedent for the symptomology. Regarding the possibility of a nonphysical basis for the condition, I cannot, of course, be completely objective about this. But I have always been a happy and well-adjusted person with no mental aberrations in childhood, adolescence, or adulthood. Friend O'Mara has my psych file and will confirm this. My hope is that these peculiar symptoms were so sudden in onset that their recession will be equally rapid."

"Perhaps Thornnastor could—" Conway began.

"The thought of that—that behemoth approaching me with investigative intent would cause me to terminate at once. And Thornnastor is busy—Friend Edanelt, be careful!"

Prilicla had switched its attention suddenly to the view-screen. It went on, "Pressure, even temporary pressure in that area causes a marked decrease in the EGCL's unconscious emoting. I suggest you approach that nerve bundle anteriorly through the opening in the..."

Conway missed the rest of it because O'Mara had gripped his arm and pulled him carefully out of the low-gravity compartment.

"That was very good advice," the Chief Psychologist said when they were some distance from Prilicla's ward. "Let's erase that tape, Doctor, and discuss our little friend's problem on the way to my office."

Conway shook his head firmly. "Not yet. Prilicla said all that could be said about its case back there. The hard facts are that the Cinrusskin species is not one of the Federation's most robust. They have no stamina, no reserves to resist over a long period the effects of any injury or disease, whatever the cause. We all know—myself, my alter ego and, I suspect, you yourself—that unless its condition is treated and relieved very quickly Prilicla will die within a few hours, perhaps ten hours at most."

The Major nodded.

"Unless you can come up with a bright idea," he went on grimly, "and I would certainly welcome it if you did, I intend to go on thinking with the Cinrusskin tape. It hasn't helped much up to now, but I want to think without constraint, without having to play mental games with myself to avoid emoting too strongly in the presence of my patient. There is something very odd about this case, something I'm missing.

"So I'm going for a walk," he ended suddenly. "I won't be far away. Just far enough, I hope, to be outside the range of Prilicla's empathy."

O'Mara nodded again and left without speaking.

Conway put on a lightweight suit and traveled upward for three levels into the section reserved for the spiney, membraneous, chlorine-breathing Illensan PVSJs. The inhabitants of Illensa were not a sociable species by Earth-human standards, and Conway was hoping to walk their foggy yellow wards and corridors without interruption while he wrestled with his problem. But that was not to be.

Senior Physician Gilvesh, who had worked with Conway some months earlier on a Dwerlan DBPK operation, was feeling uncharacteristically sociable and wanted to talk shop with its fellow Senior. They met in a narrow corridor leading from the level's pharmacy and there was no way that Conway could avoid talking to it.

Gilvesh was having problems. It was one of those days, the Illensan medic said, when all the patients were demanding inordinate amounts of attention and unnecessary quantities of palliative medication, the administration of which required its personal supervision. The junior medics and nursing staff were under pressure, therefore, and there was evident an unusual degree of verbal overreaction and sheer bad temper. Gilvesh said that it was explaining and apologizing in advance for any seeming discourtesy encountered by such an important visiting Senior as Conway. There were several of Gilvesh's cases, it insisted, which he would find interesting.

In common with the other medics trained for service in a multienvironment hospital, Conway had a thorough grounding in the basics of extraterrestrial physiology, metabolism, and the more common diseases of the Federation's member species. But for a detailed consultation and diagnosis of the kind required here he needed an Illensan physiology tape, and Gilvesh knew that as well as he did. So the Illensan Senior, it seemed, was sufficiently worried by the current state of its patients to seek a quick, other-species opinion.

With the Cinrusskin tape and his intense concern for Prilicla confusing his clinical view, Conway could do little more than make encouraging noises while Gilvesh discussed a painful intestinal tract, a visually dramatic and undoubtedly uncomfortable fungoid infection involving all eight of the spatulate limbs, and sundry other conditions to which Illensans were heir.

While the patients were seriously ill, their conditions were not critical, and the increased dosages of painkilling medication which Gilvesh was administering against its better judgment seemed to be having the desired effect, albeit slowly. Conway excused himself from the frantically busy wards as soon as he could and headed towards the much quieter MSVK and LSVO levels.

He had to pass through Level 163 again on the way, and stopped to check on the condition of the EGCL. Murchison yawned in his face and said that the operation was going well and that Prilicla was satisfied with the patient's emotional radiation. He did not call on Prilicla.

But he found that the low-gravity levels were having one of those days, too, and he was immediately trapped into further consulations. He could not very well avoid them because he was Conway, the Earth-human Senior Physician, known throughout the hospital for his sometimes unorthodox but effective methods and ideas on diagnosis and treatment. Here, at least, he was able to give some useful if orthodox advice because his Cinrusskin mind-partner was closer temperamentally and physically to the Nallajim LSVOs and the MSVKs of Euril who were fragile, birdlike, and extremely timid where the larger life-forms were concerned. But he could find no solution, orthodox or otherwise, to the problem he most desperately wanted to solve.

Prilicla's.

He thought about going to his quarters where he would have peace and quiet in which to think, but they were more than an hour's journey away at the other end of the hospital and he wanted to be close by in case there was a sudden deterioration in Prilicla's already close to critical condition. So instead he continued listening to Nallajim patients describing their symptoms and feeling a strange sadness because the Cinrusskin part of his mind knew that they were suffering, feeling, and emoting on many levels but his Earth-human mental equipment was incapable of receiving their emotional radiation. It was as if a sheet of glass lay between them, through which only sight and sound could pass.

But something more was getting through, surely? He had felt some of the aches and pains of the Illensan patients as he was feeling, to a certain extent, those of the Eurils and Nallajims around him. Or was that simply the GLNO tape fooling him into believing that he was an empath?

A *sheet of glass*, he thought suddenly, and a idea began to stir at the back of his mind. He tried to bring it out into the light, to give it form. Glass. Something about glass, or the properties of glass?

"Excuse me, Kytili," he said to the Nallijim medic who was worrying aloud about an atypical case of what should have been an easily treated and nonpainful condition. "I have to see O'Mara urgently."

It was Carrington who erased the GLNO tape because the Chief Psychologist had been called to some trouble in the chlorine-breathing level lately vacated by Conway. As O'Mara's senior assistant, Carrington was a highly qualified psychologist. He studied Conway's expression for a moment and asked if he could be of assistance.

Conway shook his head and forced a smile. "I wanted to ask the Major something. He would probably have said no, anyway. May I use the communicator?"

A few seconds later the face of Captain Fletcher flicked onto the screen and he said briskly, *"Rhabwar,* Control Deck."

"Captain," Conway said, "I want to ask a favor. If you agree to do it then it must be clearly understood that you will not be held responsible for any repercussions since it will be a medical matter entirely and you will be acting under my orders.

"There is a way that I may be able to help Prilicla," he went on, and described what he wanted done. When he finished, Fletcher looked grave.

"I'm aware of Prilicla's condition, Doctor," the Captain said. "Naydrad has been in and out of the ship so often it is threatening to wear out the boarding tube, and each time it returns we get an update on the empath's progress, or rather lack of it. And there is no need to belabor the point about our respective responsibilities. Obviously you wish to use the ship for an unauthorized mission and you are concealing the details so that any blame attached to me as a result of a future inquiry will be minimal. You are cutting corners again, Doctor, but in this instance I sympathize and will accept any instructions you care to give."

Fletcher broke off, and for the first time in Conway's experience of the man the Captain's cold, impassive, almost disdainful expression softened and the voice lost its irritatingly pedantic quality. "But it is my guess that you will order me to take *Rhabwar* to Cinruss," he went on, "so that our little friend can die among its own kind."

Before Conway could reply, Fletcher had switched him to Naydrad on the Casualty Deck.

Half an hour later the Kelgian Charge Nurse and Conway were transferring Prilicla, who was barely conscious and trembling only slightly by then, from its supporting harness to a powered litter. In the corridor leading to Lock Nine none of the medical staff questioned their action, and when any of them looked as if they might, Conway tapped irritably at the casing of his translator pack and pretended that it was malfunctioning. But when they were passing the entrance to the EGCL's room, Murchison was just leaving it. She stepped quickly in front of the litter.

"Where are you taking Prilicla?" she demanded. She sounded desperately tired and uncharacteristically angry, so much so that the empath began to twitch weakly.

"To *Rhabwar*," Conway said as calmly as he could. "How is the EGCL?"

Murchison looked at the empath, then visibly tried to control her feelings as she replied, "Very well, all things considered. Its condition is stable. There is a senior nurse continually in attendance. Edanelt is resting next door, only seconds away if anything should go wrong, but we don't expect any problems. In fact, we are expecting it to recover consciousness fairly soon. And Thornnastor has returned to Pathology to study the results of the tests we did on Prilicla. That's why you shouldn't be moving Prilicla from—"

"Thornnastor can't cure Prilicla," Conway said firmly. He looked from her to the litter and went on, "I can use your help. Do you think you can stay on your feet for another couple of hours? Please, there isn't much time."

Within seconds of the litter's arrival on Rhabwar's Casualty Deck, Conway was on the intercom to Fletcher. "Captain, take us out quickly, please. And ready the planetary lander."

"The planetary—" Fletcher began, then went on, "We haven't undocked yet, much less reached Jump distance, and you're worrying about landing on Cinruss! Are you sure you know what—"

"I'm not sure of anything, Captain," Conway said. "Take us out but be prepared to check velocity at short notice, and well within Jump distance."

Fletcher broke the connection without replying, and a few seconds later the direct vision port showed the vast metal flank of the hospital moving away. Their velocity increased to the maximum allowed in the vicinity of the establishment, until the nearest section of the gigantic structure was a kilometer, then two kilometers away. But nobody was interested in the view just then because all of Conway's attention was on Prilicla, and Murchison and Naydrad were watching him.

"Back there," the pathologist said suddenly, "you said that even Thornnastor could not cure Prilicla. Why did you say that?"

"Because there was nothing wrong with Prilicla," Conway said. He ignored Murchison's unladylike gape of surprise and Naydrad's wildly undulating fur and spoke to the empath. "Isn't that so, little friend?"

"I think so, friend Conway," Prilicla said, speaking for the first time since coming on board. "Certainly there is nothing wrong with me now. But I am confused."

"*You're* confused!" Murchison began, and stopped because Conway was again at the communicator.

"Captain," he said, "return at once to Lock Nine to take on another patient. Switch on all of your exterior lighting and ignore the traffic instructions. And please patch me through to Level One Six Three, the EGCL's recovery room. Quickly."

"Right," the Captain coldly said, "but I want an explanation."

"You'll get one—" Conway began. He broke off as the Captain's angry features were replaced by a view of the recovery room with the attending nurse, a Kelgian, curled like a furry question mark beside the EGCL. Its report on the patient's condition was brief, accurate, and, to Conway, terrifying.

He broke contact and returned to the Captain. Apologetically he said, "There isn't much time so I would like you to listen while I explain the situation, or what I think is the situation, to the others here. I had intended that the lander be fitted with remote-controlled medical servomechs and used as an isolation unit, but there isn't time for that now. The EGCL is waking up. All hell could break loose in the hospital at any minute."

Quickly he explained his theory about the EGCL and the reasoning which had led to it, ending with the proof which was Prilicla's otherwise inexplicable recovery.

"The part of this which bothers me," he concluded grimly, "is having to subject Prilicla to the same degree of emotional torture once again."

The empath's limbs trembled at the remembered pain, but it said, "I can accept it, friend Conway, now that I know the condition will be temporary."

But removing the EGCL was not as easy as had been the abduction of Prilicla. The Kelgian duty nurse was disposed to argue, and it took all of Naydrad's powers of persuasion and the combined ranks of Murchison and Conway to make it do as it was told. And while they were arguing, Conway could see the wildly rippling and twitching fur of the two nurses, the sudden, almost manic changes of facial expression in Murchison, and the emotional overreaction in all of them, in spite of his earlier warning of what would happen if they did not control their feelings. By the time the transfer of the patient to *Rhabwar's* litter was underway, so much fuss had been created that someone was sure to report it. Conway did not want that.

The patient was coming to. There was no time to go through proper channels, no time for long and repeated explanations. Then suddenly he had to find time, because both Edanelt and O'Mara were in the room. It was the Chief Psychologist who spoke first.

"*Conway!* What do you think you're doing with that patient?"

"I'm kidnapping it!" Conway snapped back sarcastically. Quickly he went on, "I'm sorry, sir, we are all overreacting. We can't help it, but try hard to be calm. Edanelt, will you help me transfer the EGCL's support systems to the litter. There isn't much time left so I'll have to explain while we work."

The Melfan Senior dithered for a moment, the tapping of its six crablike legs against the floor reflecting its indecision, then it spoke. "Very well, Conway. But if I am not satisfied with your explanation the patient stays here."

"Fair enough," said Conway. He looked at O'Mara, whose face was showing the indications of a suddenly elevated blood pressure, and went on, "You had the right idea at the beginning, but everyone was too busy to talk to you. It should have occurred to me, too, if the GLNO tape and concern for Prilicla hadn't confused me by—"

"Omit the flattery and excuses, Conway," O'Mara broke in, "and get on with it."

Conway was helping Murchison and Naydrad lift the EGCL into the litter while Edanelt and the other nurse checked the siting of the biosensors. Without looking up he went on, "Whenever we encounter a new intelligent species the first thing we are supposed to ask ourselves is how it got that way. Only the dominant life-form on a planet has the opportunity, the security and leisure, to develop a civilization capable of interstellar travel."

At first Conway had not been able to see how the EGCL's people had risen to dominance on their world, how they had fought their way to the top of their evolutionary tree. They had no physical weapons of offense, and their snaillike apron of muscle which furnished locomotion was incapable of moving them fast enough to avoid natural enemies. Their carapace was a defense of sorts in that it protected vital organs, but that osseus shell was mounted high on the body, making it top-heavy and an easy prey for any predator who had only to topple it over to get at the soft underside. Its manipulatory appendages were flexible and dexterous, but too short and lightly muscled to be a deterrent. On their home world the EGCLs should have been one of nature's losers. They were not, however, and there had to be a reason.

It had come to him slowly, Conway went on, while he was moving through the chlorine and light-gravity sections. In every ward there had been cases of patients with known and properly diagnosed ailments displaying, or at least complaining about, atypical symptoms. The demand for painkilling medication had been unprecedented. Conditions which should have caused a minor degree of discomfort were, it seemed, inflicting severe pain. He had been aware of some of this pain himself, but had put that down to a combination of his imagination and the effect of the Cinrusskin tape.

He had already considered and discarded the idea that the trouble was psychosomatic because the condition was too wide-spread, but then he thought about it again.

During their return from the disaster site with the sole sur-viving EGCL, everyone had felt understandably low about the mission's lack of success and because Prilicla was giving cause for concern. But in retrospect there was something wrong, unprofessional, about their reactions. They were feeling things too strongly, overreacting, developing in their own fashions the same kind of hypersensitivity which had affected Prilicla and which had affected the patients and staff on the Illensan and the Nallajim levels. Conway had felt it himself; the vague stomach pains, the discomfort in hands and fingers, the ov-erexcitability in circumstances which did not warrant it. But the effect had diminished with distance, because when he vis-ited O'Mara's office for the GLNO tape and later for the era-sure, he had felt normal and unworried except for the usual degree of concern over a current case, accentuated in this in-stance because the patient was Prilicla.

The EGCL was receiving the best possible attention from Thornnastor and Edanelt, so it was not on his mind to any large extent. Conway had been sure of that.

"But then I began to think about its injuries," Conway went on, "and the way I had felt on the ship and within three levels of the EGCL operation. In the hospital while I had the GLNO tape riding me, I was an empath without empathy. But I seemed to be feeling things—emotions, pains, conditions which did not belong to me. I thought that, because of fatigue and the stress of that time, I was generating sympathetic pains. Then it occurred to me that if the type of discomfort being suffered by the EGCL were subtracted from the symptoms of the medics and patients on those six levels and the intensity of the discomfort reduced, then the affected patients and staff would be acting and reacting normally. This seemed to point toward—"

"An empath!" O'Mara said. "Like Prilicla."

"*Not* like Prilicla," Conway said firmly. "Although it is possible that the empathic faculty possessed by the preintelligent ancestors of both species was similar."

But their prehistoric world was an infinitely more dangerous place than Cinruss had been, Conway continued, and in any case the EGCLs lacked the ability of the Cinrusskins quite literally to fly from danger. And in such a savage environment there was little advantage in having an empathic faculty other than as a highly unpleasant early warning system, and so the ability to receive emotions had been lost. It was probable that they no longer received even the emotional radiation of their own kind.

They had become organic transmitters, reflectors and focusers and magnifiers of their own feelings and those of the beings around them. The indications were that the faculty had evolved to the stage where they had no conscious control over the process.

"Think of the defensive weapon that makes," Conway explained. The EGCL's life support and sensors had been transferred to the litter and it was ready to leave. "If a predator tries to attack it, the anger and hunger it feels for its victim together with the fear and pain, if the victim was hurt or wounded, would be magnified, bounced back, and figuratively hit the attacker in the teeth. I can only guess at the order of emotional amplification used. But the effect on the predator, especially if there were others in the vicinity whose feelings were also being amplified, would be discouraging to say the least, also very confusing. It might have the effect of having them attack each other.

"We already know the effect of a deeply unconscious EGCL on the patients and staff three levels above and below this one," Conway went on grimly. "Now consciousness is returning and I don't know what will happen, or how far-reaching the effect will be. We have to get it away from here before the hospital's patients have their own as well as the EGCL's pain magnified to an unknown but major degree, and their medical attendants thrown into a steadily accelerating state of disorder and panic because they, too, will receive the reflected pain and—"

He broke off and tried to control his own growing panic, then he said harshly, "We have to get it away from the hospital now, without further delays or arguments."

O'Mara's face had lost its angry red coloration while Conway had been talking, until now it looked gray and bloodless. He said, "Don't waste time talking, Doctor. I shall accompany you. There will be no further delays or arguments."

When they reached *Rhabwar's* Casualty Deck the EGCL was still not fully conscious and Prilicla was again being seriously affected by the ambient emotional radiation which was being amplified and bounced off their patient. The discomfort diminished sharply with increasing distance from the hospital, the empath told them, and the awakening EGCL was radiating only a relatively low intensity of discomfort from the sites of the recent surgery—but Prilicla did not have to tell them that because they could all feel it for themselves.

"I have been thinking about the problem of communicating with these people," O'Mara said thoughtfully. "If they are all high-powered transmitters and reflectors of emotional radiation, they may not be aware of what they are doing, only that they have an automatic, nonmaterial defense against everything and everyone wishing them harm. The job of establishing communications with them may not be easy and is likely to be a long-range affair, unless our basic premise is wrong and we—"

"My first idea," Conway broke in, "was to put it in the lander with remote-controlled medical servomechs. Then I thought there should be one medic, a volunteer, inattendance—"

"I won't ask who," O'Mara said dryly, and smiled as Conway's embarrassment bounced off the EGCL and hit them.

"—because if ever there was case demanding isolation," Conway ended, "this is it."

The Chief Psychologist nodded. "What I had been about to say was that we may have miscalculated. Certainly we could never treat EGCLs in hospital where the patients surrounding them were in pain, even slight pain. But the situation here in the ship isn't too bad. I can feel pains in the equivalent sites to where the EGCL is hurting, but nothing I can't handle. And the rest of you are emoting concern for the patient, and this is not unpleasant even when magnified. It seems that if you don't think badly toward the patient, it can't bounce anything too unpleasant back at you. It's surprising. I feel just the way I always do, except more so."

"But it is regaining consciousness," Conway protested. "There should be an intensification of—"

"There isn't," O'Mara cut in. "That is very obvious, Conway. Could the reason be *because* the patient is regaining consciousness? Think about it. Yes, Doctor, we can all feel you feeling 'Eureka!'"

"Of *course*!" Conway said, and paused because his pleasure and excitement at seeing the answer, magnified by the EGCL, was causing Prilicla's wings to go into the series of slow, rippling undulations which indicated intense pleasure in a Cinrusskin. It also counteracted the aches which he and everyone else were feeling from the pateint. He thought, *What a weird experience the cultural contact specialists were going to have with this species.*

Aloud he said, "The process of reflecting and magnifying the feelings, hostile or otherwise, of the people around them is a defense mechanism which would, naturally, be at its most effective when the being is helpless, vulnerable, or unconscious. With a return to consciousness the effect seems to diminish but the empathic reflections are still strong. The result is that everyone around them will have an empathic faculty not unlike Prilicla's, and yet the EGCLs are deaf to each other's emotional radiation because they are transmitters only.

"Being like Prilicla," he went on, looking across at the empath, "is something of a mixed blessing. But the EGCL would be a nice person to have around if we were having a good time—"

"Control here," the voice of the Captain broke in. "I have some information on your patient's species. Federation Archives have signaled the hospital to the effect that this race—their name for themselves is the Duwetz—was contacted briefly by an exploring Hudlar ship before the formation of the Galactic Federation. Enough information was obtained for the basic Duwetz language to be programmed into the present-day translation computers, but contact was severed because of serious psychological problems among the crew. We are advised to proceed with caution."

"The patient," Prilicla said suddenly, "is awake."

Conway moved closer to the EGCL and tried to think positive, reassuring thoughts toward it. He noted with relief that the biosensors and associated monitors were indicating a weak but stable condition; that the damaged lung was again working satisfactorily and the bandages immobilizing the two rejoined appendages were firmly in position. The extensive suturing on the muscular apron and ambulatory pad at the base were well up to Thornnastor and Edanelt's high standards, as were the deftly inserted staples which gleamed in neat rows where the carapace fractures had been. Obviously the being was in considerable discomfort in spite of the painkilling medication Thonnastor had synthesized for its particular metabolism. But pain was not the predominant feeling it was transmitting, and fear and hostility were entirely absent.

Two of its three remaining eyes swiveled to regard them while the other one was directed toward the viewport where Sector Twelve General Hospital, now almost eight kilometers distant, blazed like some vast, surrealistic piece of jewelry against the interstellar darkness. The feelings which washed through them, so intensely that they trembled or caught their breaths or rippled their fur, were of curiosity and wonder.

"I'm not an organ mechanic like you people," O'Mara said gruffly, "but I would say that with this case the prognosis is favorable."

INVESTIGATION

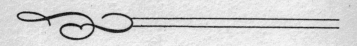

THE ambulance ship *Rhabwar* had mad the trip from Sector General to the scene of the supposed disaster in record time and with a precision of astrogation, Conway thought, which would cause Lieutenant Dodds to exhibit symptoms of cranial swelling for many days to come. But as the information was displayed on the Casualty Deck's repeater screens, it became clear to the watching medical team that this was not going to be a fast rescue—that this might not, in fact, be a rescue mission at all.

The fully extended sensor net revealed no sign of a distressed ship, nor any wreckage or components of such a ship. Even the finely divided, expanding cloud of debris which would have indicated a catastrophic malfunction in the veseel's reactor was missing. All there was to be seen was the characteristic shape of a dead and partially fused distress beacon at a distance of a few hundred meters and, about three million kilometers beyond it, the bright crescent shape which was one of this systems planets.

Major Fletcher's voice came from the speaker. The Captain did not sound pleased. "Doctor," he said. "We cannot assume

that this was a simple false alarm. Hyperspace radio distress
beacons are highly expensive hunks of machinery for one thing,
and I have yet to hear of an intelligent species who does not
have an aversion to crying their equivalent of wolf. I think the
crew must have panicked, then discovered that the condition
of the ship was not as distressed as they at first thought. They
may have resumed their journey or tried for a planetary landing
to effect repairs. We'll have to eliminate the latter possibility
before we leave. Dodds?"

"The system has been surveyed," the Astrogator's voice
replied. "G-type sun, seven planets with one, the one we can
see, habitable in the short term by warm-blooded oxygen
breathers. No indigenous intelligent life. Course for a close
approach and search, sir?"

"Yes," Fletcher said. "Haslam, pull in your long-range sensors and set up for a planetary surface scan. Lieutenant Chen,
I'll need impulse power, four Gs, on my signal. And Haslam,
just in case the ship is down and trying to signal its presence,
monitor the normal and hyperradio frequencies."

A few minutes later they felt the deck press momentarily
against their feet as the artifical gravity system compensated
for the four-G thrust. Conway, Pathologist Murchison, and
Charge Nurse Naydrad moved closer to the repeater where
Dodds had displayed the details of the target planet's gravity
pull, atmospheric composition and pressure, and the environmental data which made it just barely habitable. The empathic
Doctor Prilicla clung to the safety of the ceiling and observed
the screen at slightly longer range.

It was the Charge Nurse, its silvery fur rippling in agitation,
who spoke first. "This ship isn't supposed to land on unprepared
surfaces," Naydrad said. "That ground is—is rough."

"Why couldn't they have stayed in space like good little
distressed aliens," Murchison said to nobody in particular, "and
waited to be rescued?"

Conway looked at her and said thoughtfully, "It is possible
that their condition of distress was nonmechanical. Injury, sick-
ness, or psychological disturbances among the crew, perhaps,
problems which have since been resolved. If it was a physical
problem then they should have stayed out here, since it is easier
to effect repairs in weightless conditions."

"Not always, Doctor," Fletcher's voice cut in sharply from

the Control Deck. "If the physical problem was a badly holed hull, a breathable atmosphere around them might seem more desirable than weightless and airless space. No doubt you have medical preparations to make."

Conway felt a surge of anger at the other's thinly veiled suggestion that he tend to his medical knitting and stop trying to tell the Captain his business. Beside him Murchison was breathing heavily and Naydrad's fur was tufting and rippling as if blown by a strong wind, while above them the emotion-sensitive Prilicla's six insectile legs and iridescent wings quivered in the emotional gale they were generating. Out of consideration for the empath, Conway tried to control his feelings, as did the others.

It was understandable that Fletcher, the ship's commander, liked to have the last word, but he knew and accepted the fact that on Sector General's special ambulance ship he had to relinquish command to the senior medic, Conway, during the course of a rescue. Fletcher was a good officer, able, resourceful, and one of the Federation's top men in the field of comparative extraterrestrial technology. But there were times during the short period while responsibility was being passed to Senior Physician Conway when his manner became a trifle cool, formal—even downright nasty.

Prilicla's trembling diminished and the little empath tried to say something which would further improve the quality of the emotional radiation around it. "If the lately distressed vessel has landed on this planet," it said timidly, "then we know that the crew belongs to one of the oxygen-breathing species and the preparations to receive casualties, if any, will be relatively simple."

"That's true," Conway said, laughing.

"Only thirty-eight different species fall into that category," Murchison said, and added dryly, "that we know of."

Rhabwar's sensors detected a small concentration of metal and associated low-level radiation, which on an uninhabited planet could only mean the presence of a grounded ship, while they were still two diameters out. As a result they were able to decelerate and enter atmosphere for a closer look after only two orbits.

The ambulance ship was a modified Monitor Corps cruiser

and, as such, the largest of the Federation vessels capable of aerodynamic maneuvering in atmosphere. It sliced through the brown, sand-laden air like a great white dart, trailing a sonic shockwave loud enough to wake the dead or, at the very least, to signal its presence to any survivors capable of receiving audio stimulus.

Visibility was nil as they approached the grounded ship. The whole area was in the grip of one of the sandstorms which regularly swept this harsh, near-desert world, and the picture of the barren, mountainous surface was a sensor simulation rather than direct vision. It accurately reproduced the succession of wind-eroded hills and rocky outcroppings and the patches of thorny vegetation which clung to them. Then suddenly they were above and past the grounded ship.

Fletcher pulled *Rhabwar* into a steep climb which became a ponderous loop as they curved back for a slower pass over the landing site. This time, as they flew low over the other ship at close to stalling speed, there was a brief cessation in the storm and they were able to record the scene in near-perfect detail.

Rhabwar was climbing into space again when the Captain said, "I can't put this ship down anywhere near that area, Doctor. I'm afraid we'll have to check for survivors, if there are any, with the planetary lander. There aren't any obvious signs of life from the wreck."

Conway studied the still picture of the crash site on his screen for a moment before replying. It was arguable whether the ship had made a heavy landing or a barely controlled crash. Much less massive than *Rhabwar*, it had been designed to land on its tail, but one of the three stabilizer fins had collapsed on impact, tipping the vessel onto its side. In spite of this the hull was relatively undamaged except for a small section amidships which had been pierced by a low ridge of rock. There was no visible evidence of damage other than that caused by the crash.

All around the wreck at distances varying from twenty to forty meters there were an number of objects—Conway counted twenty-seven of them in all—which the sensor identified as organic material. The objects had not changed position between the first and second of *Rhabwar's* thunderous fly-bys, so the probability was that they were either dead or deeply unconscious. Conway stepped up the magnification until the outlines became indistinct in the heat shimmer, and shook his head in bafflement.

The objects had been, or were, living creatures, and even though they had been partly covered by windblown sand, he could see a collection of protuberances, fissures, and angular projections which had to be sensory organs and limbs. There was a general similarity in shape but a marked difference in size of the beings, but he thought they were more likely to be representatives of different subspecies rather than adults and their young at different stages of development.

"Those life-forms are new to me," the pathologist said, standing back from the screen. She looked at Conway and the others in turn. There was no dissent.

Conway thumbed the communicator button. "Captain,"he said briskly, "Murchison and Naydrad will go down with me. Prilicla will remain on board to receive casualties." Normally that would have been the Kelgian Charge Nurse's job, but nobody there had to be told that the fragile little empath would last for only a few minutes on the surface before being blown away and smashed against the rocky terrain. He went on, "I realize that four people on the lander will be a tight squeeze, but initially I'd like to take a couple of pressure litters and the usual portable equipment—"

"One large pressure litter, Doctor," Fletcher broke in. "There will be five people on board. I am going down as well in case there are technical problems getting into the wreck. You're forgetting that if the life-forms are new to the Federation, then their spaceship technology could be strange as well. Dodds will fetch anything else you need on the next trip down. Can you be ready at the lander bay in fifteen minutes?"

"We'll be there," Conway said, smiling at the eagerness in the other's voice. Fletcher wanted to look at the inside of that wrecked ship just as badly as Conway wanted to investigate the internal workings of its crew. And if there were survivors, *Rhabwar* would shortly be engaged in conducting another medical first contact with all the hidden problems, both clinical and cultural, which that implied.

Fletcher's eagerness was underlined by the fact that he rather than Dodds took the vehicle down and landed it in a ridiculously small area of flat sand within one hundred meters of the wreck. From the surface the wind-eroded rock outcroppings looked higher, sharper, and much more dangerous, but the sandstorm had died down to a stiff breeze which lifted the grains no more than a few feet above the ground. From the orbiting *Rhabwar*, Haslam reported occasional wind flurries passing through their area which might briefly inconvenience them.

One of the flurries struck while they were helping Naydrad unload the litter, a bulky vehicle whose pressure envelope was capable of reproducing the gravity, pressure, and atmosphere requirements of most of the known life-forms. Gravity nullifiers compensated for the litter's considerable weight, making it easily manageable by one person, but when the sudden wind caught it, Naydrad, Dodds, and Conway had to throw themselves across it to keep it from blowing away.

"Sorry about this," Lieutenant Dodds said, as if by studying the available information on the planet he was somehow responsible for its misdemeanors. "It is about two hours before local midday here, and the wind usually dies down by now. It remains calm until just before sunset, and again in the middle of the night when there is a severe drop in temperature. The sandstorms after sunset and before dawn are very bad and last for three to five hours, when outside work would be very dangerous. Work during the night lull is possible but inadvisable. The local animal life is small and omnivorous, but those thorn carpets on the slope over there have a degree of mobility and have to be watched, especially at night. I'd estimate five hours of daylight calm to complete the rescue. If it takes longer than that, it would be better to spend the night on *Rhabwar* and come back tomorrow."

As the Lieutenant was speaking, the wind died again so that they were able to see the wreck, the dark objects scattered around it, and the harsh, arid landscape shimmering in the heat. Five hours should be more than enough to ferry up the casualties to *Rhabwar* for preliminary treatment. Anything done for them down here would be done quickly, simple first aid.

"Did they bother to name this Godforsaken planet?" the Captain asked, stepping down from the lander's airlock.

Dodds hesitated, then said, "Trugdil, sir."

Fletcher's eyebrows rose, Murchison laughed, and they could

see agitated movements of Naydrad's fur under its lightweight suit. It was the Kelgian who spoke first.

"The trugdil," it said, "is a species of Kelgian rodent with the particularly nasty habit of—"

"I know," the astrogator said quickly. "But it was a Kelgian-crewed Monitor Corps scoutship which made the discovery. In the Corps it is customary for the Captain of the discovering ship to give his, her, or its name to the world which has been found. But in this instance the officer waived the right and offered it to his subordinates in turn, all of whom likewise refused to give their names to the planet. Judging by the name it ended with, they didn't think much of the place either. There was another case when—"

"Interesting," Conway said quietly, "but we're wasting time. Prilicla?"

Through his helmet phones, the empath's voice replied at once. "I hear you, friend Conway. Lieutenant Haslam is relaying an overall picture of the area to me through the telescope, and your helmet vision pickups enable me to see all that you see. Standing by."

"Very good," Conway said. To the others he went on, "Naydrad will accompany me with the litter. The rest of you split up and take a quick look at the other casualties. If any of them are moving, or there are indications of recent movement, call Pathologist Murchison or me at once."

As they moved off he added, "It is important that we don't waste time on cadavers at the expense of possible survivors. But be careful. This is a new life-form to us, and we are likewise strange to it. Physically we may resemble something it fears, and there is the added factor of the survivor being weak, in pain, and mentally confused. Guard against an instinctive, violent reaction from them which, in normal circumstances, would not occur." He stopped talking because the others were already fanning out and the first casualty, lying very still and partly covered by sand, was only a few meters away.

As Naydrad helped him scoop sand from around the body Conway saw that the being was six-limbed, with a stubby, cylindrical torso with a spherical head at one end and possibly a tail at the other extremity, although the severity of the injuries made it difficult to be sure. The two forelimbs terminated in long, flexible digits. There were two recognizable eyes, partially concealed by heavy lids, and various slits and orifices which were doubtless aural and olfactory sensors and the openings for respiration and ingestion. The tegument, which was pale brown shading to a deeper, reddish color on its top surface, showed many incised wounds and abrasions which had bled freely but had since congealed and become encrusted with sand—perhaps the sand had assisted in the process of coagulation. Even the large wound at the rear, which looked as if it might be the result of a traumatic amputation, was remarkably dry.

Conway bent closer and began going over the body with his scanner. There was no evidence of fracturing or of damaged or displaced organs, so far as he could see, so the being could be moved without risk of complicating its injuries. Naydrad was waiting with the litter to see whether it was a survivor for immediate loading or a cadaver for later dissection, when Conway's scanner's sensors detected cardiac activity, extremely feeble but undoubtedly present, and respiration so slow and shallow that he had almost missed it.

"Are you getting this, Prilicla?" he said.

"Yes, friend Conway," replied the empath. "A most interesting life-form."

"There is considerable tissue wastage," he went on, still using the scanner. "Possibly the result of dehydration. And there is a similarity in degree and type of the injuries which I find strange..." He trailed off into silence as Naydrad helped him lift the casualty into the litter.

"No doubt it has already occurred to you, friend Conway," Prilicla said, using the form of words which was the closest it ever came to suggesting that someone had missed the obvious, "that the dehydration and the deeper coloration on the upper areas of the epidermis may be connected with local environmental factors, and the redness is due to sunburn."

It had not occurred to Conway, but fortunately the emotional radiation associated with his embarrassment was well beyond the range of the empath. He indicated the litter and said, "Naydrad, don't forget to fit the sun filter."

In his phones he heard Murchison laughing quietly, then she said, "It hadn't occurred to me, either, so don't feel bad about it. But I have a couple of beasties over here I'd like you to look at. Both are alive, just barely, with a large number of incised wounds. There is a great disparity in mass between them, and the arrangement of the internal organs in the large one is, well, peculiar. For instance, the alimentary canal is—"

"Right now," Conway broke in, "we must concentrate on separating the living and the dead. Detailed examinations and discussions will have to wait until we're back on the ship, so spend as little time as possible on each one. But I know how you feel—my casualty has some peculiarities as well."

"Yes, Doctor," she replied coldly, in spite of his half apology. Pathologists, even beautiful ones like Murchison, he thought, were strange people.

"Captain? Lieutenant Dodds?" he said irritably. "Any other survivors?"

"I haven't been looking at them closely, Doctor," Fletcher replied. There was an odd harshness in his voice. Possibly the condition of the crash victims was distressing to a nonmedical man, Conway thought, and some of these casualties were in really bad shape. But before he could reply the Captain went on, "I've been moving around the area quickly, counting them and looking to see if any have been covered by sand or hidden between rocks. There are twenty-seven of them in all. But the positioning of the bodies is odd, Doctor. It's as if the ship was in imminent danger of blowing up or catching fire, and they used the last of their remaining strength to escape from it.

"The sensors show no such danger," he added.

Dodds waited for a few seconds to be sure that the Captain had finished speaking, then said, "Three alive and showing slight movement. One that looks dead, but you're the doctor, Doctor."

"Thank you," Conway said dryly. "We'll look at them as soon as possible. Meanwhile, Lieutenant, help Naydrad load the litter, please."

He joined Murchison then, and for the next hour they moved among the casualties, assessing the degree of injury and readying them for transfer to the lander. The litter was almost full and had space for two of the medium-sized casualties, which they had tentatively classified as belonging to physiological type DCMH, or one of the large DCOJs. The very small DCLGs, which were less than half the mass of the DCMH Conway had first examined, were left for the time being because they all showed flickerings of life. As yet neither Murchison nor Conway could make sense of them physiologically. She thought the small DCLGs might be nonintelligent lab animals or possibly ship's pets, while Conway was convinced that the large DCOJs were food animals, also nonintelligent. But with newly discovered extra-terrestrial life-forms, one could never be sure of anything, and all of them would therefore have to be treated as patients.

Then they found one of the small aliens who was quite definitely dead. Murchison said briskly, "I'll work on it in the lander. Give me fifteen minutes and I'll have something to tell Prilicla about their basal metabolism before the casualties begin arriving."

A flurry of wind blew the sand disturbed by her feet ahead of her as she moved toward the lander, the small cadaver supported by her shoulder and one arm while the other hand, carrying her med kit, acted as a counterbalance. Conway was about to suggest that a proper examination on *Rhabwar*, where the full laboratory facilities were available, would be better. But Murchison would already have considered doing that and decided against it, for two obvious reasons: If she returned to the ambulance ship with Dodds and Naydrad, some of the casualties already loaded would have to be left behind, and she needed to tell Prilicla only enough for the empath to provide emergency surgery and supportive treatment until the survivors were taken to Sector General.

"Captain, you overheard?" Conway said. "I'd like Dodds and Naydrad to take off as soon as Pathologist Murchison is through. It looks as if three trips will be necessary to lift all of them, and another for ourselves. We're going to be pushed for time if this is to be wrapped up before the sunset storm hits the area."

There was no reply from Fletcher, which usually signified assent when Conway was in command. He went on, "Murchison will stay behind and assemble another batch of casualties for the next lift. We'll collect them where there is shelter from the sun and sand. The lee side of the wreck would do, or better still, inside it if there isn't too much debris."

"No, Doctor," the Captain said. "I'm worried about what we might find on that ship."

Conway did not reply, but the sigh he gave as he continued his examination of the casualty he was working on made his impatience clear. Fletcher was one of the Monitor Corps' acknowledged experts in the field of alien ship technology. This was the reason he had been given command of Sector General's most advanced ambulance ship—it had long been recognized that a rescue mission's greatest danger was to the rescuers, who would be looking for survivors in a distressed vessel whose technology and operating principles they did not understand. Fletcher was careful, conscientious, highly competent, and did not as a rule worry out loud about his work or ability to carry it out. Conway was still wondering about the Captain's uncharacteristic behavior when a shadow fell across the casualty he was examining.

Fletcher was standing over him and looking as worried as he had sounded. "I realize, Doctor," the Captain said awkwardly, "that during rescue operations you have the rank. I want you to know that I go along with this willingly. But on this occasion I believe the circumstances are such that complete authority should revert to me." He glanced back at the wreck and then down at the badly injured alien. "Doctor, do you have any experience in forensic medicine?"

Conway sat back on his haunches and simply gaped at him. Fletcher took a deep breath and went on. "The distribution and condition of the casualties around the wreck seemed wrong to me," he said seriously. "It indicated a rapid evacuation of a relatively undamaged ship, even though our sensors showed no radiation or fire hazard. As well, all of the casualties were severely injured to varying degrees and with the same type of wounding. It seemed to me that some of them would have been able to make a greater distance from their ship than others, yet all of them collapsed within a relatively small radius from the wreck. This made me wonder whether the injuries had been sustained inside the ship or close to where they were lying."

"A local predator," Conway said, "which attacked them as

they came out already shocked and weakened as a result of the crash."

The Captain shook his head. "No life-form capable of inflicting such injuries inhabits this world. Most of the injuries I've seen are incised wounds or those caused by the removal of a limb. This suggests the use of a sharp instrument of some kind. The user of the instrument may or may not be still on board the ship. If it is on board, it may be that the beings who escaped were the lucky ones, in which case I hate to think of what we may find inside the wreck. But you can see now why I must resume overall responsibility, Doctor.

"The Monitor Corps is the Federation's law-enforcement arm," he concluded quietly. "It seems to me that a very serious crime has been committed, and I am a policeman first and an ambulance driver second."

Before Conway could reply, Murchison said, "The condition of this cadaver, and the other casualties I've examined, does not preclude such a possibility."

"Thank you, ma'am," the Captain said. "That is why I want the medical team back on *Rhabwar* while Dodds and I arrest this criminal. If things go wrong, Chen and Haslam can get you back to the hospital—"

"Haslam, sir," the Communications Officer's voice broke in. "Shall I request Corps assistance?"

The Captain did not reply at once, and Conway began thinking that the other's theory could very well explain why a previously undamaged ship had released a distress beacon and then left the scene to try for a planetary landing. Something had gotten loose among the crew, perhaps. Something which might have been confined had escaped, something very, very nasty. With an effort Conway brought his runaway imagination under control. "We can't be absolutely sure that a criminal was responsible for this. A nonintelligent experimental animal which broke loose, injured and perhaps maddened with pain, could have done—"

"Animals use teeth and claws, doctor," the Captain broke in. "Not knives."

"This is a completely new species," Conway replied. "We don't know anything about them, their culture or their codes of behavior. They may be ignorant of our particular laws."

"Ignorance of the law," Fletcher said impatiently, "has never been an acceptable excuse for committing a criminal act against another intelligent being. Just as ignorance of law by the innocent victim does not exclude the being concerned from its protection."

"I agree—" Conway began. "But I am not completely sure that a crime has been committed," he went on. "Until I am sure, you, Haslam, will not send for help. But keep a close watch on this area and if anything moves, apart from the survivors or ourselves, let me know at once. Very soon Dodds will be taking off with the lander and—"

"Naydrad and the casualties," Murchison ended for him. Quietly but firmly she went on, "Your theory scares hell out of me, Captain, but it is still only a theory. You've admitted as much yourself. The facts are that there are a large number of casualties all around us. They don't know it yet but they are entitled to the protection of Federation law. Whether their injuries are due to the crash or to being carved up by some psychopathic or temporarily deranged alien, they are also entitled, under that same law, to all necessary medical assistance."

The Captain looked toward the lander where the Pathologist was still working on the specimen, then back to the Doctor.

"I've nothing to add," Conway said.

Fletcher remained silent while Murchison completed her investigation and Dodds and Naydrad transferred two casualties into the lander. He did not speak while the vehicle was taking off or when Conway selected a spot under a large outcropping of rock which would give waiting casualties shelter from the sun and windblown sand. Neither did he offer to help them carry the injured e-ts to the assembly point even though, without the litter, it was hot, back-breaking work. Instead he moved among the e-ts with his vision pickup, recording them individually before and after the ground had been disturbed around them by Murchison and Conway, and always positioning himself between the two medics and the wreck.

Plainly the Captain was taking his strange, new role as a policeman and protector of the innocent bystanders very seriously indeed.

The cooling unit in his suit did not seem to be working very well and Conway would have loved to open his visor for a few minutes. But doing that, even in the shelter of the outcropping, would have meant letting in a lot of windblown sand.

"Let's rest for a while," he said as they placed another casualty beside its fellows. "Time we had a talk with Prilicla."

"That is a pleasure at any time, friends Murchison and Conway," the empath said promptly. "While I am, of course, beyond the range of the emotional radiation being generated down there, I sympathize and hope that your feelings of anxiety about the criminal are not too unpleasant."

"Our feelings of bewilderment are much stronger," Conway said dryly. "But maybe you can help relieve them by going over our information, incomplete as it is, before the first casualties reach you."

There was still a little doubt about the accuracy of the physiological classifications, Conway explained, but there were three separate but related types—DCLG, DCMH, and DCOJ. The wounds fell into two general categories, incised and abraded wounds which could have resulted when the ship's occupants were hurled against sharp-edged metal during the crash, and a traumatic amputation of major limbs which was so prevalent among the casualties that an explanation other than the crash was needed to explain them.

All of the survivors had body temperatures significantly greater than the norm for warm-blooded oxygen breathers, indicating a high metabolic rate and a hyperactive life-form. This was supported by the uniformly deep state of unconsciousness displayed by all of the casualties, and the evidence of dehydration and malnutrition. Beings who burned up energy rapidly rarely lingered in a semiconscious state. There were also signs that the beings had an unusual ability to control bleeding from severe wounds. Coagulation in the incised wounds, perhaps assisted by the presence of the sand, was rapid but not abnormally so, while the stumps at the amputation sites showed little evidence of bleeding.

"Supportive treatment to relieve the dehydration and malnutrition is all that can be done until we get them to the hospital," Conway went on. "Murchison has already specified the nutrients suited to their metabolism. You can also insert sutures as you see fit. If the load is too great for you, which in my opinion it is, retain Naydrad and send down only the pilot with the litter. Murchison can ride with the casualties on the next trip. She will stay with you while Naydrad comes down for the last batch."

There was a moment's silence, then the empath said, "I understand, friend Conway. But have you considered the fact that your suggestion will mean three members of the medical team being on *Rhabwar* for a lengthy period and only one, yourself, on the surface where medical assistance is most urgently needed? I am sure that, with the aid of the Casualty Deck's handling devices and the assistance of friends Haslam and Chen, I can cope with these patients."

It was possible that Prilicla could cope with the patients provided they remained unconscious. But if they came to suddenly and reacted instinctively to their strange and, to them, perhaps frightening surroundings, and to the giant but incredibly fragile insect medic hovering over them, Conway shuddered to think of what might happen to the empath's eggshell body and pipestem limbs. Before he could reply, Prilicla was speaking again.

"I am beyond the range of your emotional radiation, of course," the empath said, "but from long contact with the both of you I know of the strength of the emotional bond between friend Murchison and yourself. This, taking into account the strong possibility that there is a very dangerous life-form loose down there, is undoubtedly a factor in your decision to send her to the safety of the ship. But perhaps friend Murchison would suffer less emotional discomfort if she remained with you."

Murchison looked up from the casualty she was attending. "Is that what you were thinking?"

"No," Conway lied.

She laughed and said, "You heard that, Prilicla? He is a person utterly lacking in consideration and sensitivity. I should have married someone like you."

"I am highly complimented, friend Murchison," the empath said. "But you have too few legs."

There was the sound of Fletcher clearing his throat disapprovingly at this sudden and unseemly levity, but the Captain did not speak. He could no doubt appreciate as well as any of them the need to relieve fear tensions.

"Very well," Conway said. "Pathologist Murchison will remain with her feet, and too few legs, on Trugdil. Doctor Prilicla, you will keep Charge Nurse Naydrad with you, since it will obviously be of greater assistance in preparing and presenting the casualties for examination and treatment than would the Engineer and Communications officer. Haslam or Dodds can return with the litter and medical supplies which we will specify later. Questions?"

"No questions, friend Conway," Prilicla said. "The lander is docking now."

Murchison and Conway returned their full attention to the casualties. The Captain was examining the hull of the wreck. They could hear him tapping at the outer skin and making the metallic scraping noises characteristic of magnetic sound sensors being moved across the surfaces. The wind kept changing direction so that the casualties in the shadow of the outcropping were sheltered only from the sun and not the wind-driven sand.

From *Rhabwar* Haslam reported that the area was being affected by a small, local sandstorm which should clear before the lander returned in half an hour. He added reassuringly that nothing was moving in the area except themselves and several patches of ambulating thorn bushes, which would lose a race against a debilitated tortoise.

All but three of the casualties had been moved to the outcropping, and while Conway was bringing them in the pathologist was protecting the others from the wind and sand by loosely wrapping them in transparent plastic sheets after first attaching a small oxygen cylinder to each survivor. The tanks released a metered quantity of gas calculated to satisfy the metabolic requirements of the entity concerned. They had decided that encasing the casualties in makeshift oxygen tents could do no harm since the pure oxygen would assist the weak respiration and aid in the healing of the wounds, but with a completely new life-form one could never be sure of anything. Certainly the treatment showed no sign of returning any of the casualties to consciousness.

"The uniformly deep level of unconsciousness bothers me," Murchison said as Conway returned carrying, with difficulty, one of the large aliens they had classified as DCOJ. "The level does not bear any relation to the number or severity of the wounds. Could they be in a state of hibernation?"

"The onset was sudden," Conway said doubtfully. "They were in the process of fleeing their ship, according to the Captain. Hibernation usually occurs in a place of safety, not when the being concerned is in immediate physical danger."

"I was thinking of an involuntary form of hibernation," Murchison said, "perhaps induced by their injuries, which enables them to survive until help arrives—What was *that*?"

That was a loud, metallic screeching noise which came from the wreck. It lasted for a few seconds, then there was a moment's silence before it was repeated. They could hear heavy breathing in their suit phones so it had to be coming from Fletcher.

"Captain," Murchison said, "are you all right?"

"No trouble, ma'am," Fletcher replied at once. "I've found a hatch in what appears to be a cargo hold. It is, or was, a simple hermetically sealed door rather than an airlock. When the ship tipped over the door couldn't open fully because the outer edge dug into the sand, which I've now cleared away. The hatch opens freely now but the hinges were warped in the crash, as you probably heard. Two of the occupants were trying to escape, but couldn't squeeze through the narrow opening. They are one of the large- and one of the medium-sized types, both with amputation wounds, neither of them moving. Shall I bring them to you?"

"I'd better look at them first," Conway said. "Give me a few minutes to finish with this one."

As they were placing the last casualty inside its makeshift oxygen tent, Murchison said, "Have you found any trace of the criminal, Captain?"

"Other than the wounding on these two, no ma'am," Fletcher replied. "My sensors pick up no trace of bodily movement inside the ship, nothing but a few quiet, intermittent sounds suggesting settling debris. I'm pretty sure it is outside the ship somewhere."

"In that case," she said, looking at Conway, "I'll go with you."

The wind died and the sand settled as they neared the wreck

so that they could see clearly the black rectangular opening in
the hull just at ground level, and the arm of the Captain waving
at them from inside it. There were so many other openings
caused by sprung plating and access hatches that without Fletcher's signal they would not have known which gap was the right
one. From outside it looked as if the ship was ready to fall
apart, but when they crawled through the opening and stood
up their helmet lights showed little evidence of internal damage.

"How did the others get out?" Conway asked. He knelt and
began running his scanner over the larger of the two casualties.
There was evidence of a traumatic amputation of a major limb
but the other injuries were superficial.

"There is a large personnel hatch on the upper surface of
the hull forward," Fletcher replied. "At least it was on the
upper side after the ship toppled. Presumably they had to slide
down the curve of the hull and jump to the ground, or move
along the ship to the prow, which isn't very far from the ground,
and jump from there. These two were unlucky."

"One of them was very unlucky," Murchison said. "The
DCOJ is dead. Its injuries were not as severe as the other cases
I've seen, but there is evidence of lung damage by a corrosive
gas of some kind, according to my analyzer. What about your
DCMH?"

"This one is alive," Conway said. "Similar general condition, including the lung damage. Probably it is simply a much
tougher life-form than the other two."

"I wonder about this DCOJ life-form," Murchison said
thoughtfully. "Is it intelligent at all? The small DCLG and the
DCMH almost certainly are: The limb extremities terminate in
specialized manipulators, and the former seems to have developed six hands and no feet. But the big DCOJ has four feet
and two clawed forward appendages, and is otherwise made
up of teeth and a large system of stomachs."

"Which is empty," Conway said. After a moment he added,
"All of the cases I've examined so far had empty stomachs."

"Mine as well," Murchison said. They stared at each other
for a moment, then Conway said, "Captain."

Fletcher had been working on what seemed to be the inboard
entrance to the hold, reaching high above his head because he
was standing on a wall with the floor and ceiling on each side

of him. There was a loud click and a door swung downward and hung open. The Captain made a self-satisfied sound and joined them.

"Yes, Doctor."

Conway cleared his throat and said, "Captain, we have a theory about your criminal. We think that the condition of distress which caused this ship to release its beacon was hunger. All of the casualties we've examined so far have had empty stomachs. It is possible, therefore, that your criminal is a crew member who turned cannibal."

Before Fletcher could reply, the voice of Prilicla sounded in their phones.

"Friend Conway," the empath said timidly. "I have not yet examined all of the casualties you sent up, but those I have examined display symptoms of dehydration and tissue wastage indicative of hunger and thirst. But the condition is not far enough advanced for death to be imminent. Your hypothetical criminal must have attacked the other crew members before lack of food became a serious problem. The being was hungry but not starving to death. Are you sure that the creature is intelligent?"

"No," Conway said. "But if Murchison and I have missed it while examining the first of the casualties, and at that time we were more concerned with charting the injuries than in the contents, if any, of their stomachs, the beastie could be on *Rhabwar* now. So if you find a well-fed casualty, get Haslam and Chen to restrain it, quickly. The Captain has a professional interest in it."

"That I have," Fletcher said grimly. He was about to go on when Haslam, who had relieved Dodds as lander pilot, interrupted to say that he would be touching down in six minutes and would need help loading the litter.

By packing the litter and strapping casualties, sometimes two to a couch in the crew's positions, Haslam was able to lift just over half of the remaining survivors. There was no change in the condition of the remaining casualties. The shadow of the outcropping had lengthened, though the air was still warm; the sky remained clear and there was no wind. Murchison said that she could usefully spend the time until the lander returned investigating, so far as she was able with her portable equip-

ment, the large DCOJ cadaver they had left in the wreck. The
medium-sized DCMH survivor had gone up with Haslam.

It was obvious from the start that Fletcher found the dissection distasteful, and when Murchison told him that there
was enough light for the work from the helmet spots of Conway
and herself, he left quickly and began climbing among the
containers fastened to the now-vertical deck beside them. After
about fifteen minutes he reported that his scanner showed the
contents to be identical and, judging by the amount of packing
used, were almost certainly cargo rather than ship's stores. He
added that he intended moving into the corridor outside the
hold to explore, look for other casualties, and gather evidence.

"Do you have to do it now, Captain?" Murchison said worriedly, looking up. Conway turned to regard Fletcher, too, but
somehow his eyes did not rise above the level of the other's
waist and the weapon attached to it.

"Do you know, Captain," he said quietly, "you have been
wearing a sidearm ever since Rhabwar's first mission, and I've
barely noticed it? It was just a part of your uniform, like the
cap and insignia. Now it looks even more conspicuous than
your backpack."

Fletcher looked uncomfortable as he said, "We're taught
that the psychological effect of displaying a weapon is negligible among the law-abiding, but increases in direct proportion
to the guilt or harmful intentions of the criminal or potential
lawbreaker. However, the effect of my weapon was purely
psychological until Lieutenant Haslam brought down the charges
for it a few minutes ago." Defensively he added, "There was
no need to wear a loaded weapon on an ambulance ship, and
I'd no reason to believe that this would be a police operation."

Murchison laughed softly and returned to her work, and
Conway joined her. As the Captain turned to go, he said, "We
can't spend much time here, but I must make as full a report
as possible of the incident and all relevant circumstances. This
is a new species to the Federation, a different technology, and
the purpose of this ship might have a bearing on the case. Was
our criminal a responsible being, perhaps a captive, or an unintelligent animal? If it was intelligent was it deranged, and if
so why? And was the distressed condition of the ship and crew
a contributory factor? I know that it is difficult to conceive of

extenuating circumstances for grievous wounding and cannibalism, but until all the facts are known—"

He broke off and placed his sensor against the deck beside
him. A few seconds later he went on, "There is nothing other
than ourselves moving inside the wreck. I've left the outside
hatch open only a few inches. If anything tried to get in you
will have plenty of warning, either from the beastie itself forcing it open against the sand or from the sensors on *Rhabwar*.
I can get back to you in plenty of time in any case, so you
have nothing to worry about."

While they resumed the dissection they could follow every
step of the Captain's progress sternward, because he insisted
on verbally describing and amplifying the pictures he was sending up to Dodds. The corridor was low and not very roomy by
Earth-human standards, he reported. He had to crawl on hands
and knees and it would be difficult to turn around to come back
other than at an intersection. Cable looms and air or hydraulic
pipelines ran along the sidewalls of the corridor, and coarse-
mesh netting was attached to the floor and ceiling indicating
that the ship did not possess an artificial gravity system.

Aft of the compartment occupied by the medics there was
another cargo deck, and beyond that the unmistakable shapes
of the hyperdrive generators. Further aft the reactor and thrusters were sealed from him and heavily shielded, but the sensor
indications were that there had been a complete power shut-
down—probably an automatic safety measure built into the
design—when the ship had toppled. But he could detect a
residue of power in some of the corridor lines which he thought
might be associated with an emergency lighting circuit, and he
thought he had identified a light switch.

It was a light switch, he confirmed a few seconds later. A
large stretch of the corridor was illuminated. The lighting was
uncomfortably bright but his eyes were adjusting to it. He was
moving amidships.

They heard him pause outside their cargo hold, and suddenly
the lights came on all over the ceiling beside them. Conway
switched off his now-unnecessary helmet light.

"Thank you, Captain," he said, then continuing the discussion he had been having with Murchison, went on, "There is
capacity for a large brain in the cranium, but we cannot assume

that all of the available volume is used for cerebration. I don't
see how a beastie with four feet and two manipulators which
are little more than claws could be a tool user, much less a
crew member of a starship. And those teeth bother me. They
are certainly not those of a predator. In the distant past they
might have been fearsome natural weapons, but now their condition shows that they have not much to do."

Murchison nodded. "The stomach system is overlarge in
relation to the mass of the being," she said, "yet there is no
evidence of adipose or excess edible tissue which would be
present if it was an animal bred for food. And the stomach
resembles that of an Earth-type ruminant. The digestive system
is odd, too, but I'd have to work out the whole intake to
elimination cycle to make any sense out of it, and I can't do
that down here. I'd love to know what these things ate before
their food ran out."

"I'm passing a storage deck of some kind," Fletcher said at
that point. "It is divided into large racks with passages between
them. The racks are filled with containers of different colors
and sizes with funnellike dispensers at one end. There are
wastebins holding empties, and some of the full and empty
containers have spilled out into the corridor."

"May I have samples, please," Murchison said quickly, "of
both."

"Yes, ma'am," the Captain replied. "Considering the starved
condition of the survivors they are more likely to contain paint
or lubricant than food. But I expect you have to eliminate all
possibilities, like me. I am moving toward the next—Oh!"

Conway opened his mouth to ask what was happening but
the Captain forestalled him.

"I switched on the lighting for this section and found two
more casualties," he reported. "One is a DCMH, one of the
medium-sized ones, which was crushed by a buckled structural
member and certainly dead. The other is the small, DCLG life-
form, with one amputation wound, not moving. I'm fairly sure
that it's dead, too. This is the section of the ship which fell
across the outcropping when she tipped over.

"The internal structure is badly deformed," he went on,
"with sprung deck and wall plating all over the place. There
are also two large, wall-mounted cylinders which seem to have

been the reservoir for a hydraulic actuator system. Both have been ruptured and their connecting lines fractured, and there is a faint fog surrounding them as if some of the contents remains and is evaporating.

"Ahead the corridor is partly blocked by wreckage," he continued. "I can move it but there will be a lot of noise, so don't—"

"Captain," Conway broke in. "Can you please bring us the DCLG and a sample of the hydraulic fluid with the other samples as soon as you can." To Murchison he added, "I'd like to know if the lung damage is associated with that leakage. It would eliminate another possibility."

Fletcher sounded irritated at having to break off his investigation of the ship. He said shortly, "They'll be outside your hold entrance in ten minutes, Doctor."

By the time Conway had retrieved the samples the Captain had already returned to the midships section, but once again his investigation was interrupted, this time by Lieutenant Dodds.

"The lander is ready to leave, sir," the Astrogator said. There was a certain hesitancy in his voice as he went on, "I'm afraid there will be time for only one round trip before sunset, so would the Doctor and you decide which casualties should be lifted and which left there for retrieval tomorrow? With you three and Haslam on board just over half of the remaining casualties can be lifted, less if you bring up all portable equipment."

"I'm not leaving unattended casualties down here," Conway said firmly. "The drop in temperature and the sandstorms would probably finish them!"

"Maybe not," Murchison said thoughtfully. "If we have to leave some of them, and it seems we've no choice, we could cover them with sand. They have a high body temperature, the sand is a good insulator, and they are already sealed up with a self-contained oxygen supply."

"I've heard of doctors burying their mistakes," Conway began dryly, but Dodds broke in again.

"Sorry, there is a problem there, Ma'am," he said. "There are four large thorn patches moving toward the wreck. Slowly, of course, but we estimate their arrival just before midnight. According to my information the thorns are omnivorous and trap mobile prey by slowly encircling it, often at a distance, and allowing the animal to scratch itself on the thorns. These secrete a poison which is paralyzing or lethal, depending on the size of the prey and number of scratches. When the prey is immobilized the thorn clump inserts its roots and removes whatever nutrient material there is available.

"I don't think your buried casualties," he added grimly, "would survive till morning."

Murchison swore in very unladylike fashion, and Conway said, "We could move them into the hold here and seal the hatch. We would need heaters and a medical monitor and— I'm still not happy about leaving them unattended."

"Obviously this is something which will have to be carefully considered, Doctor," the Captain said. "Your casualties will not only have to be attended, they may have to be defended as well. Dodds, how long can you delay the launch?"

"Half an hour, sir," the Astrogator said. "Then allowing another half hour for the trip and at least an hour on the surface to load up and make provision for the other casualties. If the lander does not leave in two and a half hours there will be serious problems with the wind and sand during take-off."

"Very well," Fletcher said. "We should reach a decision in half an hour. Hold the lander until then."

But there was very little discussion and the decision was made, in spite of anything Murchison and Conway could say to the contrary, by the Captain. Fletcher stated that the two medics on Trugdil had done everything possible for the casualties and could do nothing further without the facilities of *Rhabwar*, except keep them under observation. The Captain insisted that he was capable of doing that, and of defending them in case they were attacked again.

He was sure that the criminal responsible for their injuries was not currently on the ship, but it might return to the shelter of the wreck when the cold and the sandstorms returned, or even to escape the advancing thorn clumps. He added that the proper place for all of the medical team was on *Rhabwar* where the casualties there could be given proper attention.

"Captain," Conway said angrily, unable to refute his arguments, "in the medical area I have complete authority."

"Then why don't you exercise it responsibly, Doctor?" Fletcher replied.

"Captain," Murchison broke in quickly, trying to head off an argument which could sour relations on the ambulance ship for weeks to come. "The DCLG specimen you found was not badly injured, compared with some of the others, but it was defunct, I'm afraid. Severe inflammation of the breathing passages and massive lung damage similar to the one you found in the hold. Both sets of lungs contained traces of the sample you took from the hydraulic reservoir. That is lethal stuff, Captain, so don't open your visor anywhere near a leak."

"Thank you, ma'am, I won't," Fletcher said calmly, and went on, "Dodds, you can see that the stretch of corridor ahead has been crushed almost flat. There is enough space for crew members to squeeze through, but I will have to cut away a lot of this jagged metal—"

Conway switched off his radio and touched his helmet against Murchison's so that they could speak privately. He said furiously, "Whose side are you on?"

She grinned at him through her visor, but before she could reply Prilicla's voice rustled timidly from the phones. The empath, too, was trying to calm a potentially unpleasant source of emotional radiation.

"Friend Conway," it said, "while friend Fletcher's arguments are valid, and I would personally welcome the presence of friend Murchison and yourself back on board, friend Naydrad and myself are coping adequately with the patients, all of whom are in a stable condition with the exception of three of the small DCLGs who are showing a slight reduction in body temperature."

"Deepening shock, do you think?" Conway asked.

"No, friend Conway," Prilicla replied. "There seems to be a slight improvement in their general condition."

"Emotional radiation?"

"Nothing on the conscious level, friend Conway," the empath replied, "but there are unconscious feelings of deprivation, and need."

"They are all hungry," Conway said dryly, "except one."

"The thought of that one is abhorrent to me, too," Prilicla

said. "But to return to the condition of the patients: The lung damage and inflammation of the breathing passages noted by friend Murchison is repeated, to a much lesser degree of severity, in the other survivors, and the cause is correctly attributed to the damaged reservoir. But it is possible that operating in Trugdil conditions with the less sensitive portable equipment—"

"Prilicla," Conway said impatiently, "what you mean is that we were too blind or stupid to spot an important medical datum, but you are too nice a person to hurt our feelings. But intense impatience and curiosity can be unpleasant emotions, too, so just tell us what you discovered, Doctor."

"I am sorry, friend Conway," said the empath. "It is that the food passage as well as the breathing passage is similarly inflamed. The condition is relatively mild, not obvious as are the other areas of inflammation, but is present in uniform intensity in all of the survivors regardless of physiological classification. I wondered if there was anything on their ship which would explain this.

"I am also puzzled by the amputation wounds," Prilicla went on. "I have been suturing incised wounds, none of which have penetrated to vital organs, and generally tidying up. But the stumps I have covered with sterile dressings only until the possibility of replacing the original limbs has been eliminated. Have you found anything down there which might be a missing limb or organ? Or have you given thought to the shape, size, and purpose of these missing parts?"

From amidships there were sounds of metal scraping against metal and of erratic, heavy breathing in their phones as the Captain cleared an obstruction. When it was quiet again, Murchison said, "Yes, Doctor, but I've formed no firm conclusions. There is a fairly complex nerve linkage to the stump in all three types and, in the case of the big DCOJ, a collapsed, tubular connection whose origin I have been unable to trace because of its close association with the very complex upper intestinal tract. But taking into account the positioning of these limbs or organs, which are at the base of the spine in the two smaller life-forms and on the medial underside of the large one, all I can say is that the missing parts must have been considered particularly edible by the attacker since it did not remove anything else. I have no clear idea of the size or shape of the missing parts, but my guess would be that they are probably tails, genitalia, or mammaries—"

"I'm sorry to interrupt a medical conference, ma'am," Fletcher broke in, in a tone which suggested that he was very glad to interrupt before it could go any farther. He went on quickly, "Doctor Conway, I've found another DCMH. It is tangled up in bedding, not moving, and seems to be uninjured. I thought you might like to examine it here rather than have it pulled through the wreckage in the corridor."

"I'm on my way," Conway said.

He climbed out of the hold and crawled along the corridor in the Captain's wake, listening as Fletcher resumed his commentary. Immediately forward of the cleared section of corridor the Captain had found the Dormitory Deck. It was characteristic of the early type of hyperships which did not have artificial gravity, and was filled with rows of sandwich-style double hammocks which retained the sleeper in weightless conditions. The hammocks were suspended on shock absorbers so as to double as acceleration couches for off-duty crew members.

There were three distinct sizes of hammock, so the ship had the DCLG, DCMH, and DCOJ life-forms in the crew— which proved that even the large and apparently unintelligent DCOJs were ship's personnel and not lab animals. Judging by the number and size of the hammocks, the two smaller life-forms outnumbered the large one by three to one.

He had made a quick count of the hammocks, the Captain said as Conway was passing the damaged hydraulic system reservoir, and the total number, thirty, agreed with the number of casualties found outside and inside the ship, which meant that the missing criminal was almost certainly not of any of the three species who served as the crew.

It was difficult to be precise regarding occurrences on the Dormitory Deck, Fletcher explained, because loose objects, ornaments, and personal effects had collected on the wall when the ship had fallen on its side. But one third of the hammocks were neatly stowed while the remaining two thirds looked as though they had been hastily vacated. No doubt the neat hammocks belonged to the crew members on duty, but the Captain thought it strange that if the ship operated a one-watch-on, two-off duty roster the rest of the crew were in their bunks instead of half of them being outside the dormitory on a recreation deck. But then he was forgetting the fact that the safest place during the landing maneuver would be inside the acceleration hammocks.

The Captain was backing out of the dormitory as Conway reached it. Fletcher pointed and said, "It is close to the inner hull among the DCMH hammocks. Call me if you need help, Doctor."

He turned and began crawling toward the bows again. But he did not get very far because by the time Conway reached the casualty he could hear the hiss of the cutting torch and the Captain's heavy breathing.

It took only a few minutes to piece together what had happened. Two of the hammock's supports had broken due to the lateral shock when the ship had fallen—they had been designed to withstand vertical G forces, not horizontal ones—and the hammock had swung downward throwing its occupant against the suddenly horizontal wall. There was an area of subcutaneous bleeding where the DCMH's head had struck, but no sign of a fracture. The blow had not been fatal, but it had been enough to render the being unconscious or dazed until the highly lethal vapor from the damaged reservoir had invaded its lungs.

This one had been doubly unlucky, Conway thought as he carefully drew it the rest of the way from its hammock and extended his examination. There was one wound, the usual one, at the base of its spine. Conway's scalp prickled at the thought that the attacker had been inside the dormitory and had struck even at a victim in its hammock. What sort of creature was it? Small rather than large, he thought. Vicious. And fast. He looked quickly around the dormitory, then returned his attention to the cadaver.

"That's unusual," he said aloud. "This one has what seems to be a small quantity of partially digested food in its stomach."

"You think that's unusual," Murchison said in a baffled tone. "The sample containers from the storage deck contain food. Liquid, a powdery solid, and some fibrous material, but all high-grade nutrient suited to the metabolisms of all three life-forms. What was the excuse for cannibalism? And why the blazes was everybody starving? The whole deck is packed with food!"

"Are you sure—?" began Conway, when he was cut off by a voice in his phones which was so distorted that he could not tell who was speaking.

"What *is* that thing?"

"Captain?" he said doubtfully.

"Yes, Doctor." The voice was still distorted, but recognizable.

"You—you've found the criminal?"

"No, Doctor," Fletcher replied harshly. "Another victim. Definitely another victim—"

"It's moving, sir!" Dodds voice broke in.

"Doctor," the Captain went on, "can you come at once. You too, ma'am."

Fletcher was crouched inside the entrance of what had to be the ship's Control Deck, using the cutting torch on the tangle of wreckage which almost filled the space between the ceiling and floor. The place was a shambles, Conway saw by the light coming through the open hatch above them and the few strips of emergency lighting which were still operating. Practically all of the ceiling-mounted equipment had torn free in the fall; ruptured piping and twisted, jagged-edged supporting brackets projected into the space above the control couches on the deck opposite.

The control couches had been solidly mounted and had remained in position, but they were empty, their restraining webbing hanging loose—except for one. This was a very large, deep cupola around which the other couches were closely grouped, and it was occupied.

Conway began to climb toward it, but the foothold he had been using gave way suddenly and a stub of broken-off piping dug him painfully in the side without, fortunately, rupturing his suit.

"Careful, damn it!" Fletcher snapped. "We don't need another casualty."

"Don't bite my head off, Captain," Conway said, then laughed nervously at his unfortunate choice of words.

He cringed inwardly as he climbed toward the central cupola

in the wake of the Captain, thinking that the crew on duty and those in the Dormitory Deck had had to find a way through this mess, and in great haste because of the toxic vapor flooding through the ship. They were much smaller than Earth-humans, of course, but even so they must have been badly cut by that tangle of metal. In fact, they *had* been badly cut, with the exceptions of the DCMH in the dormitory and the new life-form above them, neither of whom had attempted to escape.

"Careful, Doctor," the Captain said.

An idea which had been taking shape at the back of his mind dissolved. Irritably, Conway said, "What can it do except look at me and twitch its stumps?"

The casualty hung sideways in its webbing against the lower lip of the cupola, a great fleshy, elongated pear shape perhaps four times the mass of an adult human. The narrow end terminated in a large, bulbous head mounted on a walrus neck which was arched downward so that the two big, widely spaced eyes could regard the rescuers. Conway could count seven of the feebly twitching stumps projecting through gaps in the webbing, and there were probably others he could not see.

He braced himself against a control console which had remained in place and took out his scanner, but delayed beginning the examination until Murchison, who had just arrived, could climb up beside him. Then he said firmly, "We will have to remain with this casualty overnight, Captain. Please instruct Lieutenant Haslam to evacuate all the other casualties on the next trip, and to bring down the litter stripped of nonessential life-support equipment so that it will accommodate this new casualty. We also need extra air tanks for ourselves and oxygen for the casualty, heaters, lifting gear, and webbing, and anything else you think we need."

For a long moment the Captain was silent, then he said, "You heard the Doctor, Haslam."

Fletcher did not speak to them while they were examining the new casualty other than to warn them when a piece of loose wreckage was about to fall. The Captain did not have to be told that a wide path would have to be cleared between the big control cupola and the open hatch if the litter was to be guided in and out again carrying the large alien. It was likely to be a long, difficult job lasting most of the coming night, made more difficult by ensuring that none of the debris struck Murchison, Conway, or their patient. But the two medics were much too engrossed in their examination to worry about the falling debris.

"I won't attempt to classify this life-form," Conway said nearly an hour later when he was summing up their findings for Doctor Prilicla. "There are, or were, ten limbs distributed laterally, of varying thicknesses judging by the stumps. The sole exception is the one on the underside which is thicker than any of the others. The purpose of these missing limbs, the number and type of manipulatory and ambulatory appendages, is unknown.

"The brain is large and well developed," he want on, looking aside at Murchison for corroboration, "with a small, separate lobe with a high mineral content in the cell structure suggesting one of the V classifications—"

"A wide-range telepath?" Prilicla broke in excitedly.

"I'd say not," Conway replied. "Telepathy limited to its own species, perhaps, or possibly simple empathy. This is borne out by the fact that its ears are well developed and the mouth, although very small and toothless, has shown itself capable of modulating sounds. A being who talks and listens cannot be a wide-range telepath, since the telepathic faculty is supplemented by a spoken language. But the being did not display agitation on seeing us, which could mean that it is aware our intentions toward it are good.

"Regarding the airway and lungs," Conway continued, "you can see that there is the usual inflammation present but that the lung damage is minor. We are assuming that since the being was unable to move when the gas permeated the ship, it was able, with its large lung capacity, to hold its breath until most of the toxic vapor had dissipated. But the digestive system is baffling us. The food passage is extremely narrow and seems to have collapsed in several places, and with few teeth for chewing food it is difficult . . . to see how—"

Conway's voice slowed to a stop while his mind raced on. Beside him Murchison was making self-derogatory remarks because she, too, had not spotted it sooner, and Prilicla said, "Are you thinking what I am thinking, friends?"

There was no need to reply. Conway said, "Captain, where are you?"

Fletcher had cleared a narrow path for himself to the open hatch. While they had been talking they had heard his boots moving back and forth along the outer hull, but for the past few minutes there had been silence.

"On the ground outside, Doctor," Fletcher replied. "I've been trying to find the best way of moving out the big one. In my opinion we can't swing it down the sides of the wreck, too much sprung plating and debris, and the stern isn't much better. We'll have to lower it from the prow. But carefully. I jarred my ankles badly when I jumped from it to the sand, which is only about an inch deep over a gently sloping shelf of rock in that area. Obviously the big life-form needed a special elevator to board and debark, because the extending ladder arrangement below the hatch is usable only by the three smaller life-forms.

"I'm about to reenter the ship through the cargo hold hatch," he ended. "Is there a problem?"

"No, Captain," Conway said. "But on your way here would you bring the cadaver from the Dormitory Deck?"

Fletcher grunted assent and Murchison and Conway resumed their discussion with Prilicla, stopping frequently to verify with their scanners the various points raised. When the Captain arrived pushing the dead DCMH ahead of him, Conway had just finished attaching an oxygen tank and breathing tube to the patient and covering its head in a plastic envelope against the time when, during the night, the entry hatch would be closed and the fumes produced by the cutting torch against the metal and plastic debris might turn out to be even more toxic than those from the hydraulic reservoir.

They took the cadaver from Fletcher and, holding it above their heads, fitted it into one of the control couches designed for it. The big alien did not react and they tried it in a second, then a third couch. This time the patient's stub tentacles began to twitch and one of them made contact with the DCMH. It maintained the contact for several seconds then slowly withdrew and the big entity became still again.

Conway gave a long sigh, then said, "It fits, it all fits. Prilicla, keep your patients on oxygen and IV fluids. I don't think they will return to full consciousness until they have food as well, but the hospital can synthesize that when we get back." To Murchison he said, "All we need now is an analysis of the stomach contents of that cadaver. But don't do the dissection here, do it in the corridor. It would probably, well, upset the Captain."

"Not me," Fletcher said, who was already at work with his cutting torch. "I won't even look."

Murchison laughed and pointed to the patient hanging above them. She said, "He was talking about the other Captain, Captain."

Before Fletcher could reply, Haslam announced that he would be landing in fifteen minutes.

"Better stay with the patient while I help the Captain load the lander," Conway told Murchison. "Radiate feelings of re-assurance at it; that's all we can do right now. If we all left it might think it was being abandoned."

"You intend leaving her here alone?" Fletcher said harshly.

"Yes, but there is no danger—" Conway began, when the voice of Dodds interrupted him.

"There is nothing moving within a twenty-mile radius of the wreck, sir," he said reassuringly, "except thorn patches."

Fletcher said very little while they were helping Haslam move the casualties from the outcropping into the lander and while they were pushing the litter with its load of spare equipment to the wreck. It was unlike the Captain, who usually spoke his mind no matter who or what was bothering him, to behave this way. But Conway's mind was too busy with other things to have time to probe.

"I was thinking," Conway said when they reached the open cargo hatch, "that according to Dodds the thorn patches are attracted to food and warmth. We are going to create a lot of warmth inside the wreck, and there is a storage deck filled with food containers as well. Suppose we move as much food as we can from the wreck and scatter it in front of the thorn clumps—that might make them lose interest in the wreck for a while."

"I hope so," Fletcher said.

The lander took off in a small, self-created sandstorm as Conway was dragging the first containers of food toward the edge of the nearest thorn patch, which was about four hundred meters astern of the wreck. They had agreed that Fletcher would move the containers from the storage deck to the ground outside the hatch, and Conway would scatter them along the front of the advancing thorns. He had wanted to use the litter with its greater capacity and gravity neutralizers, but Naydrad had stated in its forthright fashion that the Doctor was unused to controlling the vehicle and if the gravity settings were wrong or a part of the load fell off, the litter would disappear skyward or blow weightlessly away.

Conway was forced to do it the hard way.

"Make this the last one, Doctor," the Captain said as he was coming in from his eighth round trip. "The wind is rising."

The shadow of the wreck had lengthened steadily as he worked and the sky had deepened in color. The suit's sensors showed a marked drop in the outside temperature, but Conway had been generating so much body heat himself that he had not noticed it. He threw the containers as far in front and to each side of him as he could, opening some of them to make sure that the thorns would know that the unopened containers also held food, although they could probably sense that for themselves. The thorn clumps covered the sand across a wide front like black, irregular crosshatching, seemingly motionless. But every time he looked away for a few minutes then back again, they were closer.

Suddenly the thorn patches and everything else disappeared behind a dark-brown curtain of sand and a gust of wind punched him in the back, knocking him to his knees. He tried to get to his feet but an eddy blew him onto his side. Half crawling and half running, he headed back toward the wreck, although by then he had no clear idea where it was. The storm-driven sand was hissing so loudly against his helmet that he could barely hear Dodds' voice.

"My sensors show you heading toward the thorns, Doctor," the astrogator said urgently. "Turn right about one hundred ten degrees and the wreck is about three hundred meters distant."

Fletcher was outside the cargo hatch with his suit spotlight turned to maximum power to guide him in. The Captain pushed him through the hatch and closed it behind him. The crash had warped the hatch so that sand continued to blow in around the edges, except near the bottom where it came through in a steady trickle.

"Within a few minutes the outside of the hatch will be sealed by a sand drift," Fletcher said without looking at Conway. "It will be difficult for our cannibal to get in. Dodds will spot it on the sensors anyway and I'll have time to take the necessary steps."

Conway shook his head and said, "We've nothing to worry about except the wind, sand, and thorn patches." Silently he added, *If that wasn't enough.*

The Captain grunted and began climbing through the hatch leading to the corridor, and Conway crawled after him. But it was not until Fletcher slowed to pass the leaking hydraulic reservoir, which was steaming very faintly now, that Conway spoke.

"Is there anything else bothering you, Captain?"

Fletcher stopped and for the first time in over an hour looked directly at the Doctor. He said, "Yes, there is. That creature in the Control Deck bothers me. Even in the hospital, what can you do for it, a multiple amputee? It will be completely helpless, little more than a live specimen for study. I'm wondering if it would not be better just to let the cold take it and—"

"We can do a great deal for it, Captain," Conway broke in, "if we can get it safely through the night. Weren't you listening to Murchison, Prilicla, and me discussing the case?"

"Yes and no, Doctor," Fletcher said, moving forward again. "Some of it was quite technical, and you might as well have been talking untranslated Kelgian so far as I was concerned."

Conway laughed quietly and said, "Then I had better translate."

The alien vessel had released its distress beacon, he explained, not because of a technical malfunction but because of serious illness on board which had affected the entire crew. Presumably the least affected crew members were on duty on the Control Deck while the rest were confined to their hammocks. It was still not clear why the ship had to put down on a planet. Possibly there were physiological reasons why a planetary gravity or atmosphere was needed, or maybe the weightless conditions on board aggravated the condition and they could not provide artificial gravity by using their thrusters because the crew were fast losing consciousness. Whatever the reason they had made an emergency landing on Trugdil. There were much better landing sites on the planet, but their degree of urgency must have been extreme and they had landed here.

Conway broke off as they entered the Control Deck because Murchison was high above them closing the personnel hatch. She said, "Don't let me interrupt you, but now that we will be using the cutting torches in a confined space, I'm going to take the patient off pure oxygen. It seems to be breathing easily now. Would one part oxygen to four inert be suitable, Doctor?"

"Fine," Conway said. "I'll help you."

The hissing of sand against the outer hull rose suddenly and the whole ship seemed to lurch sideways. There was a screeching and banging sound from amidships, which halted suddenly as a section of hull plating tore free and blew away.

"A piece of the wreck has blown away," Dodds reported unnecessarily, then went on, "The thorn patches have halted over the food containers, and those nearby are converging on the area. But there are other large clumps off to the side which are still heading directly for the wreck. They are moving quite fast. The wind is behind them and they are letting it carry them forward using only enough of their root system to maintain a loose hold on the ground. At this rate they could be at the ship in half an hour."

It was as if an enormous, soft pillow struck the side of the ship. The deck tilted under their feet, then righted itself. This time it sounded as if maniacs with sledgehammers were attacking three different sections of the hull until, a few seconds later, the banging ceased. But to the sound of the sand beating against the hull plating was added the discordant moaning and whistling of the wind as it forced its way into the wreck.

"Our defenses," the Captain said worriedly, "have become decidedly porous. But go on, Doctor."

"The ship made an emergency landing here," Conway resumed, "because they had no time to look for a better spot. It was a good landing, all things considered, and it was sheer bad luck that they toppled and as a result ruptured that hydraulic reservoir. If they hadn't done so it is possible that their illness, whatever the cause, would have run its course and in time they would have taken off again. Or maybe the first sandstorm would have knocked them over anyway. But instead they crash-landed and found themselves suddenly in a wreck which was rapidly filling with toxic fumes. Weakened by their condition as they were, they had to get out fast and, because the escape routes aft led past the source of the contaminant and were partly blocked by wreckage from the fall, they had to evacuate through the Control Deck here and along the upper surface of the hull, then slide to the ground.

"They injured themselves very seriously in doing so," Conway added.

He paused for a moment to help Murchison change over the patient's air supply. From the stern there was a clanking sound which reverberated steadily and monotonously throughout the ship. One of the pieces of wreckage was refusing to become detached. Conway raised his voice.

"The reason they did not move far from their ship was probably two-fold," he continued. "As a result of the debilitating effects of their illness, they did not have the strength to move farther, and I suspect there were strong psychological reasons for remaining close to their ship. Their physical condition, the high temperatures, and the indications of malnutrition observed, which we mistakenly assumed to be due to enforced starvation, were symptoms of the disease. The state of deep unconsciousness may also have been a symptom, or possibly some kind of hibernation mode which they adopt when injured or otherwise distressed and assistance is likely to be delayed, and which slows the metabolic rate and reduces bleeding."

Fletcher was readying his cutting torch and looking baffled. He said, "Disease and injuries caused by escaping from the wreck I can believe. But what about the missing limbs and—"

"Dodds, sir," *Rhabwar*'s astrogator broke in. "I'm afraid the midnight drop in wind strength will not affect your area. There are local weather disturbances. Three large thorn patches have reached the stern and sections of the peripheral growth are entering the food storage deck. A lot of hull plating is missing there. Once they open that concentrated store of food they'll probably lose interest in anything else." His optimism sounded forced.

Murchison said, "We're not completely sure that it was a disease that caused the trouble, Captain. From the analysis of the stomach contents of the cadaver from the dormitory deck, the indications are that it was a severe gastrointestinal infection caused by a bug native to their home planet, and the symptom which led us to suspect malnutrition was total regurgitation of stomach contents in all of the other cases. The casualty from the dormitory had been knocked unconscious before the process was complete and was asphyxiated shortly afterward so that involuntary regurgitation did not take place. But it is also possible that the ship's own food supply was contaminated and that caused the trouble."

Conway wondered if it was possible for a mobile omnivorous vegetable to get food poisoning, and if it would take effect in time to save them from the thorns. He rather doubted it.

"Thank you, Ma'am," Fletcher said, and went on, "About the missing limbs?"

"There are no missing limbs, Captain," she replied. "Or perhaps the crew are all missing the same organ, their head. The large number of the other injuries concealed the truth at first, but there are no missing limbs, and there is no criminal."

Fletcher looked at Conway, too polite to express his disbelief to the pathologist in words, and the Doctor took over the explanation. But he had to work as he talked because he and Murchison were faced with the long, difficult job of transferring the big alien from its cupola to the litter.

It was hard to imagine the set of environmental circumstances which had caused such an essentially helpless life-form to evolve, become dominant, and in time achieve a culture capable of star travel, Conway said, but these gross, limbless, and all too obviously immobile creatures had done just that. It was a host-symbiote, they now knew, who had developed multiple symbiotes specialized so as to act as short-and long-range manipulators and sensors. Its stumps and the areas which on the casualties had been mistaken for amputation sites were the interfaces which joined the host creature to its symbiotes when physical activity became necessary or the host required sustenance.

It was likely that a strong mental as well as physical bond existed between the host Captain and its crew, but continuous contact was not needed because in and around the wreck there had been three times the number of crew members as there were organic connectors on the host. It was also probable that the host entity did not sleep and provided continual, nonphysical support to its symbiotes. This was borne out by the type of emotional radiation being picked up on *Rhabwar* by Prilicla—confusion and feelings of loss. The host Captain's telepathic or empathic faculty did not reach as far as the ambulance ship's orbit.

"The smallest, DCLG life-form is independently intelligent and performs the finer, more intricate manipulative operations," Murchison joined in, clarifying the situation in her own mind as well as for the Captain, who had disappeared briefly into the corridor to check on the position of the thorns. "As is the slightly larger DCMH. But the function of the big DCOJ is purely that of eating and supplying predigested food to the host. There is evidence, however, that all three of these life-forms have their own ingestion, digestion, and reproductive systems, but one of them must figure in the transfer of sperm or ova between immobile host creatures—"

She broke off as the Captain returned, his cutter in one hand and what looked like a short, tangled piece of barbed wire in the other. He said, "The thorns have grown out of the food storage deck and are halfway along the corridor. I brought you a sample, ma'am."

She took it from him carefully and Conway joined her for a closer look. It was like a dark-brown, three-dimensional zigzag with fine green thorns growing out of every angle, except one which sprouted a long, tapering hollow tube like the vegetable equivalent of a hypodermic needle, and which was probably a root. She snipped off the thorns with surgical scissors and let them drop into her analyzer.

"Why did we have to wear lightweight suits?" she said a few minutes later. "A scratch from a thorn won't kill you, but three or four would. What are you doing, Captain?"

Fletcher was unclipping the signal flare from his backpack. He said, "You can see from the charring on the stem that they burn. I removed that sample with the cutting torch. But the flame isn't self-sustaining. Maybe this will stunt its growth for a while. Stay clear of the corridor entrance, both of you. These things were not meant to be used in a confined space."

He set the timer on the flare and threw it as hard as he could into the corridor. The beam of light which poured out of the entrance was so intense that it looked almost solid, and the hissing of the flare was louder even than the sand lashing against the outer hull. The beam maintained its intensity but began to flicker as smoke poured from the entrance. *The thorns were burning*, Conway thought excitedly, and hoped that the pyrotechnics were not worrying their patient too much. It seemed to be unusually agitated—

There was a sudden, crashing detonation. Pieces of the flare, burning thorn branches, and parts of the dissected DCMH erupted from the corridor entrance, and the cupola edge Conway was gripping seemed to jerk in his hands. He hung on desperately as the vertical deck swung toward him, accompanied by the screech of tearing metal. There was a softer shock and the metallic noises ceased. The emergency lighting had died but there was enough illumination from the sputtering pieces of flare and their helmet lights to show that the patient had fallen out of its cupola and was hanging directly above him, suspended only by its webbing, sections of which were beginning to tear.

"The litter!" Conway shouted. "Help me!"

There was so much smoke from the flare that all he could see clearly were Murchison's and the Captain's helmet lights. He let go his hold with one hand and felt around for the litter, which had been left drifting weightlessly with repulsors set to one negative G so as to make the vehicle easier to maneuver in the confined space. He found it and a few seconds later felt other hands steadying it. Above him the alien hung like a great organic tree trunk with its stumps projecting between the webbing, ready to fall and crush him and probably kill itself on the charred but still poisonous thorns below them.

Suddenly it sagged closer. Conway flinched, but the rest of the webbing was holding it. He felt for the control panel of the litter. "Get it under the things!" he shouted. "Right under its center of gravity, that's it."

Gradually he increased the repulsion until the litter was pressing firmly against the underside of the patient, and again until the being's entire weight was being supported and the webbing was simply holding it against any lateral movement. He became aware of the voice of Dodds in his phones, asking over and over again what had happened and were they all right.

"We're all right," Fletcher said angrily. "And you tell us what happened, Lieutenant. What are your sensors for?"

"An explosion at the site of the damaged hydraulic reservoir, sir," Dodds said, sounding relieved. "The stuff is highly inflammable as well as toxic, it seems, and the flare set it off. The explosion broke the back of the ship where it lies across that rock outcropping, and now the prow is lying on the sand, too. Amidships and stern sections have been stripped of plating by the explosion and the wind. The ship looks very open, sir."

The smoke had cleared but fine clouds of sand were blowing through the Control Deck from somewhere. Fletcher said dryly, "I believe you, Dodds. It is also very cold. How long until pickup?"

"Just under three hours, sir," Dodds replied. "Sunrise is in two hours and the wind should have abated an hour later."

The two portable heaters and spare cutting torch had been shaken loose by the explosion and had fallen into the thorns. One of the heaters was still functioning but its effect was severely reduced by the icy, sand-laden wind sweeping out of the corridor. Conway shivered and clenched his teeth, both to stop them chattering and in reaction to the indescribable noise of the wind screaming through the bare bones of the stern section and the irregular, thunderous din of the remaining plating shaking itself loose. He resited the portable lights, which had survived the explosion, so that they were within a few feet of the litter. They gave a little warmth.

More than an hour was spent completing the transfer of the alien from its cupola to the litter and securing it in the vehicle. The being, too, was suffering from the cold—its organic connectors twitched continuously and patterns of wrinkles marched across its smooth, featureless body. Conway tried to find something to wrap around it, but all that was available was the control cupola webbing from its own and the crew's positions. By the time he had finished, the being was virtually cocooned in the stuff and the few areas of skin visible were still twitching and wrinkling.

They moved it up to the sealed personnel hatch, hoping that the available heat would rise and it would be fractionally warmer up there. The difference, to Conway, was indetectable. He wondered if it would be possible to rescue the other heater, but when he looked down he saw that a fresh, uncharred tangle of thorns had grown in from the corridor and was climbing toward them.

"Doctor," said Fletcher quickly, indicating a large ceiling panel which was held in position by a single remaining support strut. "Hold onto that while I cut it free."

They dropped the panel onto the thorns and knotted loose pieces of webbing together into a rope so that the Captain could lower himself onto its center. The panel buckled slightly under his weight but the thorns beneath the plate were forced down by two meters or more. Fletcher kneeled carefully on his make-shift raft and unlimbered his cutting torch. With the flame focused down to a long, thin needle he attacked the thorns all around him.

After nearly six hours of constant use the power pack was exhausted. When the flame dimmed and died, Fletcher got carefully to his feet and began flexing and straightening his legs, bouncing the section of plating up and down. The thorns were forced lower. He paused for a rest and still the plate continued to sink. But now the needle-sharp thorns were grow-ing in from the edges of the raft, slowly submerging it.

The rope of webbing was barely within reach. Fletcher steadied himself, jumped, and caught the end in a double grip as the plate teetered and disappeared sideways under the thorns. Conway climbed down as far as he could and pulled the rope close so that Fletcher could get his feet onto the edge of a projecting cabinet.

"Did you see the way that thing moved itself from under the plate and surrounded you, Captain?" Murchison said when they rejoined her. "It's very slow, but do you think we are hurting a potentially intelligent vegetable life-form?"

"Yes, ma'am," the Captain said with feeling, "but not nearly enough."

"Eighty minutes to go, sir," Dodds said.

They detached the few pieces of wreckage and equipment that could be dislodged by hand and dropped them onto the thorns, but with little effect. Fletcher and Conway took turns hacking at the growth with a metal support strut, but still it grew slowly toward them. Soon there was not enough space to move around freely or exercise to keep warm, or more accurately, less cold. They could only huddle close to the personnel hatch, teeth clenched together to keep from chattering, and watch the thorns creep closer.

The scene was being relayed to *Rhabwar* and was causing increasing concern. Lieutenant Haslam said suddenly, "I can launch now, sir, and—"

"No," the Captain said firmly. "If you touch down before it is safe to do so and the lander is blown over, nobody here will get out of this mess—"

He broke off because his voice had suddenly sounded very loud.

The wind had died.

"Open up," Fletcher said. "Let's get out of here."

The dark-blue morning sky showed through the opening hatch and a negligible quantity of sand blew in. They maneuvered the litter and its trussed-up casualty through the opening and onto the upper surface of the hull.

"The lull may be temporary, sir," Dodds warned. "There are still a few squalls running through your area."

The rising sun was still hidden behind sand clouds, but there was more than enough light to see that the surface had been drastically altered overnight by the shifting of many sand drifts. From midships to stern the wreck was denuded of plating, but the skeleton had been filled out by a tightly packed tangle of thorns. The upper surface of the ship forward to the prow was intact, and the rocky shelf ahead was clear of thorns.

"One large squall will hit you in about twelve minutes," Dodds added.

They jammed the litter against the open hatch and attached its magnetic grapples to the hull. Then they secured their suit safety lines to the massive hinge and threw themselves across the litter, hooking their fingers into the webbing around the casualty. It was just one more physical indignity for the alien captain, Conway thought, but by now the being was probably past caring about such things.

Abruptly the sky was dark again and the wind and sand tore at them, threatening to lift them bodily off the hull. Conway desperately gripped the webbing as he felt the magnetic grapples begin to slide and the litter slue around. He wondered briefly if the wind would blow him beyond the surrounding thorns were he to let go his grip and his safety line. But his fingers were locked in a cramp and he felt that his arms, like those of the alien Captain, were about to be separated from his torso. Then as suddenly as it had come the wind died and it was light again.

He saw that Murchison, Fletcher, and the patient were still safely attached to the litter. But he did not move. It grew brighter and he could feel the sun warming his side when the sand lashed at them again, accompanied by a high-pitched, screaming thunder.

"Extrovert!" Murchison yelled.

Conway looked up to see the lander hovering ahead of the ship and blasting sand in all directions with its thrusters. Haslam touched down on the shelf of rock which was clear of thorns, barely fifty meters from them.

There were no problems while moving the litter to the other ship, and no shortage of time to do it even though the thorns were already inching toward it. Before loading it on board, Conway removed the extra webbing and the makeshift eye protection from the patient and gave it a thorough examination. In spite of everything it had gone through it was alive and, in Conway's opinion, very well.

"How about the others, Prilicla?" he asked.

"The temperatures of all of them have come down, friend Conway," the empath replied. "They are radiating strong feelings of hunger, but not on the level of distress. Since the food supply on the wreck has been lost, and may have been contaminated anyway, they will have to wait until the hospital's synthesizers provide some. Otherwise they are emoting feelings of confusion and loss.

"But they will feel much better," Prilicla added, "when they rejoin their Captain."

COMBINED
OPERATION

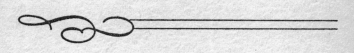

They emerged into normal space at a point whose coordinates placed them far out on the galactic rim and where the brightest object to be seen was a nearby sun burning coldly against a faint powdering of stars. But as Conway stared through Control's direct vision port, it became obvious that the emptiness was only apparent, because suddenly both the radar and long-range sensor displays were indicating two contacts, very close together and just under two thousand kilometers distant. For the next few minutes Conway expected to be ignored.

"Control, Power Room," Captain Fletcher said briskly. "I want maximum thrust in five minutes. Astrogator, give me the numbers to put us alongside that trace, and the ETA."

Lieutenants Chen and Dodds, seven decks below and a few feet away respectively, acknowledged. Then Lieutenant Haslam, from the Communications position, joined in.

"Sir," he said without taking his attention from his displays, "the sensor readings suggest that the larger trace has the mass, configuration, and antennae deployment of a scoutship engaged on survey duty. The other trace is currently unidentifiable, but their relative positions might indicate a recent collision."

"Very well," the Captain said. He touched his transmit stud and, speaking slowly and distinctly, he went on, "This is the ambulance ship *Rhabwar*, operating out of Sector Twelve General Hospital, responding to your distress beacon released six plus hours ago. We will close with you in—"

"Fifty-three minutes," Dodds supplied.

"—If you are able to communicate, please identify yourselves, specify the nature of your trouble, and list the type and number of casualties."

In the supernumerary's position Conway leaned forward intently, even though the difference of a few centimeters could not affect the clarity of any incoming message. But when the voice did come it sounded apologetic rather than distressed.

"The Monitor Corps scoutship *Tyrell* here, Major Nelson commanding," it said. "It was our distress beacon, but we released it on behalf of the wreck you see beside us. Our medical officer isn't sure, you understand, because its medical experience covers only three species, but it thinks that there may still be life on board."

"Doctor—" the Captain began, looking across at Conway. But before he could go on, Haslam was reporting again.

"Sir! Another, no, two more traces. Similar mass and configuration as the distressed vessel. Also smaller, widely scattered pieces of metallic wreckage."

"That's the other reason why we released our beacon," Nelson's voice sounded from *Tyrell*. "We don't have your long-range sensor equipment—our stuff is chiefly photooptical and computing gear associated with survey work—but this area seems to be littered with wreckage and, while I don't entirely agree with my medic that some of it must contain survivors, the possibility does exist that—"

"You were quite right to call for help, Captain Nelson," Conway said, breaking in. "We would much rather answer a dozen false alarms than risk missing one which might mean a rescue. Space accidents being what they are, most distress calls are answered too late in any case. However, Captain, as a matter of urgency we need the physiological classification of the wreck's survivors and the nature and extent of their injuries so that we can begin making preparations for accommodating and treating them.

"I am Senior Physician Conway," he ended. "May I speak to your medical officer?"

There was a long, hissing silence during which Haslam reported several more traces and added that, while the data were far from complete, the distribution of the wreckage was such that he was fairly certain that the accident had happened to a very large ship which had been blown apart into uniform pieces, and that the wreckage alongside *Tyrell* and the other similar pieces which were appearing all over his screens were lifeboats. Judging by the spread of the wreckage so far detected, the disaster had *not* been a recent occurrence.

Then the speaker came to life again with a flat, emotionless voice, robbed of all inflection by the process of translation. "I am Surgeon-Lieutenant Krach-Yul, Doctor Conway," it said. "My knowledge of other-species physiology is small, since I have had medical experience with only the Earth-human, Nidian, and my own Orligian life-forms, all of which, as you know, fall within the DBDG warm-blooded, oxygen-breathing classification."

The fact that the natives of Orligia and their planetary neighbor Nidia had a marked disparity in physical mass and one of them possessed an overall coat of tight, curly red fur was too small a difference to affect the four-letter classification coding, Conway thought as the other doctor was talking. Just like the small difference which had, in the early days of their stellar exploration, caused Orligia and Earth to fight the first, brief, and so far only interstellar war.

For this reason the Orligians and Earth-humans were more than friendly—nowadays they went out of their way to help each other—and it was a great pity that Krach-Yul was too professionally inexperienced to be really helpful. All Conway could hope for was that the Orligian medic had had sense enough to restrain its professional curiosity and not poke its friendly, furry nose into a situation which was completely beyond its experience.

"We did not enter the wreck," the Orligian was saying, "because our crew members are not specialists in alien technology and there was the danger of them inadvertently contributing to the problem rather than its solution. I considered drilling through the hull and withdrawing a sample of the wreck's atmosphere, in the hope that the survivor was a warm-blooded oxygen breather like ourselves and we could pump in air. But I decided against this course in case their atmosphere was an exotic mixture which we could not supply and we would then have reduced their ship's internal pressure to no purpose.

"We are not certain that there is a survivor, Doctor," Krach-Yul went on. "Our sensors indicate pressure within the wreck, a small power source, and the presence of what appears to be one large mass of organic material which is incompletely visible through the viewports. We do not know if it is living."

Conway sighed. Where extraterrestrial physiology and medicine were concerned this Krach-Yul was uneducated, but it certainly was not unintelligent. He could imagine the Orligian qualifying on its home planet, moving to the neighboring world of Nidia, and later joining the Monitor Corps to further increase its e-t experience and, while treating the minor ills and injuries of an Earth-human scoutship crew, hoping for something just like this to happen. The Orligian was probably one great, furry lump of curiosity regarding the organic contents of the wreck, but it knew its professional limitations. Conway was already developing a liking for the Orligian medic, sight unseen.

"Very good, Doctor," Conway said warmly. "But I have a request. Your vessel has a portable airlock. To save time would you mind—"

"It has already been deployed, Doctor," the Orligian broke in, "and attached to the wreck's hull over the largest entry port we could find. We are assuming it is an entry port, but it could be a large access panel because we did not try to open it. The wreck was spinning about its lateral axis and this motion was checked by *Tyrell*'s tractor-beams, but otherwise the vessel is as we found it."

Conway thanked the other and unstrapped himself from his couch. He could see several new traces on the radar display, but it was the picture of *Tyrell* and the wreck growing visibly larger on the forward screen which was his immediate concern.

"What are your intentions, Doctor?" the Captain asked.

Indicating the image of the wreck, Conway said, "It doesn't seem to be too badly damaged and there isn't much sharp metal in sight so, in the interests of a fast recovery, my people will wear lightweight suits. I shall take Pathologist Murchison and

Doctor Prilicla. Charge Nurse Naydrad will remain in the Casualty Deck lock with the litter, ready to pressurize it with the survivors' atmosphere as soon as Murchison analyzes it. You, sir, will come along to pick the alien airlock?"

Rhabwar was the first of its kind. Designed as a special ambulance ship, it had the configuration and mass of a Federation light cruiser, which was the largest type of Monitor Corps vessel capable of aerodynamic maneuver within a planetary atmosphere. As he pulled himself aft along the gravity-free central well, Conway was visualizing its gleaming white hull and delta wings decorated with the Occluded Sun, the Brown Leaf, the Red Cross, and the many other symbols which represented the concept of aid freely given throughout the worlds of the Federation.

It was a Traltha-built ship with all the design and structural advantages which that implied, and named *Rhabwar* after one of the great figures of Tralthan medical history. The ship had been designed for operation by an Earth-human crew, whose quarters were immediately below Control on Deck Two. The medical team occupied similar accommodation on Three except in the matter of furniture and bedding for the Kelgian Charge Nurse and reduced artificial gravity for the Cinrusskin empath.

Deck Four was a compromise, Conway thought as he pulled himself past it, a combination Messdeck and recreation room where the people who worked together were expected, regardless of physiological classification, to play together—even though there was barely enough room to play a game of chess when everyone was present. The whole of Five was devoted to the ship's consumables, which comprised not only the food required by six Earth-humans, a Kelgian, and a Cinrusskin of classifications DBDG, DBLF, and GLNO respectively, but the storage tanks whose contents were capable of reproducing or synthesizing the atmosphere breathed by any species known to the Galactic Federation.

Six and Seven, where Conway was headed, were the Casualty Deck and underlying lab and treatment ward. Here the gravity, atmospheric pressure, and composition could be varied to suit the life-support requirements of any survivors who might be brought in. Deck Eight was the Power Room, the province of Lieutenant Chen, who controlled the ship's hyperdrive gen-

erators and normal space thrusters, the power supply for the
artificial gravity grids, tractor and pressor beams, communications, sensors, and everything which made the energy-hungry
ship live.

Conway was still thinking of the diminuitive Chen and the
frightful powers available at the touch of one of his stubby
fingers when he arrived on the Casualty Deck. He did not have
to speak because his earlier conversation with the Captain had
been relayed to Casualty, as were the more interesting and
important displays on Control's screens. There was nothing for
him to do except climb into his spacesuit—he had a very good
medical team who kept their equipment and themselves at in-
stant readiness, and who tried constantly to make their leader
feel redundant.

Murchison was bending and stretching to check the seals of
her lightweight spacesuit, and Naydrad was inside the casualty
entrance lock testing a pressure litter, its beautiful silver fur
rippling in slow waves along its caterpillarlike body as it worked.
The incredibly fragile Prilicla, aided by its gravity nullifiers
and a double set of iridescent wings, was hovering close to the
ceiling where it would not be endangered by an accidental
collision with one of its more massive colleagues. Its eight,
pipestem legs were twitching slowly in unison, indicating that
it was being exposed to emotional radiation of a pleasurable
kind.

Murchison looked from Prilicla to Conway and said, "Stop
that."

Conway knew that it was Murchison, albeit indirectly, and
himself who were responsible for the Cinrusskin's twitchings.
Prilicla, like the other members of its intelligent and sensitive
race, possessed a highly developed empathic faculty which
caused it to react to the most minute changes and levels of
feeling in those surrounding it. Pathologist Murchison possessed that combination of physical attributes which made it
extremely difficult for any Earth-human male DBDG to regard
her with anything like clinical detachment—and while she was
wearing a contour-hugging lightweight suit it was downright
impossible.

"Sorry," Conway said, laughing, and began climbing into
his own suit.

* * *

The wreck looked like a long section of metal tree trunk with a few short, twisted branches sprouting from it, Conway thought as they launched themselves from *Rhabwar*'s casualty lock toward the distressed alien ship, but apart from those pieces of projecting metal the vessel seemed to have retained its structural integrity. He could see two small viewports reflecting the ambulance ship's floodlights like two tiny suns. One of the ports was set about two meters back from the bows of the wreck and the other a similar distance from the stern, although it was impossible to say just then which was which, and he had learned that there were another two viewports in identical positions on the side hidden from him.

He could also see the loose, transparent folds of *Tyrell*'s portable airlock clinging to the hull like a wrinkled limpet and, beside it, the tiny figure of what could only be the scoutship's Orligian medic, Krach-Yul.

Fletcher, Murchison, and Conway landed beside the Orligian. They did not speak and they tried hard not to think so that Prilicla, who was slowly circling the distressed vessel, would be able to feel for survivors with the minimum of emotional interference. If anything lived inside that wreck, no matter how faintly the spark of life glowed, the little empath would detect it.

"This is very strange, friend Conway," said Prilicla after nearly fifteen minutes had passed and they were all radiating feelings of impatience in spite of themselves. "There is life on board, one source only, and the emotional radiation is so very faint that I cannot locate it with accuracy. And contrary to what I would expect in these circumstances, there are no indications that the survivor is in a distressed condition."

"Could the survivor be an infant?" Krach-Yul asked, "Left in a safe place by adults who perished, and too young to realize that there is danger?"

Prilicla, who never disagreed with anyone because to do so might give rise to unpleasant emotional radiation from the other party, said, "The possibility cannot be dismissed, friend Krach-Yul."

"An embryo, then," Murchison said, "who still lives within its dead parent?"

"That is not impossible, either, friend Murchison," Prilicla replied.

"Which means," the Pathologist said, laughing, "that you don't think much of that idea, either."

"But there *is* a survivor," the Captain said impatiently, "so let's go in and get it out."

Fletcher wriggled through the double seal of the portable airlock and under the folds of tough, transparent plastic which, when inflated, would form a chamber large enough for them to work at extricating the survivor and, if necessary, provide emergency treatment. Murchison and Conway, meanwhile, spent several minutes at each of the tiny viewports, which were so deeply recessed that their helmet lights showed only areas of featureless leathery tegument.

When they joined the Captain in the lock, Fletcher said, "There are only so many ways of opening a door. It can hinge inward or outward, unscrew in either direction, slide open, or dilate. The actuator for this one appears to be a simple recessed lever which—Oh!"

The large metal hatch was swinging open. Conway tensed, waiting to feel the outward rush of the ship's air tugging at his suit and inflating the portable lock, but nothing else happened. The Captain grasped the edge with both hands, detached his foot magnets so that his legs swung away from the hull, and drew his head deep inside the opening. "This isn't an airlock but a simple access hatch to mechanisms and systems situated between the inner and outer hulls. I can see cable runs, plumbing, and what looks like a—"

"I need an air sample," Murchison said, "quickly."

"Sorry, ma'am," Fletcher said. He let go with one hand and pointed carefully, then went on, "It seems obvious that only the inner hull is airtight. It should be safe enough for you if you site your drill in the angle between that support bracket and cable loom just there. I don't know how efficient their insulation is, but that cable is too thin to carry much power. The color coding suggests that their visual range is similar to ours, wouldn't you say?"

"I would," Murchison agreed.

Conway said quickly, "If you use a Five drill it will be wide enough to take an Eye."

"I intend doing that," she said dryly.

The drill whirred briefly, the sound conducted through the metal of the hull and the fabric of Conway's suit, and a sample of the ship's atmosphere hissed through the hollow drill-head and into the analyzer.

"The pressure is a little low by our standards," she reported quietly, "but that could be dangerously low or normal so far as the survivor is concerned. Composition, the proportion of oxygen to inert gases, makes it a warm-blooded, oxygen-breathing life-form. I shall now insert the Eye."

Conway saw her detach the analyzer from the hollow drill and, so expertly that she could not have lost more than a few cubic centimeters of ship's atmosphere in the process, replace it with the Eye. Very carefully she threaded in the transparent tube containing the lens, light source, and vision recorder through the hollow center of the drill, then attached the eyepiece and magnifier which would enable her to use the instrument while wearing a space helmet.

For what seemed like an hour but was probably only ten minutes she swiveled the lens and varied the light intensity, without speaking. Then she wriggled backward out of the opening to give Conway and the others a look.

"It's big," she said.

The interior of the wreck was a hollow cylinder completely free of compartment dividers or structural crossmembers and the floor—Conway was assuming it was the floor because it was flat and ran the length of the ship—had a double line of closely spaced holes three or four inches in diameter running down the middle. Seven or eight pairs of the survivor's feet disappeared into the holes so they were probably part of the vessel's system of safety restraints, as were the broad bands of torn webbing which floated loosely about its body.

The Eye was positioned close to floor level so that Conway could see the being's flank along the section whose feet were held in the deck holes. Farther along, where the feet had been pulled free by the force of the accident to its ship, he could see in detail the double line of stubby, centipedal legs and the pale-gray underside. In the opposite direction—he could not tell whether it was toward the being's head or tail—he could make out part of the upper surface of the creature and a single line of dorsal tentacular appendages. The long, cylindrical compartment did not give the being much room to maneuver and the twists and curves of the weightless, flaccid body seriously hampered viewing, but at the limit of his vision Conway could just make out three lengths of tubing, pencil thin, transparent, and apparently flexible, which sprouted from a container attached to the wall to disappear into the body of the survivor.

Despite the multiplicity of the being's arms and legs there seemed to be very little if anything for it to do. Apart from a large number of wall-mounted storage cabinets, the interior of the ship was bare of anything resembling control and indication systems or any obvious means by which the vessel could be guided by its occupant—unless, of course, there was a small control center forward in the area concealed by the survivor's body.

Conway must have been thinking aloud because the Captain, who had just returned from an external examination of the ship, said seriously, "There *is* nothing for it to do, Doctor. Except for a very unsophisticated power cell which, at present, is not being used to power anything, there is nothing. No propulsion unit, no attitude control jets, no recognizable external sensors or communications, no personnel lock. I'm beginning to wonder if this is a ship or some kind of survival pod. This would explain the odd configuration of the vessel, which is a cylinder of constant diameter with a perfectly flat face at each end. However, when I sighted along the hull in an effort to detect minor protrusions which could have housed sensor equipment, I observed that the cylinder was very slightly curved along its longitudinal axis. This opens up another possibility which—"

"What about power sources and comm equipment mounted outboard?" Conway broke in before the Captain's observations could develop into a lecture on ship design philosophy. "We have matched hyperdrive generators on our wingtips and perhaps these people had a similar idea."

"No, Doctor," Fletcher said in the cool, formal tone he used when he thought someone was trying to tell him his business. "I examined those external spars, which have been broken off too short to give any indication of the type of structure they supported, but the wiring still attached to them is much too thin to carry power to a hyperspace generator. In fact, I seriously doubt if these people had either hyperdrive or artificial gravity, and the general level of technology displayed is pretty elementary for a star-traveling race. Then there is the apparent absence of an entry port. An airlock for this beastie would have to be almost as long as the vessel itself."

"There are a few star-traveling species who do not use them," Conway said. "For purely physiological reasons they do not indulge in extravehicular activity, entering and leaving their ships only at time of departure and arrival."

"Suppose," Murchison said, "this vehicle is the being's spacesuit."

"A nice idea, ma'am, but no," Fletcher said apologetically. "Apart from the four viewports, whose angles of vision are severely limited because of their small size and the space between the outer and inner hulls, there is no sensory input of any kind known to me and, more important, no external manipulators. But there must be some easy way of getting that beastie into and out of that thing, whether it is a ship, a survival pod, or something else."

There was a long silence, then Conway said, "I'm sorry, Captain. A few minutes ago you were about to mention a third possibility when I interrupted you."

"I was," Fletcher said in the tone of one graciously receiving an apology. "But you will understand, Doctor, that the theory is based on my initial visual observation only and not, as yet, supported by accurate measurements. Nevertheless, as I have already stated, this vessel is not a true cylinder but appears to be curved slightly along its longitudinal axis.

"Now, an explosion or collision sufficiently violent to warp the cylinder out of true," he went on, slipping into his lecturing manner, "would buckle and open up seams in the hull plating, and leave evidence of heat discoloration and indentations from flying debris. There are no such indications. So if the longitudinal axis of the vessel is, in fact, a very flat curve rather than a straight line, then the curvature was deliberate, built in. This would explain the lack of power and control linkages and an artificial gravity system because they used—"

"Of course!" Conway broke in. "The hull beneath the flat

deck was outward facing and free of structural projections, which means that they got their gravity the old-fashioned way by—"

"Will one of you," Murchison said crossly, "kindly tell me what you are talking about?"

"Certainly," Conway said. "The Captain has convinced me that this structure is not a ship or a lifeboat, but a section of a space station, an early Wheeltype of very large diameter, which suffered a collision."

"A space station away out here?" Murchison sounded incredulous. Then she began to realize the implications and added feelingly, "In that case we could have an awful lot of work ahead of us."

"Maybe not, ma'am," Fletcher said. "Admittedly there is a strong possibility of finding many more space station segments, but the survivors may be very few." His tone became suddenly forceful. "Transferring that creature to our Casualty Deck is out of the question. Instead I suggest we attach it to our hull, extend *Rhabwar*'s hyperspace envelope accordingly, and whisk it back to Sector General where their airlocks can easily handle a patient extraction problem of this size. I am not the e-t medical specialist, of course, but I think we should do this at once, leaving *Tyrell* to search for other survivors, and then return as soon as possible for the others."

"No," Conway said firmly.

"I don't understand you, Doctor." Behind his helmet visor Fletcher's face had gone red.

Conway ignored him for a moment while he addressed Murchison and Prilicla, who had drifted closer in spite of the strong emotional radiation being generated in the area. He said, "The survivor, so far as we are able to see, is linked to what appears to be some kind of life-support system by three separate sets of tubing. It is deeply unconscious but not physically distressed. There is also the fact that its vessel contains a reservoir of power which is not presently being used. Now, would either of you agree that the observed emotional radiation and apparent lack of physical injury could be the result of it being in a hibernation anesthesia condition?"

Before either of them could reply, Conway added, "Since there is no evidence of the presence of the power-hungry,

complex refrigeration systems which we associate with suspended animation techniques, just three sets of tubing entering
its body, would you also agree that the life-form is a natural
hibernator?"

There was a short silence, then Murchison said, "We are
familiar with the idea of long-term suspended animation being
associated with star travel—that used to be the only way to
do it, after all, and the cold-sleeping travelers would require
neither air nor food during their trips. In the case of a life-form
with the ability to go periodically into a state of hibernation
for planetary environmental reasons, a minimal supply of food
and air would be required. It is quite possible that the natural
process of hibernation could be artificially initiated, extended,
and counteracted by specific medication and the food supplied
intravenously, as seems to be the case with our friend here."

"Friend Conway," Prilicla said, "the survivor's emotional
radiation pattern agrees in every particular with the hypothesis
of hibernation anesthesia."

Captain Fletcher was not slow on the uptake. He said, "Very
well, Doctor. The survivor has been in this condition for a very
long time, so there is no great urgency about moving it or the
other survivors we might find to the hospital. But what are
your immediate intentions?"

Conway was aware of a multiple, purely subjective silence
as the party on the alien's hull and the communications officers
who were listening in on *Rhabwar* and *Tyrell* held their col-
lective breath. He cleared his throat and said, "We will examine
this section of space station, if that is what it is, as closely as
possible without entering it, and simultaneously make as detailed a visual examination of the survivor as we can using the
Eye, and then we will all try to *think*."

He had the feeling, very strong and not at all pleasant to
judge by the trembling of Prilicla's spidery limbs, that this was
not going to be an easy rescue.

For a little over three hours, the duration remaining to their
lightweight suits, they did nothing but think as they examined
the exterior of the wreck and what little they could see of its
occupant, slowly adding data which might or might not be
important. But they thought as individuals, increasingly baffled

individuals, so that it was not until they met on *Rhabwar*'s Messdeck and recreation level that they were able to think as an equally baffled group.

Tyrell was represented by its Captain, Major Nelson, and Surgeon-Lieutenant Krach-Yul, while Major Fletcher and the astrogation officer, Lieutenant Dodds, furnished the required military balance for *Rhabwar*. Murchison, Prilicla, Naydrad, and Conway—who were, after all, mere civilians—filled the remainder of the deck space with the exception of the empath, who was clinging to the safety of the ceiling.

It was Prilicla, knowing that nobody else felt ready to contribute any useful ideas, who spoke first.

"I feel that we are all agreed," it said in the musical trills and clicks of the Cinrusskin tongue, which emanated from their translator packs as faultless if somewhat toneless speech in the languages of Kelgia, Orligia, and Earth, "that the being is in a state of suspended animation, that there is a high probability that it is not a patient but a survivor who should be returned to its home world as soon as convenient if this planet can be found, and that the need to move it is not an urgent one."

Lieutenant Dodds looked at Fletcher for permission to speak, then said, "It depends on what you mean by urgent, Doctor. I ran a vectors and velocities check on this and the other pieces of wreckage within detector range. These bits of alien vessel or space station occupied roughly the same volume of space approximately eighty-seven years ago, which is when the disaster must have occurred. If it was a ship I don't think it was heading for the nearby sun since there are no planets, but a lot of the dispersed wreckage will either fall into the sun or pass closely enough to make no difference to any other survivors in hibernation. This will begin to occur in just over eleven weeks."

They digested that for a moment, then *Tyrell*'s Captain said, "I still say a space station way out here is impossible, especially one traveling at such a clip that its wreckage will reach the sun, there, in eleven weeks. It is far more likely that the survivor is in a lifeboat with suspended animation extending the duration of its consumables."

Fletcher glared at his fellow captain, then he noticed Prilicla beginning to tremble. He visibly calmed himself as he said,

"It is not impossible, Major Nelson, although it is unlikely. Let us suppose that the survivor's race, which is at the interplanetary flight level of technology, was beginning to experiment with hyperspace generation on its space station and inadvertently performed a random Jump and found themselves very far indeed from home, and subsequently went into hibernation for the reason you have stated. Many such accidents have occurred during early experiments with hypertravel. In any case, I think we are drawing too many conclusions from what is, after all, only one small piece of a very large jigsaw."

Conway decided to join in before this spirited exchange of technical views could devolve into a quarrel. He said placatingly, "But what conclusions, however few and tentative, can we draw from the piece you have examined, Captain? And what, however vaguely, can you see of the complete picture?"

"Very well," said Fletcher. He quickly inserted his vision spool from the wreck into the Recreation Deck's display unit and began to describe everything he had observed and deduced during his examination of the distressed vessel, which he preferred to think of as a simple, pressurized container rather than a ship. It was a cylinder just over twenty meters in length and approximately three meters in diameter, with ends which were flat except for a set of eight couplings which would enable it to be connected at either end to other similar containers. The couplings had been designed to break open before any external shock or force applied to adjacent structures could damage or deform the container. If the dimensions of the other containers or space station sections were the same as the one examined, and if the longitudinal curvature was uniform in all of them, then approximately eighty of these sections would form a Wheel just under five hundred meters in diameter.

He paused, but Major Nelson still had his lips pressed tightly together, and the others, knowing that a reaction was expected of them, kept perversely silent.

The section had a double hull with only the inner one pressurized, Fletcher resumed, but it possessed no control, sensor, or power systems other than those associated with the suspended animation equipment. The level of technology displayed was advanced interplanetary rather than interstellar, so the station had no business being where it was in the first place.

But the most puzzling feature of the container was the method used to enter and leave it.

They had already seen that there were no openings on the hull large enough to allow entry or exit by the survivor, which meant that it had to enter and leave via the flat, circular plate at each end of the cylinder. In Fletcher's opinion the creature went in one end and came out the other because physically it was too massive to turn itself around inside its container. But there was nothing resembling a door at either end of the cylinder, just the two large circular plates whose edges were set inside the thick rims which supported the couplings.

"So far as I can see there is no operating mechanism for these endplates," Fletcher went on with the hint of an apology creeping into his tone. "There are only so many ways for a door to open, and there has to be a door into and out of that thing, but I can't find one. I even considered explosive bolts, with the extraterrestrial sealed in until it arrived or was taken by its rescuers to an environmentally suitable position—either a planet or the hold of a rescue ship—whereupon it would blow the hatch fastenings and crawl out. But there are no hatch fastenings that I can see and the rim structure surrounding the hatches, if that is what they are, would not allow them to be blown open. Neither can they be opened inward because the diameter of the inner, pressurized hull is much smaller than that of the endplates."

Fletcher shook his head in bafflement and ended, "I'm sorry, Doctor. Right now I can see no way for you to get to your survivor without cutting its ship apart. What I need is another piece of this jigsaw puzzle to examine, a broken piece which will let me see how the other undamaged pieces were put together."

There was silence for a few seconds, during which Prilicla trembled in sympathy with the Captain's embarrassment, then Murchison spoke.

"I would like to examine a broken piece as well," she said quietly. "Specifically, a piece containing a nonsurvivor which would let me see how our survivor is put together."

Conway turned to Dodds. "Are there many pieces which look as if they had been broken up?"

"A few," replied the astrogator. "Most of the traces give

sensor readings similar to the first piece. That is, a vehicle of similar mass retaining internal pressure and containing a small power source. All of the pieces, including the few damaged ones, are at extreme sensor range. It is a long way to go on impulse drive, but if we jumped through hyperspace we would probably overshoot."

"How many pieces altogether?" asked Nelson.

"Twenty-three solid traces so far," said Dodds, "plus a few masses of what appears to be loose, structural debris. There is also one largish mass, unpressurized and radioactive, which I'd guess was part of a power center."

From its position on the ceiling, Prilicla said, "If I might make a suggestion, and if Major Nelson is willing to interrupt his survey mission . . . ?"

Nelson laughed suddenly and the other Corps officers present smiled. With great feeling he went on, "There isn't a scout-ship crew on survey duty anywhere in the Galaxy who would not rather be doing something, *anything*, else! You only have to ask and give me half an excuse for accepting, Doctor."

"Thank you, friend Nelson," said the empath with a slow tremor of pleasure. "My suggestion is that *Rhabwar* and *Tyrell* act independently to seek out other survivors and return them to this area, using tractor beams if the distance is short enough for impulse drive or by extending the hyperspace envelopes to include them if a Jump is necessary. My empathic faculty enables me to identify sections containing living occupants and, because of the large mass of these beings, Doctor Krach-Yul and Nurse Naydrad should accompany me to assist with treatment, should this be possible. Pathologist Murchison and you, friend Conway, are well able to identify living casualties by more orthodox means if the ship's sensors are uncertain.

"This will halve the time needed to search for other survivors," Prilicla ended apologetically, "even though the period will still be a lengthy one."

Tyrell's medical officer spoke for the first time, its whining and barking speech translating as "I always assumed that a space rescue by ambulance ship would be a fast, dramatic, and decisive operation. This one appears to be disappointingly slow."

"I agree, Doctor," said Conway. "We need help if this job is not to take months instead of a few days. Not one scoutship

but a flotilla, or better yet a squadron of them to search the
entire—"

Captain Nelson began to laugh, then broke off when he saw
that Conway was serious. He said, "Doctor, I'm just a major
in the Monitor Corps and so is Captain Fletcher. We haven't
got the rank to whistle up a flotilla of scoutships no matter
how much you think we need them. All we can do is explain
the situation and put in a very humble request."

Fletcher looked at his fellow Captain and opened his mouth
to speak, then changed his mind.

Conway smiled and said, "I am a civilian, Captain, with
no rank at all. Or considered in another way, I, as a specialist
member of the public, have ultimate authority over people like
yourselves who are public servants—"

Clearing his throat noisily, Fletcher said, "Please spare us
the political philosophy, Doctor. Do you wish me to get off a
subspace signal to Sector base requesting massive assistance
because of a large number of widely scattered potential survivors of a hitherto unknown life-form?"

"That's it," said Conway. "And would you also take charge
of assigning search areas to the scoutships if and when they
arrive? In the meantime we'll do as Prilicla suggests, except
that Murchison and I will go in *Tyrell*, if that is agreeable to
you, Captain."

"A pleasure," said Nelson, looking at Murchison.

"Because your crew aren't used to our fragile friend scam-
pering about on their ceilings and there might be an accident,"
he continued. "But right now we'll need help to transfer some
of our portable equipment to your ship."

While their gear was being moved to the scoutship and
Conway was trying hard to keep Murchison from transferring
the Casualty Deck's diagnostic and treatment equipment in toto,
Tyrell's portable airlock was detached from the alien vessel
and restowed on board in case it would be needed on one of
the other widely scattered sections. Several times as they worked,
Rhabwar's lighting and gravity control fluctuated in momentary
overload, indicating that Conway's subspace signal was going
out.

He knew that Fletcher was keeping the signal as brief as
possible because the power required to punch a message through

the highly theoretical medium of subspace from a vessel of *Rhabwar*'s relatively small size would have Lieutenant Chen in the Power Room chewing his nails. Even so, that signal would be splattered with interstellar static and have audible holes blown through it by every intervening cloud of ionized gas, star, or quasistellar object, and for that reason the message had been speeded up many times and repeated so that the people at the receiving end would be able to piece together a normal-speed coherent message from the jumble reaching them.

But their response to the signal was an entirely different matter, Conway thought worriedly. Despite his seeming confidence before the others, he did not know what would happen because this was the first time he had made such a request.

Nelson had invited Murchison and Conway to Control so that they could observe *Tyrell*'s approach to the second section of alien space station to be investigated, and so that his crew could observe the pathologist. Since the subspace signal had gone out six hours earlier, the Captain had been regarding Conway with a mixture of anxiety and awe as if he did not know whether the Doctor was seriously self-deluded or a highly potent individual indeed.

The messages which erupted from his Control Room speaker shortly afterward, and which continued with only a few minutes' break between them for the best part of the next hour, resolved his doubts but left him feeling even more confused.

"Scoutship *Tedlin* to *Rhabwar*. Instructions please."

"Scoutship *Tenelphi* to *Rhabwar*, requesting reassignment instructions."

"Scoutship *Torrance*, acting flotilla leader. I have seven units and eighteen more to follow presently. You have work for us, *Rhabwar*?"

Finally Nelson muted the speaker and the sound of Captain Fletcher assigning search areas to the newly arrived scoutships, which were being ordered to search for sections of the alien space station and bring them to the vicinity of *Rhabwar*. With so much help available, Fletcher had decided that the ambulance ship would not itself join in the search but would instead remain by the first section to coordinate the operation and give medical assistance. Confident that the situation was under control, Conway relaxed and turned to face Captain Nelson, whose curiosity had become an almost palpable thing.

"You—you *are* just a doctor, Doctor?" he said.

"That's right, Captain," Murchison said before Conway could reply. She laughed and went on, "And stop looking at him like that, you'll give him an inflated sense of his own importance."

"My colleagues are constantly on guard against the possibility of that happening," Conway said dryly. "But Pathologist Murchison is right. I am not important, nor are any of the Monitor Corps officers or the medical team on *Rhabwar*. It is our job which is important enough to command the reassignment of a few flotillas of scoutships to assist."

"But it requires the rank of subfleet Commander or higher to order such a thing—" Nelson began, and broke off as Conway shook his head.

"To explain it I must first fill in some background, Captain," he said. "Some of this information is common knowledge. Much of it is not because the relevant decisions of the Federation Council and their effects on Monitor Corps operational priorities are too recent for it to have filtered down to you. And you'll excuse me, I hope, if some of it is elementary, especially to a scoutship Captain on a survey mission..."

Only a tiny fraction of the Galaxy had been explored by the Earth-humans or by any of the sixty-odd other races who made up the Galactic Federation, so that the member races were in the peculiar position of people who had friends in far countries but had no idea who was living in the next street. The reason for this was that travelers tended to meet each other more often than the people who stayed at home, especially when the travelers exchanged addresses and visited each other regularly.

Visiting was comparatively easy. Providing there were no major distorting influences on the way and the exact coordinates of the destination were known, it was almost as easy to travel through hyperspace to a neighboring solar system as to one at the other side of the galaxy. But first one had to find a system containing a planet with intelligent life before its coordinates could be logged, and finding new inhabited systems was proving to be no easy task.

Very, very slowly a few of the blank areas in the star maps were being surveyed and explored, but with little success. When a survey scoutship like *Tyrell* turned up a star with planets it was a rare find, even rarer if one of the planets harbored life. And if one of these life-forms was intelligent then jubilation, not unmixed with concern over what might possibly be a future threat to the Pax Galactica, swept the worlds of the Federation, and the cultural contact specialists of the Monitor Corps were assigned the tricky, time-consuming, and often dangerous job of establishing contact in depth.

The cultural contact people were the elite of the Monitor Corps, a small group of specialists in extraterrestrial communications, philosophy, and psychology. Although small, the group was not, regrettably, overworked.

"During the past twenty years," Conway went on, "they have initiated first-contact procedure on three occasions, all of which were successful and resulted in the species concerned joining the Federation. There is no need to bore you with such details as the fantastically large number of survey missions mounted, the ships, personnel, and material involved, or shock you with the cost of it all. I mention the cultural contact group's three successes simply to make the point that within the same period Sector Twelve General Hospital, our first multienvironment medical treatment center, became fully operational and initiated first contacts which resulted in seven new species joining the Federation.

"This was accomplished," he explained, "not by a slow, patient buildup and widening of communications until the exchange of complex philosophical and sociological concepts became possible, but by giving medical assistance to a sick alien."

This was something of an oversimplification, Conway admitted. There were the medical and surgical problems inherent in treating a hitherto unknown life-form. Sector General's translation computer, the second largest in the Federation, was available, as was the assistance of the Monitor Corps' hospital-based communications specialists, and the Corps had been responsible for rescuing and bringing in many of the extraterrestrial casualties in the first place. But the fact remained that the hospital, by giving medical assistance, demonstrated the Federation's goodwill toward e-ts much more simply and directly than could have been done by any time-consuming exchange of concepts.

Because all Federation ships were required to file course and passenger or crew details before departure, the position of a distress signal was usually a good indication of the ship and therefore the physiological classification of the beings who had run into trouble, and an ambulance ship with matching crew and life-support equipment was sent from Sector General or from the ship's home planet to assist it. But there had been instances, far more than was generally realized, when the disasters involved beings unknown to the Federation in urgent need of help, help which the would-be rescuers were powerless to give.

Only when the rescue ship concerned had the capability of extending its hyperspace envelope to include the distressed vessel, or the survivors could be extricated safely and a suitable environment provided for them within the Federation ship, could they be transported to Sector General for treatment. The result was that many hitherto unknown life-forms, entities of high intelligence and advanced technology, were lost except as interesting specimens for dissection and study.

But an answer to this problem had been sought and, hopefully, found.

"It was decided to build and equip a very special ambulance ship," Conway continued, "which would give priority to answering distress signals whose positions did not agree with the flight plans filed by Federation vessels. The First Contact people consider *Rhabwar* to be the near-perfect answer in that we involve ourselves only with star-traveling species, beings who are *expecting* to encounter new and to them alien life-forms and who, should they get into trouble, would not be expected to display serious xenophobic reactions when we try to help them. Another reason why the cultural contact people prefer meeting star travelers to planetbound species is that they can never be sure whether they are helping or hindering the newly discovered culture's natural development, giving them a technological leg up or a crushing inferiority complex.

"Anyway," Conway said, smiling as he pointed at Nelson's main display where the newly arrived scoutships covered the screen, "now you know that it is *Rhabwar* which has the rank and not any member of its crew."

Nelson was looking only slightly less impressed, but before

he could speak the voices of two scoutship commanders reporting to *Rhabwar* sounded in quick succession. Both vessels had emerged from hyperspace close to sections of alien space station and were already returning to the rendezvous point with them in tow on long-focus tractor beams. In both cases the sections gave sensor indications of life on board.

"The news isn't all good, however," Nelson said, pointing at his main display where an enlarged picture of the section toward which they were heading filled the screen. "That one has taken a beating and I don't see how the occupant could have survived."

Conway nodded, and as the wrecked section turned slowly to present an end view, Murchison added, "Obviously it didn't."

The alien cylinder had been dented and punctured by multiple collisions with some of the structural members which had furnished the supporting framework of the original space station and which was still drifting nearby. Amid the loose tangle of debris was one of the section's circular endplates, and from the open end of the compartment the body of its occupant protruded like an enormous, dessicated caterpillar.

"Can you relay this picture to *Rhabwar*?" Conway asked.

"If I can get a word in edgewise," Nelson replied, glancing at his speaker, which was carrying a continuous, muted conversation between Fletcher and the scoutships.

Murchison had been staring intently at the screen. She said suddenly, "It would be a waste of time examining that cadaver out here. Can you put a tractor on it, Captain, and take us back to *Rhabwar*?"

"We'll need to bring back the wreck for study as well," Conway said. "The life-support and suspended animation systems will give us important information on the being's physiology and—"

"Excuse me, Doctor," Nelson said. For several seconds the voices from *Rhabwar* and the scoutships had been silent and the Captain had seized the chance to send a message of his own. He went on, "*Tyrell* here. Will you accept a visual relay, *Rhabwar*? Doctor Conway thinks it's important."

"Go ahead, *Tyrell*," Fletcher's voice said. "All other traffic wait out."

There was a long silence while *Rhabwar*'s Captain studied

the image of the slowly rotating wreck and the attached cadaver, long enough ,for it to make three complete revolutions, then Fletcher spoke. The tone and words were so uncharacteristic that they scarcely recognized his voice. "I'm a fool, a stupid damned fool for not seeing it!"

It was Murchison who asked the obvious question.

"For not seeing how that endplate opened," Fletcher replied. He made several more self-derogatory remarks in an undertone, then went on, "It *drops* out, or there is probably a spring-loaded actuator which pushes it out through the slot which you can see behind the coupling collar. No doubt there is an internal air pressure sensor linked to the actuator to keep the endplate from popping out accidentally when the section is in space or the adjoining section is airless. Do you intend returning with this section and not just the cadaver?"

The tone of the question suggested that if such was not the Doctor's intention, then forceful arguments would be forthcoming to make him change his mind.

"As quickly as possible," Conway said dryly. "Pathologist Murchison is just as keen to look inside that alien as you are to look inside its ship. Please ask Naydrad to stand by the Casualty Lock."

"Will do," Fletcher said. He paused for a moment, then went on seriously, "You realize, Doctor, that the manner in which these cylinders open means that their occupants were sealed into their suspended animation compartments while in atmosphere, almost certainly on their home planet, and the cylinders were not meant to be opened until their arrival on the target world. These people are members of a sublight colonization attempt."

"Yes," Conway said absently. He was thinking about the probable reaction of the hospital to receiving a bunch of outsize, hibernating e-ts who were not, strictly speaking, patients but the survivors of a failed colonization flight. Sector General was a hospital, not a refugee camp. It would insist, and rightly, that the colonists be transferred either to their planet of origin or destination. Since the surviving colonists were in no immediate danger there might be no need to involve the hospital at all—or the ambulance ship—except in an advisory capacity. He added, "We are going to need more help."

"Yes," Fletcher said with great feeling. It was obvious that his thinking had been parallelling Conway's. "*Rhabwar* out."

By the time *Tyrell* had returned to the assembly area, it was beginning to look congested. Twenty-eight hibernation compartments—all of which, according to Prilicla, contained living e-ts—hung in the darkness like a gigantic, three-dimensional picture showing the agglutinization of a strain of rod-shaped bacilli. Each section had been numbered for later identification and examination. There were no other scoutships in the area because they were busy retrieving more cylinders.

Even with the Casualty Deck's artificial gravity switched off and tractor beams aiding the transfer, it took Murchison, Naydrad, and Conway more than an hour to extricate the cadaver from its wrecked compartment and bring it into *Rhabwar*. Once inside it flowed over the examination table on each side and on to intrument trolleys, beds, and whatever else could be found around the room to support its massive, coiling body.

Fletcher paid them a visit some hours later to see the cadaver at close range, but he had chosen a moment when Murchison's investigation was moving from the visual examination to the dissection stage and his stay was brief. As he was leaving he said, "When you can be spared here, Doctor, would you mind coming up to Control?"

Conway nodded without looking up from his scanner examination of one of the alien's breathing orifices and its tracheal connection. The Captain had left when he straightened up a few minutes later and said, "I just can't make head or tail of this thing."

"That is understandable, Doctor," Naydrad said, who belonged to a very literal-minded species. "The being appears to have neither."

Murchison looked up from her microscopic examination of a length of nerve ganglia and rubbed her eyes. She said, "Naydrad is quite right. Both head and tail sections are absent and may have been surgically removed, although I cannot be certain of that even though there are indications of minor surgery having taken place at one extremity. All that we know for sure is that it is a warm-blooded oxygen breather and probably an adult. I say 'probably' despite the fact that the creature in the first cylinder was relatively more massive. Genetic factors gen-

erally make for size differences among the adults of most species, so I cannot assume that it is an adolescent or younger.
Of one thing I am sure—Thornnastor is going to enjoy itself
with this one."

"So are you," Conway said.

She smiled tiredly and went on, "I don't wish to give the
impression that you are not helping, Doctor. You are. But I
had the distinct feeling back there that the Captain was just
being polite, and he wants to see you very urgently."

Prilicla, who had been resting on the ceiling between trips
outside to monitor the emotional radiation of newly arrived
survivors, made trilling and clicking noises which translated
as "For a nonempath, friend Murchison, your feeling was remarkably accurate."

When Conway entered Control a few mintues later, both
captains were present and they looked relieved to see him. It
was Nelson who spoke first.

"Doctor," he said quickly, "I think this rescue mission is
getting out of hand. So far thirty-eight contacts have been made
and the sensors report the presence of life on all but two of
them, and more cylinders are being reported every few minutes.
They are all uniform in size and the present indications are that
there are many more sections out there than would be necessary
to complete one Wheel."

"If, for technical or physiological reasons, the alien vessel
had to have the configuration of a Wheel," Conway said
thoughtfully, "then it could have been built, as were some of
our early space stations, in a series of concentric circles, as
wheels within wheels."

Nelson shook his head. "The longitudinal curvature on all
sections is identical. Could there have been two Wheels, separate but identical vessels, which were in collision?"

"I disagree with the collision theory," Fletcher said, joining
in for the first time. "At least between two or more Wheels.
There are far too many survivors and undamaged sections for
that. Their vessel seems to have fallen apart. I think there was
a high-velocity collision with a natural body, the shock of which
shook the hub and central support structure apart."

Conway was trying to visualize the finished shape of this

alien jigsaw puzzle. He said, "But you still think there was more than one Wheel?"

"Not exactly," Fletcher replied. "Two of them mounted side by side, with a different alien or set of aliens in each. Right now we don't know whether we are retrieving single aliens who have been surgically modified for travel or pieces of much larger creatures, and we won't know how many we are dealing with until the scoutships begin bringing back heads and tails. I'm assuming that all of the occupants were in suspended animation and their ship ran itself, accelerating or decelerating along its vertical axis. If I'm right then the hub wreckage should contain the remains of just one propulsion unit and one section which contained the automatic navigation and sensor equipment."

Conway nodded. "A neat theory, Captain. Is it possible to prove it?"

Fletcher smiled and said, "All of the pieces are out there, even though some of them will be smashed into their component parts and difficult to identify, but given time and the necessary assistance we could fit them together."

"You mean *reconstruct* it?"

"Perhaps," Fletcher replied in an oddly neutral tone. "But is it really any of our business?"

Conway opened his mouth, intending to tell the other exactly what he thought of a damn fool question like that, then closed it again when he saw the expressions on both captains' faces.

For the truth was that the situation which was developing here was no longer any of their business. *Rhabwar* was an ambulance ship, designed and provisioned for short-duration missions aimed at the rescue, emergency treatment, and transfer to the hospital of survivors of accident or disease in space. But these survivors did not require treatment or fast transport to the hospital. They had been in suspended animation for a long time and would be capable of remaining in that condition without harm for a long time to come. Reviving them and, more important, relocating them on a suitable planet would be a major project.

The sensible thing for Conway to do would be to bow out gracefully and dump the problem in the laps of the cultural contact specialists. *Rhabwar* could then return to its dock and the medical team could go back to treating the weird and wonderful variety of patients who turned up at Sector General while they waited for the next distress call for their special ambulance ship.

But the two men watching him so intently were a scoutship commander on survey duty, who would be lucky if he turned up one inhabited system in ten years of searching, and Major Fletcher, *Rhabwar*'s Captain and a recognized authority in the field of extraterrestrial comparative technology—and the rescue of this e-t sublight colonization transport could well be the biggest problem to face the Federation since the discovery and treatment of the continent-girdling strata creature of Drambo.

Conway looked from Nelson to Fletcher, then said quietly, "You're right, Captain, this isn't our responsibility. It is Cultural Contact's problem, and they would not think any the less of us, in fact they would expect us to hand it over to them. But I get the impression that you don't want me to do that."

Fletcher shook his head firmly and Nelson said, "Doctor, if you have any friends in authority, tell them I would willingly give an arm or a leg to be allowed to stay on this one."

A cool, logical portion of Conway's mind was urging him to do the sensible thing, to think about what he was letting himself in for and to remember who would be blamed if things went wrong, but it never had any hope of winning that argument.

"Good," Conway said, "that makes it unanimous."

They were both grinning at him in a manner totally unbefitting their rank and responsibilities, as if he had bestowed some great favor instead of condemning them to months of unremitting mental and physical hard labor. He went on, "As the ship responsible for making the original find, *Tyrell* would be justified in remaining, and as the medical team in attendance, the same applies to *Rhabwar*. But we are going to need a lot of help, and if we are to have any hope of getting it you will have to give me detailed information on every aspect of this problem, not just the medical side, and answers to the questions which are going to be asked.

"To begin with, I shall need to know a great deal more about the physiology of the survivors, and you will have to find me a couple of additional cadavers for Thornnastor, the hospital's Diagnostician-in-Charge of Pathology. It has six feet and weighs half a ton and if Murchison and I don't come up with some sensible conclusions about this life-form, and specimens for Thorny to investigate independently, it will walk all over me. And what O'Mara and Skempton will do——"

"They're public servants, Doctor," Nelson said, grinning. "You have the rank."

Conway got to his feet and said very seriously, "This is not simply a matter of whistling up another flotilla of scoutships, gentlemen, and something more than a hyperspace signal will be needed this time. To get the help we need I'll have to go back to the hospital and argue and plead, and probably thump the table a bit."

As he entered the gravity-free central well and began pulling himself toward the Casualty Deck he could hear Fletcher saying, "That wasn't much of an inducement, Nelson. Most of his highly placed friends have more arms and legs than they know what to do with."

Leaving *Rhabwar* and the rest of the medical team at the disaster site, Conway traveled to Sector General in *Tyrell*. He had requested an urgent meeting with the hospital's big three— Skempton, Thornnastor, and O'Mara—as soon as the scoutship had emerged into normal space. The request had been granted but Chief Psychologist O'Mara had told him curtly that there would be no point trying to start the meeting prematurely by worrying out loud over the communication channel, so Conway had to curb his impatience and try to marshal his arguments while Sector General slowly grew larger in the forward viewscreen.

When Conway arrived in the Chief Psychologist's office, Thornnastor, Skempton, and O'Mara were already waiting for him. Colonel Skempton, as the ranking Monitor Corps officer in the hospital, was occupying the only other chair, apart from O'Mara's own, which was suitable for the use of Earth-humans; Thornnastor, like the other members of the Tralthan species, did everything including sleeping on its six, elephantine feet.

The Chief Psychologist waved a hand at the selection of e-t furniture ranged in front of his desk and said, "Take a seat if you can do so without injuring yourself, Doctor, and make your report."

Conway arranged himself carefully in a Kelgian relaxer frame and began to describe briefly the events from the time *Rhabwar* had arrived in response to *Tyrell*'s distress beacon. He told of the investigation of the first section of the fragmented alien vessel which was the product of a race in the early stage of spaceship technology, possessing sublight drive and gravity furnished by rotating their ship. Every undamaged section found had contained an e-t in suspended animation. For this reason additional scoutships had been requested to help find and retrieve the remaining survivors as a matter of urgency because the majority of these widely scattered suspended animation compartments would, in just under twelve weeks' time, fall into or pass so close to a nearby sun that the beings inside them would perish.

While Conway was speaking, O'Mara stared at him with eyes which opened into a mind so perceptive and analytical that it gave the Chief Psychologist what amounted to a telepathic faculty. Thornnastor's four eyes were focused equally on Conway and Colonel Skempton, who was staring down at his scratch pad where he was drawing a circle and going over it repeatedly without lifting his stylus. Conway found himself watching the pad as well, and abruptly he stopped talking.

Suddenly they were staring at him with all of their eyes, and Skempton said, "I'm sorry, Doctor, does my doodling distract you?"

"To the contrary, sir," Conway said, smiling, "you have helped a lot."

Ignoring the Colonel's baffled expression, Conway went on, "Our original theory was that a sublight vessel with the configuration of a rotating wheeltype space station suffered a catastrophic malfunction or collision which carried away its hub-mounted propulsion and navigation systems, and jarred the rim structure apart; the subsequent dispersal of the suspended animation containers was aided by the centrifugal force which furnished their ship with artificial gravity. But the number of sections found just before I left the area were more than enough to form three complete Wheels and, because I have been bothered by the fact that no head segments have been found so far,

I have decided to discard the Wheel or multiple Wheel theory in favor of the more simple configuration suggested by the Colonel's sketch of a continuous—"

"Doctor," Thornnastor broke in firmly. As the Diagnostician-in-Charge of Pathology it had a tendency toward single-mindedness where its specialty was concerned. "Kindly describe in detail and give me the physiological classification of this life-form and, of course, your assessment of the number of casualties we will be required to treat. And are specimens of this life-form available for study?"

Conway felt his face reddening as he made an admission no Senior Physician on the staff of Sector General should ever have to make. He said, "We cannot classify this life-form with complete certainty, sir. But I have brought you two cadavers in the hope that you may be able to do so. As I have already said, the survivors are still inside their suspended animation compartments and the relatively few who did not survive are in a badly damaged condition—in several pieces, in fact."

Thornnastor made untranslatable noises which probably signified approval, then it said, "Had they not been in pieces, I would soon have rendered them so. But the fact that neither Murchison nor yourself are sure of their classification surprises and intrigues me, Doctor. Surely you are able to form a few tentative conclusions?"

Conway was suddenly glad that Prilicla was still on board *Rhabwar* because his embarrassment would have given the little empath a bad fit of the shakes. He said, "Yes, sir. The being we examined was a warm-blooded oxygen breather with the type of basic metabolism associated with that physiological grouping. The cadaver was massive, measuring approximately twenty meters in length and three meters in diameter, excluding projecting appendages. Physically it resembles the DBLF Kelgian life-form, but many times larger and possessing a leathery tegument rather than the silver fur of the Kelgians. Like the DBLFs it is multipedal, but the manipulatory appendages are positioned in a single row along the back.

"There were twenty-one of these dorsal limbs, all showing evidence of early evolutionary specialization. Six of them were long, heavy, and claw-tipped and were obviously evolved for defense since the being was a herbivore, and there were fifteen in five groups of three spaced between the six heavier tentacles. Each of the thinner limbs terminated in four digits, two of which were opposable, and were manipulatory appendages originally evolved for gathering and transferring food to the mouths, of which there are three on each flank opening into three stomachs. Two additional orifices on each side open into a very large and complex lung. The structure inside these breathing orifices suggests that expelled air could be interrupted and modulated to produce intelligence-bearing sounds. On the underside were three openings used for the elimination of wastes.

"The mechanism of reproduction was unclear," he continued, "and the specimen showed evidence of possessing both male and female genitalia on the forward and rear extremities respectively. The brain, if it was the brain, took the form of a cable of nerve ganglia with localized swellings in three places, running longitudinally through the cadaver like a central core. There was another and much thinner nerve cable running parallel to the thicker core, but below it and about twenty-five centimeters from the underside. Positioned close to each extremity were two sets of three eyes, two of which were mounted dorsally and two on the forward and rear flanks. They were recessed but capable of limited extension and together gave the being complete and continuous vision vertically and horizontally. The type and positioning of the visual equipment and appendages suggest that it evolved on a very unfriendly world.

"Our tentative classification of the being," Conway ended, "was an incomplete CRLT."

"Incomplete?" Thornnastor said.

"Yes, sir," Conway said. "The cadaver we examined had sustained minimum damage since it had died during a slow decompression while in suspended animation. We could be wrong, but there were signs of some kind of radical surgery having taken place, a double removal of what may have been the head and tail of the being. This was not a traumatic amputation caused by the disaster to their ship, but a deliberate procedure which may have been required to fit the being into its suspended animation container for the colonization attempt. The body tegument overall is thick and very tough, but at the extremities the only protection is a hard, transparent layer of organic material, and the underlying protrusions, fissures, orifices, and musculature look raw. This suggests—"

"Conway," O'Mara said sharply, with a glance toward the suddenly paling Colonel. "With respect to Thornnastor, you have moved too quickly from the general to the particular. Please confine yourself at this stage to a simple statement of the problem and your proposed solution."

Colonel Skempton was the man responsible for making Sector General function as an organization— but, as he was fond of telling his medical friends when they started to talk shop in grisly detail, he was a glorified bookkeeper, not a bloody surgeon! The trouble was that there was no way Conway could state his problem simply without offending the sensibilities of the overly squeamish Colonel.

"Simply," Conway said, "the problem is a gigantic, wormlike entity, perhaps five kilometers or more in length, which has been chopped into many hundreds of pieces. The indicated treatment is to join the pieces together again, in the correct order."

The Colonel's stylus stopped in mid-doodle, Thornnastor made a loud, untranslatable sound, and O'Mara, normally a phlegmatic individual, said with considerable vehemence, "Conway, you are not considering bringing that—that Midgard Serpent to the hospital?"

Conway shook his head. "The hospital is much too small to handle it."

"And so," Skempton said, looking up for the first time, "is your ambulance ship."

Before Conway could reply, Thornnastor said, "I find it difficult to believe that the entity you describe could survive such radical amputation. However, if Prilicla and yourself state that the separate sections so far recovered are alive, then I must accept it. But have you considered the possibility that it is a group entity, similar to the Telphi life-form which are stupid as individuals but highly intelligent as a gestalt? Physical fragmentation in those circumstances would be slightly more credible, Doctor."

"Yes, sir, and we have not yet discarded that possibility—" Conway began.

"Very well, Doctor," O'Mara broke in dryly. "You may restate the problem in less simple form."

The problem . . . thought Conway.

He began by asking them to visualize the vast, alien ship as it had been before the disaster—not the multiple Wheel shape first discussed but a great, continuous, open coil of constant diameter and similar in configuration to the shape on the Colonel's pad. The separate turns of the coil had been laced together by an open latticework of metal beams which held the vessel together as a rigid unit and provided the structural support needed along the thrust axis during take-off, acceleration, and landing. Assembled in orbit, the ship had been approximately five hundred meters in diameter and close on a mile long, with its power and propulsion system at one end of an axial support structure and the automatic guidance system and sensors at the other.

The exact nature of the accident or malfunction was not yet known, but judging by the observed effects it had been caused by a collision with a large natural object which, striking the vessel head-on, had taken out the guidance system forward, the axial structure, and the stern thrusters. The shock of the collision had shaken the great, rotating coil into its component suspended animation compartments, and centrifugal force had done the rest.

"This being—or beings—is so physiologically constituted," Conway went on, "that to assist it we must first rebuild its ship and land it successfully. Fitting the pieces together again can be done most easily in weightless conditions. The fact that the twenty-meter sections of the coil have flown apart but retained their positions with respect to each other will greatly assist the reassembly operation—"

"Wait, wait," the Colonel said. "I cannot see this operation being possible, Doctor. For one thing, you will need a very potent computer indeed to work out the trajectories of those expanding sections accurately enough to return them to their original positions in this—this jigsaw puzzle—and the equipment needed to reassemble it would be—"

"Captain Fletcher says it is possible," Conway said firmly. "Piecing together the remains of an extraterrestrial ship has been done before, and much valuable knowledge was gained in the process. Admittedly, on previous occasions there were no living survivors to be pieced together as well and the work was on a much smaller scale."

"Much smaller," O'Mara said dryly. "Captain Fletcher is a theoretician and *Rhabwar* is his first operational command. Is he happy ordering three scoutship flotillas around?"

The Chief Psychologist was considering the problem in the terms of his own specialty, Conway knew, and as usual O'Mara was a jump ahead of everyone else.

"He seems to enjoy worrying about it," Conway said carefully, "and there are no overt signs of megalomania."

O'Mara nodded and sat back in his chair.

But the Colonel could jump to correct conclusions as well, if not always as quickly as the Chief Psychologist. He said, "Surely, O'Mara, you are not suggesting that *Rhabwar* direct this operation? It's too damned big, and expensive. It has to be referred up to—"

"There isn't time for committee decisions," Conway began.

"—the Federation Council," the Colonel finished. "And anyway, did Fletcher tell you how he proposed fitting this puzzle together?"

Conway nodded. "Yes, sir. It is a matter of basic design philosophy . . ." Captain Fletcher was of the opinion—an opinion shared by the majority of the Federation's top designers—that any piece of machinery beyond a certain degree of complexity, be it a simple groundcar or a spaceship one kilometer long, required an enormous amount of prior design work, planning and tooling long before the first simple parts and subassemblies could become three-dimensional metal on someone's workbench. The number of detail and assembly drawings, wiring diagrams, and so on for even a small spaceship was mind-staggering, and the purpose of all this paperwork was simply to instruct beings *of average intelligence* how to manufacture and fit together the pieces of the jigsaw without knowing, or perhaps even caring, anything about the completed picture.

If normal Earth-human, Tralthan, Illensan, and Melfan practice was observed—and the engineers of those races and many others insisted that there was no easier way—then those drawings and the components they described must include instructions, identifying symbols, to guide the builders in the correct placing of these parts within the jigsaw.

Possibly there were extraterrestrial species which used more exotic methods of identifying components before assembly, such as tagging each part with an olfactory or tactile coding system, but this, considering the tremendous size of the coil ship and the number of parts to be identified and joined, would represent a totally unnecessary complication unless there were physiological reasons for doing things the hard way.

The cadaver had possessed eyes which operated within the normal visible spectrum, and Captain Fletcher was sure that the alien shipbuilders would do things the easy way by marking the surface of the components with identifying symbols which could be read at a glance. Following a detailed examination of a damaged suspended animation cylinder and the remains of its supporting framework, Fletcher found that the system of identification used was groups of symbols vibro-etched into the metal, and that adjoining components bore the same type and sequence of symbols except for the final letter or number.

"Clearly they think, and put their spaceships together, much the same as we do," Conway concluded.

"I see," the Colonel said. He sat forward in his chair. "But decoding those symbols and fitting the parts together will take a lot of time."

"Or a lot of extra help," Conway said.

Skempton sat back, shaking his head. Thornnastor was silent also, but the slow, impatient thumping of its massive feet indicated that it was not likely to remain so for long. It was O'Mara who spoke first.

"What assistance will you need, Doctor?"

Conway looked gratefully at the Chief Psychologist for getting straight to the point as well as for the implied support. But he knew that O'Mara would withdraw that support without hesitation if he had the slightest doubt about Conway's ability to handle the problem. If Conway was to be confirmed in this assignment, he would have to convince O'Mara that he knew exactly what he was doing. He cleared his throat.

"First," he said, "we should initiate an immediate search for the vessel's home world so that we can learn as much as possible about this entity's culture, environment, and food requirements, as well as having somewhere to put it when the rescue is complete. It is almost certain that the disaster caused a large deviation in the coilship's course, and it is possible that the vessel suffered a guidance malfunction not associated with the accident which fragmented it, and it has already overshot the target world. This would complicate the search and increase the number of units conducting it."

Before the Colonel could react, Conway went on quickly, "I also need a search of the Federation Archives. For many centuries before the Federation came into being there were species who possessed the startravel capability and did a lot of independent exploration. There is a slight chance that one of them may have encountered or heard reports of an entity resembling an intelligent Midgard Serpent—"

He broke off, then for Thornnastor's benefit he explained that the Midgard Serpent was a creature of Earth-human mythology, an enormous snake which was supposed to have encircled the planet with its tail in its mouth. Thornnastor thanked him and expressed its relief that the being was mythological.

"Until now," the Colonel said sourly.

"Second," Conway went on, "comes the problem of rapid retrieval and placement of the scattered suspended animation cylinders. Many more scoutships will be required, supported by all of the available specialists in e-t languages and technical notation systems, and computer facilities capable of analyzing this material. A large, ship-borne translation computer should be able to handle the job—"

"That means *Descartes*!" Skempton protested.

"—In the time remaining to us," Conway resumed, "and I hear *Descartes* recently completed its first contact program on Dwerla and is free. But the third and most technically difficult part of the problem is the reassembly. For this we need fleet auxiliaries with the engineering facilities and space construction personnel capable of rapidly rebuilding those parts of the alien vessel's supporting framework which cannot be salvaged from the wreckage. Ideally the people concerned should be experienced Tralthan and Hudlar space construction teams.

"Four," he continued, allowing no time for objections, "we need a ship capable of coordinating the reassembly operation, and mounting a large number of tractor and pressor beam batteries with officers highly trained in their use. This will reduce the risk of collision in the assembly area between the retrieved sections and our own ships. The coordinating vessel will have its own computer capable of handling the logistic—"

"Vespasian, he wants," Skempton said dully.

"Yes, its tactical computer would be ideal," Conway replied. "It also has the necessary tractor and pressor batteries and, I believe, a very large cargo lock in case I have to withdraw some of the CRLTs from their suspended animation compartments. Remember, several segments of the entity were destroyed and surgery may be required in these areas to close the gaps. But until we know a great deal more about this entity's physiology and environment I have no clear idea of the type and quantity of medical assistance which will be needed."

"At last," Thornnastor growled through its translator, "you are about to discuss the needs of the patient."

"The delay was intentional, sir," Conway said, "since we must repair the ship before we can help the occupant. Regarding this entity, or entities, Pathologist Murchison and myself have examined one cadaver and we seek confirmation of our preliminary findings and as much additional physiological data as you can provide from the specimens brought back in *Tyrell,* and from the contents of the intravenous infusion equipment which is used, apparently, to induce, extend, and reverse the suspended animation process. Specifically, we require much more information on the nervous system, the linkages to the voluntary and involuntary musculature, the degree and rapidity of tissue regeneration we can expect if surgical intervention is necessary and additional data on the transparent material which covers and protects the raw areas at the forward and rear extremities. Naturally, sir, this information is required the day before yesterday."

"Naturally," Thornnastor growled. Its six elephantine feet, which had been silent while Conway was speaking, resumed their slow thumping. Clearly the Tralthan was eager to go to work on those specimens of the completely new life-form.

O'Mara waited for precisely three seconds, then he scowled up at Conway and said, "And that is all you require, Doctor?"

Conway nodded. "For the present."

Colonel Skempton leaned forward and said caustically, "*For the present* he needs the services of a Sector subfleet, including *Descartes* and *Vespasian*. Before we can recommend the deployment of so many Service units we should refer the matter to the Federation Council for—" He broke off because the thumping of Thornnastor's feet was making conversation difficult.

"Your pardon, Colonel," the Tralthan said, "but it seems to me that if we refer this matter to the Council they will ponder on it at great length and then decide to make it the responsibility of the beings best able to understand and solve the problem, who are the entities comprising the technical and medical crew of *Rhabwar*. The special ambulance ship program was designed to deal with the unexpected, and the fact that this problem is unexpectedly large is beside the point.

"This is an entity, or entities, of a hitherto unknown species," it went on, "and I recommend that Senior Physician Conway be given the assistance he requires to rescue and treat it. However, I have no objection to you recommending this course and referring the matter to the Council for discussion and ratification, and for amendment should they come up with a better idea. Well, Colonel?"

Skempton shook his head. He said doggedly, "It's wrong, I know it's wrong, for a newly appointed ship commander and a medic to be given so much authority. But the *Rhabwar* people are the only ones who know what they are doing at the moment. Reluctantly, I agree. O'Mara?"

All their eyes, the Colonel's and Conway's two and Thornnastor's four, were on the Chief Psychologist, who kept his steadily on Conway. Finally he spoke.

"If you have nothing else to say, Doctor," he said dryly, "I suggest you return to *Rhabwar* as quickly as possible before the area becomes so congested that you can't find your own ship."

The reaction time of the Monitor Corps to an emergency large or small was impressively fast. In *Tyrell*'s forward viewscreen the area resembled a small, untidy star cluster in which *Rhabwar*'s beacon flashed at its center like a short-term variable. Apart from acknowledging their arrival and giving them permission to lock on, Fletcher did not speak to them because, he explained, fifteen more scoutships had arrived unexpectedly and he was busy fitting them into his retrieval program. For this reason Conway did not get an opportunity to tell him about the other unexpected things which were about to happen until he was back on board the ambulance ship, and by that time it was too late.

"Rhabwar," a voice said from the wall speaker as Conway entered Control, "this is the survey and cultural contact vessel *Descartes,* Colonel Okaussie commanding. I'm told you have work for us, Major Fletcher."

"Well, yes, sir," the Captain said. He looked appealingly at Conway, then went on, "If I might respectfully suggest, sir, that your translation specialists—"

"I'd rather you didn't," Colonel Okaussie broke in. "Respectfully suggest, I mean. When I know as much about this situation as you do I'll accept suggestions, respectful or otherwise. But until then, Major, stop wasting time and tell me what you want us to do."

"Yes, sir," Fletcher said. Speaking quickly, concisely, and, out of habit, respectfully, he did just that. Then a few seconds after he broke contact the radar screen showed a new trace which was even larger than *Descartes.* It identified itself as the Hudlar-crewed depot ship *Motann,* a star-going engineering complex normally used to bring technical assistance to vessels whose hyperdrive generators had failed noncatastrophically leaving them stranded in normal space between the stars. Its captain, who was not a Monitor Corps officer, was also happy to take his instructions from Fletcher. But then an even larger blip appeared on the screen, indicating that a very large ship indeed had just emerged from hyperspace. Automatically Lieutenant Haslam fed the bearing to the telescope and tapped for maximum magnification.

The tremendous, awe-inspiring sight of an Emperor-class battlecruiser filled the screen.

"Rhabwar, this is *Vespasian . . ."*

Fletcher paled visibly at the thought of giving instructions to the godlike entity who would be in command of *that* ship, whose communications officer was relaying the compliments of Fleet Commander Dermod and a request for full vision contact as soon as convenient. Conway, who had not had time to tell the Captain what to expect because it was already happening, got to his feet.

"I'll be in the Casualty Deck lab," he said. Grinning, he reached across to clap Fletcher reassuringly on the shoulder and added, "You're doing fine, Captain. Just remember that, a long, long time ago, the Fleet Commander was a major, too."

The conversation between Fletcher and the Fleet Commander, complete with visuals, was on the Casualty Deck's repeater when he arrived, but the sound was muted because Prilicla was on another frequency giving instructions to one of the scoutship medical officers regarding a cadaver the other had found and which Murchison wanted brought in for examination. Murchison and Naydrad were still working on the first specimen, which had been reduced to what seemed to be its component parts.

Murchison nodded toward the repeater screen and said, "You seem to have been given everything you needed. Was O'Mara in a good mood?"

"His usual sarcastic, helpful self," Conway said, moving to join her at the dissection table. "Do we know anything more about this outsize boa constrictor?"

"I don't know what we know," she said crossly, "but I know a little more and feel more than a little confused by the knowledge. For instance . . ."

The thick pencil of nerve ganglia with its localized bunchings and swellings which ran through the center of the cylindrical body was, almost certainly, the CRLT's equivalent of a brain, and the idea of a missing head or tail was beginning to seem unlikely—especially since the transparent material which covered the raw areas fore and aft was, despite its appearance, equally as tough as the being's leathery body tegument.

She had been successful in tracing the nerve connections between the core swellings and the eyes, mouths, and manipulatory appendages, and from both ends of the axial nerve bundle to the puzzling system of muscles which underlay the raw areas on the forward and rear faces of the creature.

The specimen appeared to be male—at least, the female genitalia at the other end were shrunken and seemed to be in a condition of early atrophy—and she had identified the male sperm generator and the method of transfer to a female.

"... There is evidence of unnatural organ displacement," she went on, "which can only be caused by weightlessness. Gravity, real or artificial, is a physiological necessity for this life-form. During hibernation the absence of weight would not be fatal, but weightlessness while conscious would cause severe nausea, sensory impairment, and, I feel sure, intense mental and physical distress."

Which meant that the being would have to be in position on the rim of its rotating vessel or affected by natural gravity, that of its target world, when it was revived. *It isn't a doctor this patient needed,* Conway thought wryly, *it's a miracle worker!*

"With the Captain's help," Murchison continued, "we have established that the medication which produces and or extends the hibernation anesthesia occupies the larger volume of a dispenser mechanism which also contains a smaller quantity of the complex organic secretion which can only be the reviver. Fletcher also traced the input to the automatic sensor and actuator which switches the mechanism from the hibernation to the resuscitation mode and found that it reacted to the combined presence of gravity and external pressure. The same actuator mechanism is also responsible for ejecting the endplates of its hibernation compartment which would enable the CRLT to disembark.

"Sooner or later we're going to have to revive one of these things," she ended worriedly, "and we'll have to be very sure that we know what we are doing."

Conway was already out of his spacesuit and climbing into his surgical coveralls. He said, "Anything in particular you'd like me to do?"

They worked on the cadaver while the hours flickered past on the time display to become days, then weeks. From time to time a terse, subspace message from Thornnastor would arrive confirming their findings or suggesting new avenues of investigation, but even so it seemed that their rate of progress was slow to nonexistent.

Occasionally they would look up at the Control Room repeater, but with decreasing frequency. Fletcher, a Hudlar space construction specialist, and variously qualified Monitor Corps officers were usually showing each other pieces of twisted metal via their vision channels, comparing identification symbols and talking endlessly about them. No doubt it was all vitally important stuff, but it made boring listening. Besides, they had their own organic jigsaw puzzle to worry about.

A pleasant break in the routine would occur when they had to go outside to look at one of the other cadavers which had been brought in and attached to the outer hull, there being room for only one CRLT at a time inside *Rhabwar*. On these occasions the investigations were conducted in airless conditions and only the organic material which was of special interest to them was excised for later study. As a result they found a bewildering variety of age and sex combinations which seemed to indicate that the older CRLTs were well-developed males whose raw areas at each extremity had a brownish coloration, while the younger beings were clearly female and the areas concerned were a livid pink under the transparent covering.

Once there was a break in the investigative routine which was not pleasant. For several hours they had been studying a flaccid, purplish lump of something which might have been the organic trigger for the being's hibernation phase, and making very little progress with it, when Prilicla broke into their angry, impatient silence.

"Friend Murchison," the empath said, "is feeling tired."

"I'm not," the pathologist said, with a yawn which threatened to dislocate her firm but beautifully formed lower mandible. "At least, I wasn't until you reminded me."

"As are you, friend Conway—" Prilicla began, when there was an interruption. The furry features of Surgeon-Lieutenant Krach-Yul replaced the pieces of alien hardware which had been filling the repeater screen.

"Doctor Conway," the Orligian medic said, "I have to report an accident. Two Earth-human DBDGs, simple fractures, no decompression damage—"

"Very well," said Conway, clenching his teeth on a yawn. "Now's your chance to get in some more other-species surgical experience."

"—And a Hudlar engineer, physiological classification FROB," Krach-Yul went on. "It has sustained a deep, incised,

and lacerated wound which has been quickly but inadequately
treated by the being itself. There has been a considerable loss
of body fluid and associated internal pressure, diminished sen-
soria, and—"

"Coming," Conway said. To Murchison he muttered, "Don't
wait up for me."

While *Tyrell* was taking him to the scene of the accident,
an area where three of the coilship sections were being fitted
together, Conway reviewed his necessarily scant surgical experience with the Hudlar life-form.

They were a species who rarely took sick, and then only
during preadolescence, and they were fantastically resistant to
physical injury, with eyes which were protected by a hard,
transparent membrane, tegument like flexible armor, and no
body orifices except for the temporary ones opened for mating
and birth.

The FROBs were ideally suited to space construction projects. Their home planet, Hudlar, pulled four Earth gravities,
and its atmospheric pressure—if that dense, soupy mixture of
oxygen, inerts, and masses of microscopic animal and vegetable nutrient in suspension could be called an atmosphere—
was seven times Earth-normal. At home they absorbed the food-
laden air through their incredibly tough yet porous skin, while
offplanet they sprayed themselves regularly and frequently with
nutrient paint. Their six flexible and immensely strong limbs
terminated in four-digited hands which, when the fingers were
curled inward and the knuckles presented to the ground, served
also as feet.

Environmentally, the Hudlars were a very adaptable species,
because the physiological features which protected them against
their own planet's crushing gravity and pressure also enabled
them to work comfortably in any noncorrosive atmosphere of
lesser pressure right down to and including the vacuum of
space. The only item of equipment a Hudlar space construction
engineer needed, apart from its tools, was a communicator
which took the form of a small, air-filled blister enclosing its
speaking membrane and a two-way radio.

Conway had not bothered to ask if there was an FROB
medic on the Hudlar ship. Curative surgery had been a completely alien concept to that virtually indestructible species until

they had joined the Federation and learned about places like
Sector General, so that medically trained Hudlars were about
as rare outside the hospital as physically injured ones inside it.

Captain Nelson placed *Tyrell* within fifty meters of the scene
of the accident. Conway headed for the injured Hudlar. Krach-
Yul had already reached the Earth-human casualties, one of
whom was blaming himself loudly and unprintably for causing
the accident and tying up the suit frequency in the process.

Conway gathered that the two Earth-humans had been saved
from certain death by being crushed between two slowly closing
ship sections by the Hudlar interposing its enormously strong
body, which would have escaped without injury if the jagged-
edged stump of an external bracing member had not snagged
one of the FROB's limbs close to the point where it joined the
body.

When Conway arrived, the Hudlar was gripping the injured
limb with three of its hands, tourniquet fashion, while the two
free hands remaining were trying to hold the edges of the wound
together—unsuccessfully. Tiny, misshapen globules of blood
were forming between its fingers to drift weightlessly away,
steaming furiously. It could not talk because its air bag had
been lost, leaving its speaking membranes to vibrate silently
in the vacuum.

Conway withdrew a limb sleeve-piece, the largest size he
carried, from his Hudlar medical kit and motioned for the
casualty to bare the wound.

He could see that it was a deep wound by the way the dark
red bubbles grew suddenly larger before they broke away, but
he was able to snap the sleeve-piece in position before too
much blood was lost. Even so there was a considerable leakage
around both ends of the sleeve as the Hudlar's high internal
pressure tried to empty its body fluids. Conway quickly attached circlips at each end of the sleeve and began to tighten
one while the Hudlar itself tightened the other. Gradually the
fluid loss slowed and then ceased, the casualty's hands drifted
away from the injured limb, and its speaking membrane ceased
its silent vibrating. The Hudlar had lost consciousness.

Ten minutes later the Hudlar was inside *Tyrell*'s cargo lock
and Conway was using his scanner to search for internal damage
caused by the traumatic decompression. The longer he looked

the less he liked what he saw, and as he was concluding the examination Krach-Yul joined him.

"The Earth-humans are simple fracture cases, Doctor," the Orligian reported. "Before setting the bones I wondered if you, as a member of their own species, would prefer to—"

"And rob you of the chance to increase your other-species experience?" Conway broke in. "No, Doctor, you treat them. They're on antipain, I take it, and there is no great degree of urgency?"

"Yes, Doctor," Krach-Yul said.

"Good," Conway said, "because I have another job for you—looking after this Hudlar until you can move it to Sector General. You will need a nutrient sprayer from the Hudlar ship, then arrange with Captain Nelson to increase the air pressure and artificial gravity in this cargo lock to levels as close to Hudlar-normal as he can manage. Treatment will consist of spraying the casualty with nutrient at hourly intervals and checking on the cardiac activity, and periodically easing the tightness of the sleeve-piece if your scanner indicates a serious reduction of circulation to the injured limb. While you are doing these things you will wear *two* gravity neutralizers. If you were wearing one and it failed under four-G conditions there would be another seriously injured casualty, you.

"Normally I would travel with this patient," he went on, stifling a yawn, "but I have to be available in case something urgent develops with the CRLT. Hudlar surgery can be tricky so I'll tape some notes on this one for the operating team, including the suggestion that you be allowed to observe if you wish to do so."

"Very much," Krach-Yul said, "and thank you, Doctor."

"And now I'll leave you with your patients and return to *Rhabwar*," Conway said. Silently he added, *to sleep*.

"*Tyrell* was absent for eight days and was subsequently assigned to courier duty, taking specimens to Sector General and returning with information, advice, and detailed lists of questions regarding the progress of their work from Thornnastor. The great, spiral jigsaw puzzle which was the alien ship was beginning to take shape—or more accurately, to take a large number of semicircular and quarter-circular shapes—as the hibernation cylinders were identified, positioned, and coupled. Many of the cylinders were still missing because they had been so seriously damaged that their occupants had died or they had still to be found and retrieved by the scoutships.

Conway was worried because the incomplete coilship and the motley fleet of Monitor Corps vessels and auxiliaries were on a collision course with the nearby sun, which was growing perceptibly brighter every day. It was clearly evident that the growth rate of the alien vessel was much less perceptible. When he worried about it aloud to the Fleet Commander, Dermod told him politely to mind his own medical business.

Then a few days later *Tyrell* returned with information which made it very much his medical business.

Vespasian's communications officer, who was usually a master of the diplomatic delaying tactic, put him through to the Fleet Commander in a matter of seconds instead of forcing him to climb slowly up the ship's entire chain of command. This was not due to any sudden increase in Conway's standing with the senior Monitor Corps officer, but simply that while Conway was trying to reach Dermod, the Fleet Commander was trying to contact the Doctor.

It was Dermod who spoke first, with the slight artificiality of tone which told Conway that not only was the other in a hurry and under pressure but that there were other people present beyond the range of the vision pickup. He said, "Doctor, there is a serious problem regarding the final assembly phase and I need your help. You are already concerned over the limited time remaining to us and, frankly, I was unwilling to discuss the problem with you until I was able to present it, and the solution, in its entirety. This can now be done, in reverse order, preferably. My immediate requirement is for another capital ship. *Claudius* is available and—"

"Why—" Conway began, shaking his head in momentary confusion. He had been about to list his own problems and requirements and found himself suddenly on the receiving end.

"Very well, Doctor, I'll state the problem first," The Fleet Commander said, frowning as he nodded to someone out of sight. The screen blanked for a few seconds, then it displayed a black field on which there was a thick, vertical gray line. At the lower end of the line a fat red box appeared and on the opposite end a blue circle. Dermod went on briskly, "We now have a pretty accurate idea of the configuration of the alien ship, and I am showing you a very simple representation because I haven't time to do otherwise right now.

"The ship had a central stem, the gray line," Dermod explained, "with the power plant and thrusters represented by the red box aft and the forward-mounted sensors and navigation systems shown as a blue circle. Since the ship's occupant was unconscious, all of these systems were fully automatic. The stem also provided the anchoring points for the structure which supported the inhabited coil. You will see that the main supports are angled forward to compensate for stresses encountered while the vessel was under power and during the landing maneuver."

A forest of branches grew suddenly from the stem, making it look like a squat, cylindrical Christmas tree standing in its red tub and with a bright-blue fairy light at the top. Then the continuous spiral of linked hibernation compartments was attached to the ends of the branches, followed by the spacing members which separated each loop of the coil, and the picture lost all resemblance to a tree.

"The coil diameter remains constant throughout at just under five hundred meters," the Fleet Commander's voice continued. "Originally there were twelve turns of the coil and, with each hibernation cylinder measuring twenty meters in length, this means there were roughly eighty hibernating CRLTs in every loop of the coil and close on one thousand of the beings on the complete ship.

"Every loop of the coil was separated by a distance of seventy meters, so that the total height of the coilship was just over eight hundred meters. We were puzzled by this separation since it would have been structurally much simpler laying one on top of the other, but we now believe that the open coil configuration was designed both to reduce and localize meteorite collision damage and remove the majority of the hibernation compartments as far as possible from radiation leakage from the reactor at the stern. While encased in its rather unusual vessel we think the creature traveled tail-first so that its thinking end was at the stern to initiate disembarkation following the landing. Unfortunately, the stern section had to be heavier and more rigid than the forward structure since it had to support the weight of the vessel during deceleration and landing, and so it was the stern which sustained most of the damage when the collision occurred, and most of the CRLT casualties were from the sternmost loop of the coil."

According to *Vespasian*'s computer's reconstruction, the vessel had been in direct head-on collision with a large meteor, and the closing velocities involved had been such that the whole central stem had been obliterated, as if an old-time projectile hand weapon had been used to remove the core of an apple. Only a few scraps of debris from the power unit and guidance system remained—enough for identification purposes but not for reconstruction—and the shock of the collision had shaken the overall coil structure apart.

On the screen the widely scattered hibernation compartments came together again into a not quite complete coil: There were several sections missing, particularly near the stern. Then the stem, its power and guidance systems, and the entire support structure disappeared from the display leaving only the incomplete coil.

"The central core of that vessel is a mass of pulverized wreckage many light-years away," Dermod continued briskly, "and we have decided that trying to salvage and reconstruct it would be an unnecessary waste of time and materiel when there is a simpler solution available. This requires the presence of a second Emperor-class vessel to—"

"But why do you want—?" Conway began.

"I am in the process of explaining why, Doctor," the Fleet Commander said sharply. The image on the screen changed again and he went on, "The two capital ships and *Descartes* will take up positions in close line-astern formation and lock onto each other with matched tractor and pressor beams. In effect this will convert the three ships into a single, rigid structure which will replace the alien vessel's central stem, and the branching members which supported the coil will also be non-material but equally rigid tractors and pressors.

"In the landing configuration *Vespasian* will be bottom of the heap," Dermod continued, with a tinge of pride creeping into his voice. "Our thrusters are capable of supporting the other two ships and the alien coilship during deceleration and landing, with *Claudius* and *Descartes* furnishing lateral stability and taking some of the load with surface-directed pressors.

After touchdown, the power reserves of all three vessels will be sufficient to hold everything together for at least twelve hours, which should be long enough, I hope, for the alien to leave its ship. If we can find somewhere to put it, that is."

The image flicked off to be replaced by the face of the Fleet Commander. "So you see, Doctor, I need *Claudius* to complete this—this partly nonmaterial structure and to test its practicability in weightless conditions before working out the stresses it will have to undergo during the landing maneuver. Of equal urgency are the calculations needed to extend the combined hyperspace envelope of the three ships to enclose the coil and Jump with it out of here before this damn sun gets too close."

Conway was silent for a moment, inwardly cringing at the thought of some of the things which could go catastrophically wrong when three linked ships performed a simultaneous Jump. But he could not voice his concern because ship maneuvers were most decidedly the Fleet Commander's and not the Doctor's business, and Dermod would tell him so with justification. Besides, Conway had his own problems and right now he needed help with them.

"Sir," he said awkwardly, "your proposed solution is ingenious, and thank you for the explanation. But my original question was not regarding the reason why you wanted *Claudius*, but why you needed my help in the matter."

For a moment the Fleet Commander stared at him blankly, then his expression softened as he said, "My apologies, Doctor, if I seemed a trifle impatient with you. The position is this. Under the new Federation Council directive covering extraterrestrial rescue operations by *Rhabwar*, I am required in a large-scale combined medical and military operation of this kind to obtain your approval for additional personnel and materiel, specifically another capital ship. I assume it is forthcoming?"

"Of course," Conway said.

Dermod nodded pleasantly despite his obvious embarrassment, but the lines of impatience were beginning to gather again around his mouth as he said, "It will be sufficient if you tape a few words as the physician-in-charge of the case to the effect that *Claudius* is urgently required to ensure the present safety and continued well-being of your patient. But you were calling me, Doctor. Can I help you?"

"Yes, sir," Conway said, and went on quickly, "You have been concentrating on joining the coilship sections in proper sequence. Now I have to begin putting the patient together, with special emphasis on the joining of segments which are not in sequence. That is, the ones which were separated by the hibernation compartments whose occupants died. We are now sure that the being is a group entity whose individual members are independently intelligent and may be capable of linking up naturally to their adjoining group members when the conditions are right. This is the theory, sir, but it requires experimental verification.

"The entities who are out of sequence could pose serious problems," Conway concluded. "They will have to be removed from their hibernation compartments and presented to each other so that I may determine the extent of the surgical work involved in reassembling the group entity."

"Sooner you than me, Doctor," Dermod said with a brief grimace of sympathy. "But what exactly do you need?"

He is like O'Mara, Conway thought, *impatient with confused thinking.* He said, "I need two small ships to bring in the CRLT segments I shall specify and to return them to their places in the coil. Also a large cargo hold which can accommodate two of the hibernation cylinders joined end to end and the two beings which will be withdrawn from them. The hold is to be fitted with artificial gravity grids and nonmaterial restraints in case the conscious CRLTs become confused and aggressive, and personnel to operate this equipment. I know this will mean using the cargo lock and hold in one of the largest ships, but I require only the hold; the vessel can go about its assigned duties."

"Thank you," the Fleet Commander said dryly, then paused while someone offscreen spoke quietly to him. He went on, "You may use the forward hold in *Descartes,* which will also provide the personnel and its two planetary landers for fetching and carrying your CRLTs. Is there anything else?"

Conway shook his head. "Only an item of news, sir. The Federation archivists think they have found the CRLTs home planet, although it is no longer habitable due to major orbital changes and associated large-scale seismic disturbances. The Department of Colonization has a new home for them in mind and will give us the coordinates as soon as they are absolutely sure that the environment and the CRLTs physiological classification are compatible. So we have somewhere to take Humpty-Dumpty when we've put it together again.

"However," Conway ended very seriously, "all the indications are that this was not simply a colony ship which ran into trouble, but a planetary lifeboat carrying the last surviving members of the race."

Conway stared anxiously around the enormous interior of *Descartes*'s forward hold and thought that if he had known there were going to be so many sightseers he would have asked for a much larger operating theater. Fortunately one·of them was the ship's commanding officer, Colonel Okaussie, who kept the others from getting in the way and ensured that the area of deck containing the two joined hibernation cylinders was clear except for Murchison, Naydrad, Prilicla, Fletcher, and Okaussie himself. Conway was sure of one thing: Whether the initial CRLT link-up attempt was a success or a failure, there would be no chance at all of keeping the result a secret.

He wet his lips and said quietly, "Uncouple the cylinders and move the joined faces three meters apart. Bring the artificial gravity up to Earth-normal, slowly, and the atmosphere to normal pressure and composition for the life-form. You have the figures."

The fabric of his lightweight spacesuit began to settle against Conway's body and there was mounting pressure against the soles of his feet as he watched the facing ends of the two cylinders. Then abruptly the circular endplates jumped out of their slots to clank onto the deck and come to rest like enormous, spinning coins. The hibernation cylinders were now open at both ends, enabling the two CRLTs to move toward or away from each other, or from one compartment to the next.

"Neat!" Fletcher said. "When the coilship is spinning in its space-traveling mode, centrifugal force holds the being against the outboard surface of the cylinder, and when the spin ceases in the presence of real gravity and an atmosphere the airtight seals drop away, the individual compartments are opened to all of the others and the beastie, the complete group entity, that is, exits by working down the stern-facing wall until all of it reaches the surface. The gravity and pressure sensors are linked to the medication reservoirs, Doctor, so you have just reproduced the conditions for resuscitation following a planetary landing."

Conway nodded. He said, "Prilicla, can you detect anything?"

"Not yet, friend Conway."

They moved closer so as to be able to look into the two opened cylinders, dividing their attention between the occupants who were lying flaccidly with their dorsal manipulators hanging limply along their sides. Then one of the enormous, tubular bodies began to quiver, and suddenly they were both moving ponderously toward each other.

"Move back," Conway said. "Prilicla?"

"Consciousness is returning, friend Conway," the empath replied, trembling with its own as well as everyone else's excitement. "But slowly; the movements are instinctive, involuntary."

As the forward extremity of one CRLT approached the rear of the other, the organic film which protected the raw areas on each creature softened, liquefied, and trickled away. At the center of the forward face a blunt, conical shape began to form surrounded by systems of muscles which twitched themselves into mounds and hollows and deep, irregular fissures. The rear face of the other CRLT had grown its own series of hollows and orifices which exactly corresponded with the protuberances of the other, as well as four large, triangular flaps which opened out like the fleshy petals of an alien flower. Then all at once there was just one double-length creature with a join which was virtually invisible.

And I was worried about joining them together, Conway thought incredulously. *The problem might be to keep them apart!*

"Are we observing a physical coupling for the purpose of reproduction?" Murchison said to nobody in particular.

"Friend Murchison," Prilicla said, "the emotional radiation of both creatures suggests that this is not a conscious or involuntary sex act. A closer analogy would be that of an infant seeking the physical reassurance of its parent. However, both beings are seeking physical and mental reassurance, and have feelings of confusion and loss, and these feelings are so closely matched that the only explanation is shared mentation."

"Tractor beamers," Conway said urgently. "Pull them apart, *gently!*"

He had been delighted to find that the beings who made up the vast group entity would link together naturally when the conditions were right, although that might not be the case if too many intervening segments had been destroyed in the accident, but he most certainly did not want a premature and permanent link-up between these two at this stage. They would have to be returned to a state of hibernation and resume their positions in the coil, otherwise they might find themselves permanently separated, orphaned, from the group entity.

Even though the tractor beamers were no longer being gentle, the two CRLTs stubbornly refused to separate. Instead they were becoming more physically agitated, they were trying to emerge completely from their hibernation cylinders, and their emotional radiation was seriously inconveniencing Prilicla.

"We must reverse the process—" Conway began.

"The sensors react to gravity and air pressure," Fletcher broke in quickly. "We can't evacuate the hold without killing them, but if we cut the artificial gravity only it might—"

"The endplate release mechanism was also linked to those sensors," Conway said, "and we can't replace them in their slots without chopping the two beasties apart, in the wrong place."

"It might stop the flow of resuscitation medication," Fletcher went on, "and restart the hibernation sequence. The needles are still sited in both creatures and the connecting tubing is flexible and still unbroken, although it won't be for long if we don't stop them from leaving their cylinders. If we put a clamp on the resuscitation line of each beastie, Doctor, I believe I could bypass the endplate actuator and restart the hibernation medication."

"But you will be working inside the cylinders," Murchison said, "beside two very massive and angry e-ts."

"No, ma'am," the Captain said. "I am neither foolhardy nor a xenophobe, and I shall work through an access panel in the outer skin. It should take about twenty minutes."

"Too long," Conway said. "They will have disconnected

themselves from the tubing by then. We can calculate the dosage needed to put them back to sleep. Can you drill through the wall of the container, ignoring the sensors and actuators, and withdraw the required quantity of medication directly?"

For a moment there was silence while Fletcher's features fell into an angry, why-didn't-I think-of-that? expression, then he said, "Of course, Doctor."

But even when injections of the CRLTs own hibernation medication were ready their troubles were far from over. The pressor beam operators who were responsible for immobilizing the creatures could not hold down the two joined e-ts without also flattening the medics who were trying to work on them. Their best compromise was to leave a two-meters clearance on each side of the operative field wherein the medical team would not be inconvenienced by the pressors. But this meant that there was no restraint placed on the movements of the creature along a four-meter length of its body, which wriggled and humped and lashed out with its dorsal appendages and generally made it plain that it did not want strange beings climbing all over it and sticking it with needles.

Several times Conway was knocked away from the patient and once, if it had not been for a warning from Fletcher, he would have lost his helmet and probably the head inside it. Murchison observed crossly that the big advantage in dealing with cadavers was that, regardless of their physiological classifications, they did not assault the pathologist and leave her normally peachlike skin pigmentation black and blue. But with Naydrad's long, caterpillarlike body wrapped around one appendage and both Fletcher and Colonel Okaussie hanging onto the other limb which threatened the operative field, and with Murchison steadying the scanner for him while he sat astride the creature like a bareback horserider, Conway was able to guide his hypo into the correct vein and discharge its contents before a particularly violent heave pulled the needle free.

Within a few seconds Prilicla, whose fragile body had no place in this violent muscular activity announced from its position on the ceiling that the being was going back to sleep. When they withdrew to turn their attention to its companion, its movements were already growing weaker.

By the time they had dealt similarly with the other CRLT,

the two creatures had separated. The hollows and protuberances
and flaps of muscle had collapsed and smoothed themselves
out, and the raw interface areas began exuding the clear liquid
which congealed into a thin, transparent film. Gently the tractor
and pressor beam men lifted and pushed the two beings back
into their respective hibernation cylinders. Conway signaled
for the artificial gravity to be reduced to zero and, as expected,
they were able to replace the cylinder endplates without trouble.
The cargo hold's air pressure was reduced gradually so that
they could check whether the premature opening of the hibernation compartments had caused a leak. It had not.

"So far so good," Conway said. "Return them to their positions in the coil and bring in the next two."

The first two had been the occupants of adjoining cylinders
and their linking up had been automatic, a natural process in
all respects. But the second two had been separated by a compartment which had been ruptured by a piece of flying debris
and its occupant killed. The affinity between these two might
not be so strong, Conway thought.

However, they merged as enthusiastically and naturally as
had the first two. The resuscitation process was reversed before
they were fully conscious so as to eliminate the multispecies
wrestling match needed to put them into hibernation again.
Prilicla reported a minor variation in the emotional radiation
associated with the initial body contact—a feeling, very faint
and temporary, of disappointment. But the two segments of
the group entity were compatible and that particular break in
continuity in the coil could be closed up.

Conway felt uneasy. Too much good luck worried him.
Something was bothering Prilicla, too, because he had long
since learned to recognize the difference between the little
empath's reaction to its own feelings and those of the beings
around it.

"Friend Conway," Prilicla said, while they were awaiting
the arrival of the third set of CRLTs. "The first two beings
were relatively immature and taken from the forward section
of the coil, that is, from the tail segments of this multiple
creature, and the second two came from a position considerably
aft of amidships. Our own deductions, supported by the information on the creatures' probable planet of origin which

arrived with *Tyrell*, suggest that the tail segments are immature beings, perhaps very young adults, and the head segments aft to be composed of the older, more experienced, and most highly intelligent of the beings since they are responsible for ship operations and disembarkation following a stern landing."

"Agreed," Conway said, wishing Prilicla would get to the point, no matter how unpleasant it was, instead of talking all around it.

"Aft of amidships, friend Conway," Prilicla went on, "the CRLTs should be older. The two who have just left us, judging by their emotional radiation, were even less mature than the first set."

Conway looked at Murchison, who said defensively, "I don't know why that should be, I'm sorry. Do the data on their home planet, if it *is* their home planet, suggest an answer?"

"I'm pretty sure it was their home planet," Conway replied thoughtfully, "because there couldn't possibly be another like it. But the data are old and sparse and predate the assembly and launching from orbit of the coilship, and we've been too busy since *Tyrell* brought back the information to discuss it properly."

"We have half an hour," Murchison observed, "before the next two CRLTs arrive."

Many centuries before the formation of the Galactic Federation, the Eurils had ranged interstellar space, driven by a curiosity so intense and at the same time hampered by a caution so extreme that even the Cinrusskin race to which Prilicla belonged was considered brave, even foolhardy, by comparison. Physiologically they were classification MSVK—a low-gravity, tripedal, and vaguely storklike life-form, whose wings had evolved into twin sets of multidigited manipulators. They had been and still were the galaxy's prime observers, and they were content to look and learn and record through their long-range probes and sensors without making their presence known to the large and dangerously overmuscled specimens, intelligent or otherwise, who were under study.

During their travels the Eurils had come upon a system whose single, life-bearing planet pursued a highly eccentric orbit about its primary which forced its flora and fauna to adapt to environmental conditions ranging from steaming polar jungles in summer to an apparently lifeless winter world of ice. Seeing it for the first time in its frigid, winter mode, the Eurils had been about to dismiss it as being uninhabitable until their probes showed evidence of a highly technical culture encased in the winter ice. Closer investigation revealed that the civilization was current and was awaiting the spring, like every other animal and vegetable life-form on the planet, to come out of hibernation.

It was not until the polar spring was far advanced that the members of this hibernating culture were identified as the large, loglike objects which had been lying in and around the cities under the ice.

"It is clear from this that the overall being is a group entity which, for reasons we do not yet understand, must separate into its individual parts before hibernation can take place," Conway went on. "Since hibernation is natural to them, the problem of artificially extending it and reversing the process for the purpose of interstellar migration was, medically speaking, relatively easy to solve.

"The following year a number of the beings were observed by the Eurils in a fully conscious state," he continued, "going about their business in small group gestalts inside heated domes under the winter ice, which indicates that they do not go into hibernation unless or until it is forced on them. It is unnecessary, therefore, to duplicate the extremes of temperature of their planet of origin on their new home since any world closely resembling their summer environment would suit them. Had this not been so, the near impossibility of finding another and identical planetary environment to the one they were trying to leave would have made the migration hopeless from the start. And the reasons for the CRLT life-form becoming a group entity, initially a small-group entity, are also becoming clear."

Even at the time of the Eurils' visit the CRLTs, despite their advanced technology, were not having things all their own way. They lived on an incredibly savage world which had no clear division between its animal and vegetable predators. In order to have any chance of survival at all, the young CRLTs had to be born physically well developed and remain under the protection of the parent for as long as possible. In the CRLT's case, parturition was delayed until the offspring was a young adult who had learned how to survive and how to aid the continued survival of its parent.

Separation took place every winter, when everything went to sleep and there was no physical threat, and the young one rejoined its parent in the spring to continue its lessons in survival. The young one, who at this stage was invariably female, reached physical maturity early and produced a child of its own. And so it went with the original adult, who had begun to change its sex to male, trailing a long tail of beings of diminishing degrees of masculinity and experience behind it as it moved up the chain of the group entity toward the head.

"The CRLT brain forms part of the central nerve core which during fusion is linked to the brains of the individuals ahead of and behind it via the interfaces at each end of the body," Conway went on, "so that an individual segment learns not only by its own experience but from those of its predecessors farther up the line. This means that the larger the number of individuals in the group, the smarter will be its male head and forward segments. Should the head segment, who is the elder of the group and probably its decision maker, die from natural or other causes, the male next in line takes over."

Murchison cleared her throat delicately and said, "If anyone wishes at this juncture to make a general observation regarding the superiority, physical or intellectual, of the male over the female, be advised that I shall spit in his, her, or its eye."

Conway smiled and shook his head. He said seriously, "The male head will, naturally, fertilize a number of young female tail segments of other group entities, but there is a problem. Surely there would be serious psychological difficulties, sex-based frustrations, with so many of the intervening segments neither fully male or female and unable to—"

"There is no problem," Murchison broke in, "if all mentation and, presumably, the pain and pleasure stimuli are shared by every individual in the group."

"Of course, I'd forgotten that aspect," Conway said. "But there is another. Think of the *length* of our survivor. If mentation and experience are shared, then this could be a very long-lived and highly intelligent group entity indeed—"

The discussion was cut short at that point by the lock cycling warning. The third pair of CRLTs had arrived.

These two had been taken from the sternmost loops of the coilship where the casualties among the most senior and intelligent CRLTs had been heaviest. According to *Vespasian*'s tactical computer and the findings of *Descartes*'s specialists in e-t written languages and numerical systems, fifty-three of the CRLT hibernation cylinders—and their occupants—had been destroyed as a result of the collision, and between these two segments there had been seventeen members of the group entity who had not made it.

The other breaks in the coil were much smaller—the largest missing five segments and the rest only three or four each. Conway hoped that if the largest gap could be closed successfully, then the smaller ones should pose fewer problems.

As with the previous two CRLTs, the combination of artificial gravity and atmospheric pressure triggered the actuators which opened the cylinders and reversed the hibernation process. Conway had already sited the IV needles which would put them back to sleep again should they become disorderly, and Prilicla reported that they were reviving and their emotional radiation indicated that they were beings who were fully mature, healthy, and highly intelligent. As consciousness returned they began moving out of their cylinders and toward each other.

They touched, and jerked apart.

"What?" Conway began. But Prilicla was already answering the question.

"There are feelings of intense discomfort, friend Conway," the empath said, trembling violently. "Also of confusion, disappointment, and rejection. There is background emotion, a combination of anxiety and curiosity, which is probably regarding their present surroundings."

Because he could think of nothing to say, Conway moved to a position directly between the forward and rear interfaces of the two CRLTs. He did not consider the position dangerous because, if Prilicla's emotional readings were correct, they were unlikely to come together. He began examining the two interfaces, both visually and with his x-ray scanner, and taking measurements. A few minutes later Murchison joined him, and

Prilicla dropped to hover cautiously a few meters above the area.

"Even with unaided vision you can see that the two interfaces are not compatible," Conway said worriedly. "There are three areas which cannot be made to join without surgical intervention. But I am reluctant to start cutting without having a clearer idea of how to proceed. I wish I could obtain the consent and cooperation of the patients."

"That might be difficult," Colonel Okaussie said. "But I could have my men try to—"

"Lift them on tractor beams and force another contact," Conway finished for him. "I need one more attempted joining, at least, with vision recorders catching it in close-up from the anterior, posterior, and lateral aspects. I also need Prilicla to monitor their emotional radiation closely during the attempt so that we will know which particular areas give the most discomfort and are, therefore, most in need of surgical attention. During surgery, instead of using an anesthetic, we can return them into hibernation. Yes, Doctor?"

"Have you considered, friend Conway—" began Prilicla, but Conway cut it short.

"Little friend," he said, "I know of old your roundabout manner of expressing disagreement as well as your feelings regarding the causing of unnecessary discomfort to patients, and you know that I share those feelings. But much as I dislike causing pain, in this case it is necessary."

"Doctor Conway," Colonel Okaussie said, with an impatient edge to his tone, "a few moments ago I had been about to suggest that since the beings are fully conscious, intelligent, and their visual range is similar to our own, we should be able to obtain their cooperation by explaining the situation to them graphically. I think it is worth a try."

"It most certainly is," Conway said. He caught Fletcher's eye and muttered, "Now why didn't I think of that?"

Descartes's commanding officer smiled and said, "I'll have a projection screen set up as quickly as possible, Doctor." Conway began assembling the instruments he would need while Murchison and Naydrad took over the job of measuring the interfaces and Prilicla hovered above them radiating reassurance to the patients.

*   *   *

It was a large screen, set between the angle of the ceiling
and the aft wall of the hold so that the dorsally mounted eyes
of both CRLTs would be able to view it without distortion.
Descartes's officers were specialists in e-t communications and
the presentation was short, simple, and very much to the point.

The opening sequence was familiar since it was part of the
material the Fleet Commander had used during his recent brief-
ing to Conway. It showed a diagrammatic reconstruction of
the CRLTs great, coillike interstellar transport complete with
central stem, coil supporting structure, thrusters, and guidance
system moving slowly against a starry backdrop. Suddenly a
large meteor appeared at the edge of the screen, heading directly
for the coilship. It struck, moving along the inside of the coil
and carrying away the thrusters, guidance system, and all of
the central supporting structure for the continuous spiral of
hibernation compartments. The impact shook the coil apart,
and the individual hibernation cylinders, because of the vessel's
rotation, went flying off in all directions like shrapnel from a
slow-motion explosion.

Because of the greater rigidity of the structure aft, the shock
in this area was much more severe and the casualties among
the hibernating CRLTs were heavy; the cylinders whose occupants had not survived were shown in red. Then there was
a two-minute shot of the scene as it actually was, with *Vespasian, Claudius* and *Descartes* with a shoal of smaller vessels
busy reassembling the coil followed by a longer sequence,
displayed graphically, which showed a modified coilship coming in to land on a fresh, green world with the two capital ships
and *Descartes* linked together so as to replace the missing
support structure and thrusters.

The presentation ended by showing the coilship with the
missing segments indicated in throbbing red, then with the red
sections removed and the gaps closed up to make a slightly
shorter coil, and the final scene showed the successful link-up
of the first two CRLTs.

As a piece of visual communication it left very little room
for misunderstanding, and Conway did not need Prilicla's empathic faculty to tell him that the message had been under-

stood — the two CRLTs were already moving cautiously toward each other.

"Recorders?" Conway said urgently.

"Running," Murchison said.

Conway held his breath as once again the two massive creatures attempted fusion. The movements of their stubby, caterpillarlike legs were barely perceptible and their dorsal appendages were tensely still, making them resemble two enormous, alien logs being pushed together by the current of an invisible river. When they were separated by about six inches, the forward face of the rearmost creature had grown the pattern of bumps and fleshy projections which they had seen during the first two link-ups, and the rear interface of its companion had twitched itself into a pattern of fissures and a single deep recess. Around the periphery of the interface four wide, triangular flaps of muscle tipped with osseus material, features which had not appeared to be of any importance when examined on sleeping or dead CRLTs, had grown suddenly to nearly four times their size in the unconscious state and opened out like fleshy, horn-tipped petals. But with these two the interfaces did not correspond. They touched, held contact for perhaps three seconds, then jerked apart.

Before Conway could comment, they were coming together again. This time the forward creature remained still while the second twisted its forward interface into a slightly different position to try again, but with the same result.

It was obvious that the contacts were intensely uncomfortable, and the resultant pain had triggered off the involuntary movement which had jerked them apart. But the CRLTs were not giving up easily, although it appeared at first as if they had. They withdrew until their bodies were again inside their hibernation cylinders, then their stubby legs blurred into motion as they drove themselves at each other seeking, it seemed, by sheer brute force and bodily inertia to force a fusion. Conway winced as they came together with a sound like a loud, multiple slap.

But to no avail. They broke contact to lie a few feet from each other with their dorsal appendages twitching weakly and air hissing loudly as it rushed in and out of their breathing orifices. Then slowly they began to move together again.

"They are certainly *trying*," Murchison said softly.

"Friend Conway," Prilicla said, "the emotional radiation from both creatures has become more complex. There is deep anxiety but not, I would say, personal fear. Also a feeling of understanding and great determination, with the determination predominating. I would say that both entities fully understand the situation and are desperately anxious to cooperate. But these unsuccessful attempts at fusion are causing great pain, friend Conway."

It was characteristic of the little empath that it did not mention its own pain, which was only fractionally less severe than that of the emoting CRLTs. But the uncontrollable trembling of its pipestem legs and fragile eggshell of a body spoke more eloquently than words.

"Put them to sleep again," Conway said.

There was silence while the hibernation medication was taking effect, broken finally by Prilicla who said, "They are losing consciousness, but there is a marked change in the emotional radiation. They are feeling both anxiety and hope. I think they are expecting us to solve their problem, friend Conway."

They were all looking at him, but it was Naydrad, whose mobile, silvery fur was registering its bafflement and concern, who put the question everyone else was too polite to ask.

"How?"

Conway did not reply at once. He was thinking that two highly intelligent elder CRLTs from the coilship's stern, following their first abortive attempt at fusion, would have realized that a link-up was impossible for them. But they had made two further attempts—one when the rearmost creature had tried to twist itself and its interface into a new position, and again when it had tried to achieve fusion by sheer brute force. He was beginning to wonder whether the recent attempt at communicating with the aliens had been strictly one way. Until the *Descartes* linguists could be given the opportunity to learn the CRLTs language, an accurate exchange of ideas was impossible. But it had already been shown that pictures were very effective in putting across a message, and they were all forgetting that actions, like pictures, often spoke louder than words.

Recalling those three unsuccessful attempts at fusion, Conway wondered if the two CRLTs had in fact been trying to demonstrate that the link-up was impossible for them without assistance, but that by changing the positions and perhaps the dimensions of some of the surface features on the interfaces and forcing things a little, then a join might be achieved.

"Friend Conway," Prilicla announced, "is having feelings of optimism."

"Perhaps," Murchison said, "in his own good time, of course, he will explain to us nonempaths the reason for his optimism."

Ignoring the sarcasm, Conway briefly outlined his recent thinking, although he personally would have described his feeling as one of forlorn hope rather than optimism. He went on, "So I believe that the CRLTs were trying to tell us that surgical intervention is necessary for them to achieve fusion, not brute force. And it has just occurred to me that there is a precedent for this procedure. One of the cadavers examined on *Rhabwar* showed evidence of surgery on its forward interface and this could mean—"

"But that was a very youthful, although physically mature CRLT," Murchison broke in, "and the surgery was minor. We agreed that it had probably been performed for cosmetic reasons."

"I think we were wrong," Conway said. Excitedly he went on, "Consider the physical organization of this group entity. At the head is the most mature, male adult and at the tail the most recently born infant, although as we know the infant grows to physical maturity without separating from the parent. Between the head and the tail there is a gradual and steady progression from the most elderly and intelligent male entities down to the increasingly youthful and female segments which form the tail sections. But Prilicla has reported an anomaly in this progression. Young CRLTs positioned relatively close to the tail show evidence of greater physical age and brain development than entities in the midsections. Until now I could see no reason for this anomaly.

"But now let us suppose that this group entity," he continued quickly, "forming as it does a complete colonization project, has been artificially lengthened. The extraordinarily large number of individuals in this group entity has always bothered me, and now there is a simple explanation for it. Let us assume that there is one head or, more accurately, a fairly large number of linked elders forming the leading segments, and several tails connected one behind the other. These would be very youthful tails because it must be much easier to carry out the surgical modifications on young CRLTs which enable them to link up. So we have this colonist group entity with intelligence and experience at its head and linked to a number of young and inexperienced subgroups forming an artificially lengthened tail. The joins between these subgroups are surgically assisted and, I feel sure, temporary, because once established on the target planet they would be able to separate again, and in time the young heads would grow to full adulthood and the dangers from inbreeding would be avoided.

"Perhaps the head on this group entity has also been artificially extended," Conway added, "so as to include elder CRLTs with specialist experience relating to the colonization project who would be available initially to protect the younger group entities, and subsequently to teach and train them and pass on the knowledge of their race's history and science."

Prilicla had flown closer while Conway had been speaking and was hovering a few inches above the Doctor's head. It said happily, "An ingenious theory, friend Conway. It fits both the facts as we know them and the type of emotional radiation received from the beings."

"I agree," Murchison said. "I, too, found difficulty in accepting the extreme length of this group entity, but the idea of a wise old head acting as guide and mentor to an as yet unknown number of young tails is much easier to believe. However, I can't help remembering that it was the head segments which suffered most of the casualties. Perhaps the head is no longer as wise as it should have been and an awful lot of vital knowledge has been lost to this multiplegroup entity."

Colonel Okaussie waited for a moment to see if anyone in the medical team would speak, then he cleared his throat and said, "Maybe not, ma'am. Most of the head segments who were killed in the collision were very close to the stern and to the ship's control and propulsion centres. One could reasonably expect that these segments were the beings charged with the responsibility for operating the ship and carrying out the landing maneuvers, functions which are now the responsibility of the Monitor Corps. It is likely that the scientist and teacher segments were positioned a little farther back in the chain and the majority of the casualties were suffered by the vessel's crew, whose specialist knowledge would no longer be of vital importance to the colonization project after the vessel had landed."

Before Murchison could reply Naydrad gave an impatient, modulated growl which translated as "Why don't we stop talking and get on with the job?"

The screen which had been used to communicate with the CRLTs was continuously displaying distant and close-up views of spacesuited figures of various physiological classifications busily at work on the final stages of the coilship's reassembly. Conway could not decide whether *Descartes*'s commanding officer was screening the material to be helpful and informative or as a means of suggesting, very subtly, that the medical team display a similar degree of industry. The attempt was a failure in either event, Conway thought, because the *Rhabwar* medics were far too busy to look at Okaussie's pictures. They were concentrating instead on measuring and remeasuring the features on the CRLT interfaces and charting with their scanners the paths of underlying blood vessels and the distribution of the nerve ganglia. And with great care and accuracy they were marking the areas where surgical intervention was possible without causing either a major hemorrhage or sensory impairment.

It was slow, tedious work and visually not very dramatic. Colonel Okaussie could be forgiven for thinking that the ambulance ship personnel had gone to sleep on the job.

"Friend Conway," Prilicla said at one particularly awkward stage, "the physical differences between these two entities are so marked that I cannot help wondering if they belong to different subspecies."

All of Conway's attention at that moment was concentrated on what seemed to be the main sphinctor muscle on the rear interface of the forward CRLT, so that by the time he was ready to reply Murchison had done it for him.

"In a sense you are right, Doctor Prilicla," she said. "It is a natural result of their method of reproduction. Think of this forward CRLT when it was the last and female link in its group-entity chain. In due time it grew to maturity and, still attached to its parent, it was fertilized by the male head of another group entity. Its own infant grew and became mature and in turn produced another, and the process continued with different male heads adding their individual sets of genes at every stage.

"The physical connection between any given CRLT and its offspring is perfect," she continued, "and perfect fusion may even be possible between a parent and its grandchild or great-grandchild. But the effect of different males fertilizing each new endlink in the chain would be cumulative. So it is understandable when you think about it, Doctor, that the differences between the fusion interfaces of these two, which were separated by seventeen intervening segments, are considerable."

"Thank you, friend Murchison," Prilicla said. "My brain seems not to be functioning properly."

"Probably," Murchison replied in a sympathetic tone, "because your brain is more than half asleep, like mine."

"And mine," Naydrad joined in.

Conway, who had been trying not to think of how long it had been since he had last eaten or slept, decided that the best way to deal with an impending mutiny among his overworked medics was to ignore it. He indicated a small area on the rear interface of the first alien, midway between the central conical depression and the upper rim of the interface, then pointed to the corresponding area on the forward face of the second one. He said, "We can safely ignore these reproductive organs in both creatures, since this kind of link-up is temporary and physiologically independent of the parent-offspring fusion mechanism. As I see it the three areas we must concentrate on are the central conical projection and its corresponding recess, which are the connecting points for the central nerve core and our primary concern. Second is this narrow, semirigid tongue with the fleshy mushroom at its tip which locates with this slit in the other—"

"That connection is also of vital importance," Murchison broke in, "since it links up the nerve networks controlling the voluntary and involuntary muscles which move each CRLTs legs and enable the group entity to walk in unison. There would be small advantage to the group entity if it could share mentation but a number of its segments were unable to walk."

"Friend Murchison," Prilicla said timidly, "it seems to me

that the original nerve impulse from the head segment, or whichever individual CRLT was responsible for initiating the movement, would not be sufficiently strong to trigger the ambulatory muscles throughout the enormous length of this group entity."

"That is true," the pathologist replied. "But there is an organic amplifier, consisting of a bunching of nerve ganglia situated just above the womb, or the position where the womb had been in the males, in an area where the surrounding tissue has a high mineral content and is particularly rich in copper salts. This biological booster ensures that the ambulatory muscles receive their signals with undiminished strength throughout the length of the chain."

"Third," Conway said, raising his voice slightly to discourage further interruptions, "there are these four flaps of muscle which terminate at their apexes in osseous hooks which locate in these four bone-reinforced orifices in the second creature. This is the primary mechanism by which the individual segments are held together nose to tail, and in this instance—"

"It is also the method by which the CRLT female at the end of the line held onto its developing offspring," Murchison broke in again. "At that stage the offspring had no choice in the matter. But as it matured, produced its own offspring, and moved farther up the line I feel sure that voluntary separation became possible. In fact, separation would be necessary during activities which did not require the entire group entity for their performance."

"That is most interesting, friend Murchison," Prilicla said. "I should think that the first time such a voluntary separation took place a certain amount of psychological trauma would be present. It would be analogous to a coming-of-age ceremony, perhaps, even though the separation might not be permanent—"

Before Conway could speak, Prilicla fell silent and began trembling in reaction to the Doctor's feelings of irritation and impatience. He said, "This is all very interesting, friends, but we do not have the time just now for a general discussion. In any case, following the type of temporary separation you mentioned, the young adult would rejoin its original parent segment and not a—I suppose you could describe it as an ancestor seventeen times removed, which is the problem currently facing us. And now, if you don't mind, we will concentrate on this problem and on the surgical procedures necessary to solve it.

"Feel free to interrupt at any time," he added dryly.

But the interruptions were few and pertinent, and very soon it became obvious even to the watching tractor beamers, *Descartes*'s commanding officer, and Fleet Commander Dermod, whose face appeared briefly but with increasing frequency on the overhead screen, that the medical team was also working hard.

Because Sector General was the Federation's foremost emergency hospital, the kind of surgery performed there, whether the patient was Earth-human or extraterrestrial, tended to be curative rather than cosmetic. It felt very strange to Conway, and he knew that his feelings were being shared by the other members of the team, to be operating on a perfectly healthy e-t with the purpose of simply modifying the size and contours of certain physiological features. But the operation itself was far from simple.

The greater proportion of the surgical work had to be performed on the second alien whose forward nerve coupling cone was too wide at its base to be retained by the sphinctor muscle surrounding the corresponding orifice in the first CRLT. With the semiflexible tongue and groove connection which joined the two beings' locomotor nerve networks, the solution was much simpler. The deep recess in the first alien was surgically widened until measurement showed that it would accommodate the tongue comfortably, after which reinforcing sutures were inserted to prevent further accidental widening. But the four triangular flaps with their bony, hooklike extensions posed a completely different and more difficult problem.

Together the four members formed the principal organic coupling which held the considerable mass of the second e-t against the first, and they did not fit because the hooks did not quite reach the apertures meant to receive them.

Elongating the four triangular members was contraindicated since this would have entailed surgical interference and consequent serious weakening of the muscle systems concerned, and they could not foresee the effect on the network of blood vessels which became engorged and extended the members to quadruple their size when the being returned to consciousness.

Instead they made molds of the four hooks and made artificial ones using a hard, biologically neutral plastic at the tips and a wide band of thinner, more flexible material around the bases. The result was a set of hollow, hook-tipped gloves which, when a little of the original hooks were filed away to make them fit, were slipped over the original members and secured in position with rivets and sutures.

Suddenly there was nothing left to do, but hope.

Above the two unconscious CRLTs the vision screen was displaying an overall picture of their coilship, complete now except for the segments whose occupants were awaiting surgical attention, and the dense but orderly mass of shipping moving in and around it. The thought came to Conway, no matter how hard he tried to avoid it, that the tremendous fleet of Monitor Corps and other units, from the great capital ships and auxiliaries down to the swarms of scoutships and the army of specialists in engineering and communications they represented, were all wasting their time here if this particular operation was not a success.

For this responsibility he had argued long and eloquently with Thornnastor, O'Mara, and Skempton at Sector General. He must have been mad.

Harshly, he said, "Wake them up."

They watched anxiously as once again the two CRLTs came out of hibernation and began moving toward each other. They touched once, a brief, exploratory contact, then they fused. Where there had been two massive, twenty-meter caterpillarlike creatures there was now one of twice that length.

The join was visible, of course, but one had to look very carefully to see it. Conway forced himself to wait for ten interminable seconds, and still they had not pulled away from each other.

"Prilicla?"

"They are feeling pain, friend Conway," the empath replied, trembling slightly. "It is within bearable limits. There are also feelings of acceptance and gratitude."

Conway gave a relieved sigh which ended in an enormous, eye-watering yawn. He rubbed his eyes and said, "Thank you, everyone. Put them back to sleep, check the sutures, and reseal them in their hibernation cylinders. They will not have to link

up again until after the landing, by which time the wounds
should have healed to a large extent so that the fusion will be
more comfortable for them. As for ourselves, I prescribe eight
hours solid sleep before—"

He broke off abruptly as the features of Fleet Commander
Dermod appeared on the screen.

"You appear to have successfully repaired a major break in
our alien chain, Doctor," he said seriously, "but the time taken
to do so was not short. There are many other breaks and we
have three days during which a concerted Jump is possible,
Doctor, after which the gravitational distortion effects caused
by that rapidly approaching sun will make an accurate Jump
out of the question even for single ships.

"Should we overrun the three-day deadline," he went on
grimly, "single-ship Jumping within operational safety limits
will be possible for an additional twenty hours. During this
twenty-hour period, if the coilship is not to be abandoned to
fall into the sun, it will have to be dismantled into sections
small enough to be accommodated by the hyperspheres of the
units available in the area. This, you will understand, would
of necessity be a very hurried operation and our own accident
casualties as well as those of CRLTs would be heavy.

"What I am saying, Doctor," he ended gravely, "is that if
you cannot complete your organic link-ups within three days,
tell me now so that we can begin dismantling the coilship in
a safer and more orderly fashion."

Conway rubbed his eyes and said, "There were seventeen
missing segments between the join which we have just effected,
and this makes it the most difficult job of the lot. The remaining
breaks are of two, three, or at most five segments, so that those
linking operations will be correspondingly easier. We know
the drill now and three days should be ample time, barring an
unforeseen catastrophe."

"I cannot hold you responsible for one of those, Doctor,"
the Fleet Commander said dryly. "Very well. What are your
immediate intentions?"

"Right now," Conway said firmly, "we intend to sleep."

Dermod looked vaguely surprised, as if the very concept of
sleep was one that had become alien to him over the past few
days, then he nodded grudgingly and broke contact.

* * *

Feeling rested, alert, and much more human—and, of course, more Kelgian and Cinrusskin—they returned to *Descartes*'s cargo hold to find another two CRLTs already waiting for them and the remaining segments to be joined clamped to the outer hull. The Fleet Commander, it was clear, was a man who believed in maintaining the pressure.

But achieving fusion with these two was remarkably easy. Only two intervening segments were missing so that the surgery required was minor indeed. The next pair were more difficult, nevertheless a satisfactory link-up was achieved within two hours and, with their growing confidence and expertise, this was to become the average time required for the job. So well did they progress that they became almost angry with themselves when they were forced to break for meals or sleep.

Then suddenly they were finished and there was nothing to do but watch the screen while the last gap in the coil was being closed and hundreds of spacesuited figures swarmed all over it to give a final check to the sensor actuators on each hibernation cylinder which would expel their endplates and initiate resuscitation on landing.

With the exception of *Rhabwar* and one of *Descartes*'s planetary landers, the great fleet of scoutships and auxiliaries withdrew to a distance of one and a half thousand kilometers, which was far enough to relieve the traffic congestion in the area but close enough for them to return quickly should anything go wrong.

"I do not foresee anything going seriously wrong at this end," the Fleet Commander said when the coilship was in one tremendous, spiral piéce. "You have given us enough time, Doctor, to carry out all the necessary pre-Jump calculations and calibrations. This will be a time-consuming process since our three vessels, whose hyperspace envelopes will have to be extended to enclose the coilship, are Jumping in concert. Should a problem arise and we are unable to make this Jump, the units standing by will move in, dismantle the coilship as quickly as possible, and Jump away with the pieces and salvage what we can from this operation.

"There will be enough Monitor Corps medics on these ships

to deal with the expected casualties," he went on, "and for this reason I would like *Rhabwar* to leave at once and position itself close to the CRLTs new target planet. If trouble develops it is much more likely to be at that end."

"I understand," Conway said quietly.

The Fleet Commander nodded. "Thank you, Doctor. From now on this is purely a transport problem and my responsibility."

Sooner yours than mine, Conway thought grimly as Dermod broke contact.

He was thinking about the Fleet Commander's problem while they were wishing Colonel Okaussie and the *Descartes*'s tractor beam crew good-by and good luck, and it remained in his mind after the medical team boarded *Rhabwar* and the ambulance ship was heading out to Jump distance from the combined CRLT and Federation vessels.

Conway understood Dermod's problem all too well and the strong but unspoken reason why the Fleet Commander wanted the ambulance ship positioned in the target system. They both knew that the majority of single-ship accidents occurred because of a premature emergence into normal space when one of the unfortunate vessel's matched set of hyperdrive generators was out of synchronization. A single generator pod emerging into normal space while the rest of the vessel was in the hyperdimension could tear the ship apart and leave wreckage strewn across millions of kilometers. Timing, therefore, was critical even on a single ship where only two or perhaps four generators had to be matched. The Fleet Commander's problem was that *Vespasian, Claudius,* and *Descartes* together with the enormous coilship of the CRLTs were linked together by tractor and pressor beams into a single rigid structure.

The Emperor-class cruisers were the largest ships operated by the Monitor Corps, and each required six generators to move its tremendous mass into and out of hyperspace, while the survey and cultural contact vessel *Descartes* needed only four. This meant that sixteen generators in all would be required to perform a simultaneous Jump and subsequent emergence into normal space. And the problem was further complicated by the fact that all of the generators would be operating under controlled overload conditions because their combined hyperspace envelope had to be extended to enclose the coilship.

As *Rhabwar* made its Jump into hyperspace Conway was overcome by such an intense, gnawing anxiety that even Prilicla could not reassure him out of it. He had the awful feeling that they were about to witness the worst space disaster in Federation history.

The new home chosen for the CRLTs had been known to the Federation for nearly two centuries and was listed as a possible colony world for the Chalders. However, the denizens of Chalderescol Three—a water-breathing life-form resembling an outsize, tentacled crocodile which combined physical inaction with mental agility—were not very enthusiastic about it since they already possessed two colony worlds and their home planet was far from overcrowded. So when they learned of the plight of the CRLT colonists they willingly relinquished their claim to a planet which was of marginal interest to them anyway.

It was a warm, pleasant world with a continent, largely desert, encircling its equator like a wide, ragged belt and two relatively small bands of ocean separating the equatorial landmass from the two large continents centered at each pole; these were green, temperate, and free of icecaps.

Following exhaustive investigations of the cadavers available to them at Sector General both Murchison and Thornnastor were firmly of the opinion that this would be an ideal home for the CRLT life-form—moreover it was an environment which would not force them into periodic hibernation.

The landing area, a large clearing on the shore of a vast, inland sea, had already been marked with beacons. It awaited only the arrival of the CRLTs—as, with mounting anxiety, did the personnel on board *Rhabwar*. On the Casualty Deck Conway and the other members of the medical team each picked a direct visionport, hoping in some obscure fashion that by watching and worrying hard they might ensure the safe arrival of the coilship.

It was no surprise, considering the distances involved, that they learned of its emergence from the Control Room repeaters.

"Trace, sir!" Haslam's voice sounded excitedly. "The bearing is—"

"Are you sure it's them?"

"A single trace that size couldn't be anything else, sir. And yes, the sensors confirm."

"Very well," the Captain's voice replied, trying unsuccessfully to hide its relief. "Lock the scope on your radar bearing and give me full magnification. Dodds, contact astrogation on *Vespasian* and arrange a rendezvous. Power Room, stand by."

The rest of the crewmen's conversation was ignored as the medical team crowded around the Casualty Deck's repeater screen. One look was enough to tell them that their preparations to receive large numbers of casualties from the expected emergence accident had been wasted effort, but they did not care because it was immediately obvious that the concerted Jump had been completely successful.

Centered on the repeater screen was a small, sharp image of the coilship with its three Monitor Corps vessels spaced along its axis, looking like an exercise in alien three-dimensional geometry. *Vespasian*, the stern component, was already applying thrust, and the three linked ships were beginning to turn around their longitudinal axes in order to reproduce the original rate of rotation and centrifugal force conditions of the coilship before its accident. Gradually a voice from Control made itself heard above the sound of the medics' human and extraterrestrial jubilation.

". . . Rendezvous in four hours thirteen minutes," Haslam was saying. "No preliminary orbital maneuvering, sir. They intend going straight in."

Rhabwar, in its hypersonic glider configuration, circled the descending coilship at a distance of three kilometers using its thrusters only when necessary to maintain the same rate of descent. Rotating slowly and illuminated to near-incandescent brightness by the system's sun and noontime reflection from the planet's cloud blanket, it seemed to Conway as if it were boring its way into the lower reaches of the atmosphere like some gigantic, alien drill. Inside the enormous, dazzling coil the three Federation ships in their drab service liveries were virtually invisible except for the flare of *Vespasian*'s thrusters, which were supporting the weight not only of the coilship but the two vessels stacked above it. The great alien and Monitor Corps composite continued its descent until, three kilometers from the surface, tangential thrust was applied to begin killing its spin.

Vespasian's flare lengthened suddenly and brightened, slowing the descent until the ship was hovering a meter above the ground. Then simultaneously the coilship's rotation ceased, *Vespasian*'s stabilizers came to rest on the fused and blackened soil, and the sternmost segment of the coilship touched down.

For perhaps five seconds nothing happened, then, reacting to the cessation of spin and the presence of a suitable atmosphere, the sensor-actuators on every hibernation cylinder performed their function. The endplates which kept the individual CRLTs apart were ejected to fall like a shower of giant coins to the ground, and resuscitation of the group entity was initiated. Conway could imagine the individual CRLTs awakening, stretching, and linking up, the occupants of close on nine hundred hibernation compartments which had survived the eighty-seven years past collision. Then he began to worry in case some of them could not link up and there was an organic log-jam somewhere inside the coil trapping CRLTs above it . . .

But within a surprisingly short time the great group entity was leaving its ship, the leading head segments walking carefully around the fused earth under *Vespasian*'s stern and toward the vegetation on the edge of the clearing. And, like an endless, leathery caterpillar the younger segments emerged carrying equipment and stores and following the tracks of their elders.

When at last the tail was clear of the coilship, the power to the supporting tractor and pressor beams was gradually reduced so that the towering, open spiral collapsed slowly onto itself to lie like a great, loose coil of metal rope on the ground. A few minutes later *Vespasian*, *Claudius*, and *Descartes* took off and separated, the two capital ships to go into orbit and *Descartes* to land again a few kilometers along the shoreline to await formal contact with the CRLT group entity. Contact would occur, they knew, because the individual CRLTs who had undergone surgery knew that the beings inside the Fed-

eration ships wished them well and, since the CRLT life-form
had shared mentation, the whole group would be aware of these
good intentions.

By this time *Rhabwar*'s lander had also touched down and
its medics were on the surface standing as close as they possibly
could to the being who was marching endlessly past them.
Ostensibly they were there to furnish any medical assistance
which might be required. Actually they were simply satisfying
their curiosity regarding a being which must surely have been
the strangest life-form yet encountered.

Conway, as was his wont, was indulging in a bout of post-
operative worrying. He waved, indicating the endless line of
dorsal appendages which were either gathering pieces of edible
vegetation or waving back at him, and said, "I realize that one
or more of the head segments must have tried the local vegetation with no ill effects, and now the whole group entity knows
what is safe to eat, but the procedure seems a bit slapdash to
me. And I haven't been able to spot any of our surgical joins
going past. There is bound to be a certain amount of muscular
weakness in those areas, and perhaps an impairment in sensory
communication and—What the blazes is *that*!"

That was a low, moaning and caterwauling sound which
ran up and down the length of the kilometers-long entity, rising
in volume suddenly until it became deafening. It sounded as
if each and every CRLT was suffering intense physical or
mental anguish. But strangely the outpouring of emotional radiation which must have accompanied it was not bothering
Prilicla.

"Do not feel concern," the little empath said. "It is an expression of group pleasure, gratitude, and relief. They are cheering,
friend Conway."

THE RIVER OF DANCING GODS

Jack L. Chalker

BEYOND THE SEA OF DREAMS

Life had not been kind to Joe and Marge. Now, according to the stranger who met them on a road that wasn't there, they were due to die in nineteen minutes, eighteen seconds. But the ferryboat that waited to take them across the Sea of Dreams could bring them to a new and perhaps better life.

There lay a world where fairies still danced by moonlight and sorcery became real. Joe could become a mighty-thewed barbarian warrior. Marge could be more beautiful and find her magical self.

But there was much more than they realised to this strange land.

This was a world where Hell still strove to win its ancient war and demon princes sent men into battles of dark magic. It was a world where Joe and Marge must somehow help prevent the coming of Armageddon.

Futura Publications
Fantasy
An Orbit Book
0 7088 8163 7

THE SPELLSINGER SERIES

Alan Dean Foster

Jonathan Meriweather is an indolent student and aspiring rock guitarist – until he's snatched from his own world to a world where animals walk and talk as men, armed with sword and dagger. He's been summoned there for a mission – to save the peace-loving (well, fairly peace-loving) animals from the evil forces emanating from the dreaded Greendowns.

And so Jonathan forms a strange fellowship which includes Clothahump, a sorcerous turtle, Mudge, a lecherous otter, and a fire-breathing Marxist dragon and sets out to combat the deadly enemy.

Soldier and crusader, fighting with sword and song, Jonathan Meriweather is the SPELLSINGER.

But even if he can lead his motley band to victory, what other perils lie in wait for him? And will he ever be able to return to earth?

THE SPELLSINGER SERIES

SPELLSINGER
THE HOUR OF THE GATE
THE DAY OF THE DISSONANCE
THE MOMENT OF THE MAGICIAN
PATHS OF THE PERAMBULATOR

All Futura Books are available at your bookshop or
newsagent, or can be ordered from the following address:
Futura Books, Cash Sales Department,
P.O. Box 11, Falmouth, Cornwall TR10 9EN.

Please send cheque or postal order (no currency), and
allow 60p for postage and packing for the first book
plus 25p for the second book and 15p for each additional
book ordered up to a maximum charge of £1.90 in U.K.

B.F.P.O. customers please allow 60p for
the first book, 25p for the second book plus 15p per
copy for the next 7 books, thereafter 9p per book

Overseas customers, including Eire, please allow £1.25
for postage and packing for the first book, 75p for the
second book and 28p for each subsequent title ordered.